THE

Join my mailing list at timelore123@gmail.com to get updates.

1

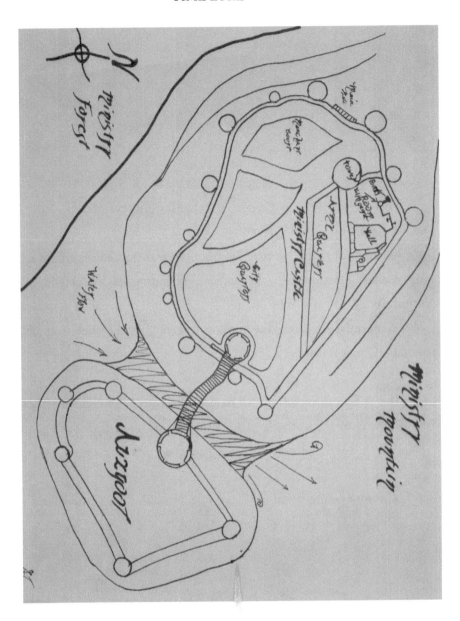

Time Lore

The Order of Pastel

Book 1

Gaven TUCKER

2021

1 CONTENTS

2 BOOK SUMMARY

Time Lore takes place during an age millions of years before our common era. Humans existed for eons, yet it has been a well-kept secret by the Ministry, the government at the time. Not all secrets can be kept completely in the dark, however. They live in a society with technology comparable to our medieval era and the 1800s, however, with extensive knowledge of the planetary bodies and galaxies, including a great understanding of time and its applications. Not originating from the parallel universe that they now occupy gives them this knowledge and a way to combat the lies of the Ministry and other foes that appear from the darkness.

3 PROLOGUE

*R*emember—*I must remember,* Cypress thought to herself as she sculpted the water into the figure of a face hovering in the air. It was the image of her father right before he had died, the last moment that she had seen him alive. Not many people could remember that far into their past; but as for Cypress Yayls, she lived in the past, present, and future. The water formed and flowed continually while she held the thought of her dead father locked in the confines of the universe and with an outstretched hand, his memory. She sat there at the table, near the fireplace, in a room that was cold and expressionless. She was not an impartial woman, as she would view other girls her age; she survived excessive turmoil. A young woman of twenty and yet she had seen so much, experienced pain that only the strongest could describe, and was not about to shrink back now. She would push forward just as she had done before and would triumph. The closed lids of her eyes twitched as her eyes roamed about behind them whilst she formed the picture in her mind. Suddenly her concentration was interrupted with the door of her room being opened.

"It's time," said Galen as he entered the room.

The water lost cohesion, splashed to the floor, and Cypress gasped and swung her arm across the table, knocking the empty goblet against the stone of the raging fireplace. Cypress was prone to anger when in demanding situations, and she was about to be subjected to one. Galen looked at her sorrowfully as he opened the door to her room, gesturing for her to do what she knew she must do.

It is common for young ones to have to bear the troubles of others, but that did not make the task any easier for anyone who could be considered an adult with an innocent disposition. Cypress was a seamless balance between the two and she was weary of accomplishing the accomplishments of an adult and being viewed as a sniveling little girl. Galen, however, was the only one that did not treat her that way. He saw a young, scared individual with the heart of a lion, and the finesse of an exceptionally beautiful woman. He often took pity on her as though she were his own offspring.

Cypress had long red hair and she was very tall and mildly skinny, but one of the most beautiful females of her time. She stood in the middle of the room, staring at the pool of water that lay on the floor, and was breathing heavily when Galen asked,

"Have I not done all that I can do?"

He knew that she would be too proud to answer him truthfully. He was surprised to see her quickly gain her composure. This was unusual. What looked like a tear from her eye had begun to emerge and she answered him with a sharp tongue,

"Perhaps if you were no longer an old man, I would not have to complete your missions for you!"

She was, however, unable to anger Galen as she so often tried. She knew he would be too softhearted to entertain such foolish actions as an ill-spoken word. The thought of this allowed her to vent at times. Galen knew of this need in Cypress and considered it a necessary step in her mental development, paying it no superficial attention.

4 THE CELLAR DOOR

CAN YOU SEE THE SCENE? Look there, far off in the distance, a castle tall and strong mounted on the side of the cliff. Look closer. Can you see it? There in the open window, the owl standing on the stone ledge of the opening. It stares down through the open stained-glass window into the poorly lit room of stone and purple tile. Yes, you can see it can't you as though you were the owl. There, in the middle of the court hall, there stands a woman partially concealed by her cloak in front of a long table as eight judges sit there on one side listening to her. It's Cypress. Shhh, she is saying something. Let's listen in, shall we?

"Our peace is reaching a climax, and there is no hiding from it. Are you prepared to face the consequences of your own inaction?"

The men and women who sat on the other side of the table stared at her with suspicion in their eyes but said nothing.

"I will not stand by and allow the human race to be extinguished. All our culture, all our history will be forgotten. All of it will be just a memory to a vicious race that will pass on through the ages as a lie, a tale of that once-forgotten age when the worthless men roamed the earth."

She now turned, facing away from them as she gestured with conviction.

"What is it that we expect from ourselves? Where is the will to fight not with one another but with the growing threat that is coming? Men once yearned for the times in which we live. Peaceful times where there is very little wrong in the world. However, these times are ending, and if we do not act now, we will be destroyed," she said, turning and slamming her fist against the foot of the table. "Do we expect ourselves to lie down where we have stood? Or do we raise our countenance and become strong against an enemy that we, in the near future, will face? We can no longer think that the wax will sustain the flame through dark gale forces. And when it becomes the time to die for what we believe in, will we?" She paused for a moment to look at every one of their faces. "If we aren't willing, we will become like refuse, scattered throughout the land and hiding against a foe that has overtaken us. If we prepare now, we will have a chance against them."

"I look down at my sword that has been through many battles that I have not seen, and I do regret having used it to do what was necessary. Neither have I forgotten the faces of those I have destroyed. We do not lust for blood, but are we to betray ourselves shrinking back at the sudden smell of our own blood being poured out? Are we to drink of our own cup of wrath? Is our righteous indignation so righteous that it demands the blood of our children and our children's children? When are we to learn from the failings of our fathers and our brothers? Possibly, our children will live to see the times that we have created for them. However, we need to act, and we need to act now!"

Cypress paused once more to pass a slow, long, piercing glare to each man and woman in the court hall. Slowly the faces of the council's members turned from confused scowls to softer and more respectful acknowledgment. Some of the members pushed themselves away from the large table as if to evade her striking words of wisdom. One of the men stood up to reveal himself in the light of the moon coming from a window. The light flickered on his face as small particles of dust passed through the air. His name was Sol. He stood there weak in his stature, as a man that had sat for too long a time in a chair. His gaunt face was frightening, and he stared at Cypress with sad eyes. He could recall a time when he once had long black hair, but that time had long since passed only to be replaced with gray-headedness.

"I see nothing that concerns us, my dear," the man said softly and gently. "And quite frankly, it sounds as though you're speaking of things that couldn't possibly pertain to the times in which I live. I look around, and I see no danger except for the lies that are coming out of your mouth. I am in no spirit to entertain such things as danger, and the extinction of the human race. These things are in the past. It is best that we do not concern ourselves with events that are out of our control. I am a tired old man, and the things you speak of are of a different time and place. There is absolutely no reason to create an army of men at this time. I'm afraid you have miscalculated, my dear, for there are not enough men on the earth to accomplish such an astronomical thing."

He paused for a response from Cypress, her expression filled with anger as she responded,

"If you cannot see past your own life and time, then you truly are a fool, but you are not a fool, for I know you well. Why do you choose to cover your face?"

"It is none of your concern how far I can or cannot see, Cypress," said the old man. "It is that there is no survival now or in our future. I do believe that the time of man has now ended and that the parallels can sense our destruction. It is a useless battle. The race of man would survive as slaves, and we would be alive. That is as good as it can come for us."

Cypress shook her head in disbelief at his words.

"So, I do see. It is not foolishness that I sensed in you, it is fear," she said in a loud and forceful voice as she slowly revealed her hand from beneath her cloak, threatening him with her power. "And is it that you would wish for man to fight against man also? I doubt that you would even protect yourself for fear that you would destroy your masters when they come. Then who would hold out their hand to feed you?"

The old man's face grew angry as the light that once shone on it warped, cloaking him in darkness. But the old man said nothing and slowly returned himself to his chair.

Two men emerged from hidden places in the room, but before they could seize her, the old man lifted his hand and gestured for the men to halt.

"What would you have me do, lead a revolt against an office that I occupy?"

He sat relaxed in his chair, not looking at her.

"I have been here too long. I have dealt with too much in this life to not have any place to rest my head. Is that what you wish of me Cypress? Do you wish for me to go into hiding with you and to live the life that a vibrant young man could hardly withstand? Any judgment that I make today is judged by someone higher than me. I have no place in this world or the next, and I am content with that reality. You must understand that it did not come easy for me, however. It was not easy for me to grow old and see my friends and family die. They too died for the cause of the Ministry. What would you have me do, Cypress?"

Cypress could see that he was beginning to relent, so her tone softened.

"I only ask that you listen to my plea and respect the decision that Galen has made, concerning what we are about to do. This involves you signing a law of noninterference."

The old man stood still in the room of the Ministry court hall. This was a place that all dreaded to enter, for the tales of the Ministry's judicial decisions was that of legendary cruelty. However, it was not Cypress that was being judged, it was the Ministry and its actions that were being put to the question. There was nothing that the man could say or do to refute the argument of Cypress, and he was facing imminent defeat. The man was beginning to regret ever allowing her to have an audience; it was he who would suffer for her words, not her. Sol looked at her with sad eyes and continued to speak.

"I did not know that I could be so fearful. I assume that it is in my old age that a man can be so consumed with the emotions that we could or could not have had. If only we would have controlled ourselves with more urgency. Often, we say this to ourselves with sudden and swift deliberation. Do we always weigh the consequences of our actions? Or do we leap into the fire, hoping not to be scorched? All of us are ready to die for what we believe to be the truth. Or is it simply the most advantageous interpretation of fact which has been distorted, hidden? Do you really think that we deserve the life that we have been given, the life of man? In the times of greed, lust, and happiness of man, yes, in the darkest day of man created by man, there lay in the depths of his mind his conscience that is trained to be pushed aside for bloodlust and other beastly things. However, in times of hardship and love, these things become paramount in our lives. The love that we did not have for other men's loved ones has created a labyrinth of bloodshed between us all. The round stone of revenge has, in the hardship of man, ceased. We, even as a scattered nation, come together now only in love and the pursuit of a more meaningful future that we will probably never look upon. You have given me no choice but to consider your proposal and it will likely end in bloodshed and may claim our lives. It is the cause of man to become more than what he really is. I will need some time. I suppose that you do not have a choice either."

Sol got up out of his chair into the light again.

"We will send to you our decision in two days' time, Cypress. This meeting is adjourned." The minister turned to the two men in the darkness and said, "Could you please show her out of the hall?"

The two men acknowledged Sol and quickly walked over to Cypress as the old minister exited through a door toward the back of the hall of the Ministry. Light rained through the stained-glass windows of the castle, casting shadows on the stone floor and tables. At this point, Cypress could see that the defeat of the Ministry was very clear; however, whether they would choose to accept that defeat or not was not in her power to see. She and the others would have to wait.

"Please come with us, professor," said one of the men in black.

The men led her through the Ministry hallway to the Ministry exit. There were two guards at the entrance. Cypress exposed her hand from beneath her cloak, and the doors opened with a loud crash. There was a storm outside the Ministry. As she stepped through the doorway, she clenched the hood of her cloak. The cold wind blew hard against her face. She could feel the pain growing as the wind pushed against her when she walked.

Cypress was an incredibly beautiful woman. Her eyes were the color of a green sea, and her face, white porcelain. She had a healthy disposition, rarely getting sick, but it was her personality that everyone loved the most. They would often say that she was equally beautiful on the outside as she was on the inside. Cypress didn't really care about other people's opinions of her. She was who she was, and if anyone didn't like her at first, they would grow to like her eventually.

Cypress lived in a time when there was much peace for the human race. However, she could recall a time when there was no peace at all when there was no good, a time when man fought against the beast and when men fought against themselves. She knew that the peacefulness humans were enjoying was not going to last much longer, and she wasn't the only one.

The cold wind continued to toss her cloak back and forth as she took a path down the mountainside. She looked out past the hills and into the valley of Paradoxtom. She could see the flashes of lightning shooting across the night sky, and the rain clouds looked as though there was a large waterfall coming down and across the valley. When she looked, she paused for a moment and stared at the beautiful sight. The wind whipped her cloak toward the storm. She felt at peace because of her subjection to the elements of nature. She imagined the experience of being swept away by them to a restful place free from all problems. Eventually, she pulled herself out of her fantasy to the reality that she was not the kind of person that would give up, even if she wanted to. It wasn't possible for her. No matter how hard she tried, she would push on to the end just as she would push on through the storm. It reminded her of the problems that she would be facing, and it made her uneasy.

She turned and headed toward the mountains, and it was not long before she could hear a carriage in the distance and the carriage master calling out to the horses, using his whip. Just as the carriage began to pass, it came to a halt. The door sprang open, and a hand reached out from the cab. Cypress grabbed hold of the man's hand and got into the carriage. She could hear the wind whistling outside the cab. She pulled back her cloak hood, looked over to the man sitting beside her concealed by the darkness from the light, and thanked him.

"My name is Cypress Yayls."

"I know," said the man, and then there was a short silence.

"It's beautiful, isn't it?" said Cypress.

"Very dangerous too," said the man. "So where should we drop you?" he asked bluntly.

"Do you know the mountain Pastel?" Cypress asked as she turned to take a look outside the window of the cab.

"As a matter of fact, I do indeed. However, first I must introduce myself, I am Talon Barrett." Cypress turned to him and faintly smiled.

Talon quickly grabbed his cane and tapped the roof of the cab and shouted, "Mountain Pastel."

"May I ask you why you are traveling to such a remote area? Wouldn't you rather come to Fable with me and rest the night?" asked Talon with a smile.

"I must see a friend about an important matter," Cypress said as she looked at him questioningly.

"So be it," he said begrudgingly.

Talon pulled out a small box of matches, struck one, and lit the candle in the front of the cab. There were flashes of lightning outside, and they had come under the rain. Cypress leaned her head against the cab window, trying to keep it steady from the violent shaking, and then realized that it was more advantageous to not sleep during the journey. She put her hand on the cold window, reaching out toward the sky in her mind.

"It is so beautiful; it won't be this way much longer."

"No, I suppose that it won't." Talon paused to look at her closer. "I'm on my way back to Fable. I have a house there. However, because where I am taking you is so far out of my way, I may need a place to stay for the night if that's alright with you. I can pay."

"You won't have to pay. There is a place that you can stay for the night, but you must promise that you will be on your way in the morning," Cypress said in a forceful manner.

"I can do that. You were going to walk to the mountain?" he asked.

"No, I was admiring the storm."

"How were you going to get there?" asked Talon.

"Never mind that," said Cypress as she turned to ignore him.

She looked out the window longingly. She, surprisingly to herself, felt very calm and safe in the cab of the stranger. She had felt as if she had known him all her life. It may have been that he had a young and warm face, or possibly, it was the way in which he looked at her. The storm had affected her profoundly too. Life was influencing her in a very peculiar way. The cab was extremely comfortable. She could feel the soft velvet seats and enjoyed the deep maroon color. It was a gentle atmosphere. *Gentle in here, harsh out there*, she thought to herself.

Cypress turned toward Talon, ready to relinquish her thoughts to him, and she knew that he could see it in her. His eyes turned from a stranger's to an empathetic friend.

"Are you all right?" asked Talon. Cypress needed time to breathe before she answered him.

"I was only five when the Requiem entered the city Heris." She paused for a moment and looked out the window once more. "It was a great city that bordered upon the Fondland. It was the most beautiful city that I had ever seen, tall trees, magnificent gardens, a dream in a world where there had seemed to be no more beauty to dream, and even that was taken away. My father was killed when the Requiem invaded. They were men as tall as the trees and super strong. We didn't have a chance against them. My father barely had enough time to get me out of the house when one of the Requiem grabbed hold of him."

A tear had begun to fall down her face when before she could turn her head or wipe the tear, Talon's hand was already there to comfort her. She quickly pulled away.

"I'm sorry about your troubles. I do not enjoy watching a beautiful woman cry. Please forgive me if I am being too friendly. It is my weakness, I suppose," said Talon.

"A strength possibly but not a weakness," said Cypress.

Talon smiled and returned his hand to the head of his cane.

"I know that life can be very hard for many people, I was raised by my mother. I saw the life that she led, the trials that she faced. She always managed to protect me from the effects of it. She was a very loving woman, and I will always remember her for that. There were times when I would cry on my pillow, many times for nothing that made any sense. I suppose that I was an easy child. I know, however, that it was not an easy job to protect me from the world that we were living in at that time. I see her face sometimes looking down on me as if I were her little boy again. Sometimes it is too much for me, and I begin to act, as some sorts would say, not that which is becoming of a man. After which I am forced to forcefully remind them that I was a boy only but a few years from the time that I am standing in now.

"Someone once told me that in order to show true pity, love, and compassion, it is a necessity that one must experience the pity, love, and compassion of another. I unreservedly believe that that is the truth. In my life at every turn, I experienced such things. It has made me into the person that I am today."

Talon looked at Cypress, smiled, and then turned his attention to the storm that was raging outside the cab.

"I think I do understand how such events as this magnificent storm could stir up the intimate feelings in all of us," said Talon.

Cypress looked at him and wondered: *what would possess a stranger to reveal so much to me.*

Perhaps it is her young gentle face or the way that she looks at me, he thought to himself.

The lights from the small city could be seen from the carriage window.

"We're nearly there," said Talon.

Cypress could see the smoke from the chimneys. The carriage ride smoothed as it came off the dirt road and onto the stone street leading to the city gate. They slowly passed a sign that said "City of Pastel" in three different languages. The gates were very large, and there were guards. The carriage slowed to a stop and a well-dressed man came to meet them.

"What is your business here in Pastel?" the young man asked as he covered his face from the wind and rain.

"We are here to meet a friend," said Talon.

"What do you mean 'we,' sir?" the young man asked.

Talon looked at the boy questioningly and turned his head to look at Cypress. There was, however, no one sitting in the side seat where Cypress had been the whole trip to the city. Talon improvised and turned to the young man and said,

"Me and my carriage master."

"Right, sir, in you go then," said the young man. And the gates were opened.

Have I been talking to Cypress at all, or was it my imagination?

"She was quite beautiful," he mumbled to himself out loud as the cab was sped through the large gate of the city of Pastel.

The city was not at all quiet. There were people in every alley and street. The city spiraled up the mountain with long streets. Bars and taverns were hustling and bustling. People were dancing and drinking the night away. The carriage passed an incredibly old hotel and bar. Talon hit his cane against the roof of the cab, gesturing for the carriage master to stop for the night.

The rain from the storm had stopped by the time Talon was ready to get out of the carriage.

"Would you like for me to get your luggage, sir?" said a man that was standing at the entrance of the hotel bar.

"Yes, please do, and tell the clerk that my coach master and I will be staying for the night. I will meet you there shortly," Talon said as he gracefully stepped out of the carriage and onto the stone street.

He took a deep breath of the brisk clean air and made his way to the bar. The door was already open when he reached it, and there was someone in the doorway, smoking a large pipe as Talon passed through it. The bar smelled of hard liquor and rosemary. There was a hint of cinnamon too. Talon mounted the chair and pushed his fancy overcoat behind him. The bartender was a woman, and she noticed him before he entered the bar.

"I suppose you'll be staying the night, will you then?" asked the woman.

"Yes, I will," said Talon.

"You don't look as if you're from around these parts, are you then?" said the woman as she gave him a pint of ale.

Talon picked up the drink and tasted it.

"No, I'm not from these parts." Talon was not paying attention to the bartender though; he was studying the people that were in the pub. He enjoyed watching people and how they reacted with one another. He was unsettled though by the person watching him from the far end of the pub.

"Who is the man in the corner on the left?" Talon asked the bartender as he tried to make his noticing the man imperceptible by not moving his head.

"That *man* paid for your drink," said the spirits master.

"What is his name?" asked Talon.

"I suggest that you ask *him* yourself. I'm not in the habit of giving out names," said the bartender.

Talon could hardly make out that there was a person sitting there at all. He didn't like questioning his own perceptive powers. Just as he was ready to raise himself, his carriage master came and sat next to him. He had surprised Talon on account of Talon's being so preoccupied with the man in the dark corner.

"Why have we come to this place, and where was the woman that we stopped for?" asked the carriage master.

Talon didn't answer the man instantaneously; he was glad that he had not dreamt the whole event during the ride.

"I suppose she had another place to be," said Talon.

The subject had taken his mind off the man in the corner of the pub for just a moment; however, he quickly refocused on the mystery.

"Have you secured the rooms for the night?" Talon asked the carriage master as he stared at the man in the corner.

He was now unable to resist the temptation to reveal the fact that he knew the man was occupying the little space cloaked in shadow at the far end of the pub.

"Yes, I did, but the clerk told me that I would not have to pay for the rooms," said the carriage master.

"Wouldn't have to pay?" asked Talon.

"Yes, the man said that the rooms had already been paid for and that they were expecting us," he said in a confident tone.

The mystery was too much for Talon. Now he had to find out what was going on. He quickly put his drink to the table bar and dismounted from his stool. He had in mind that he was going to forcefully walk to the man in the corner but found himself in an easy stroll. He made his way through the dancing crowd and loud singing to finally reach the table in the far corner of the pub. He stood there for a moment, leaning on his gentleman's cane, not saying a word, and then he spoke.

"I feel I must thank you for your great generosity. It is much appreciated," said Talon to the figure partially covered in darkness.

The figure said nothing. It did, however, momentarily lift its drink to its mouth to take a drink.

"I told you that you wouldn't need to pay for your rooms, didn't I?" said the voice of a young woman.

Talon was surprised and startled, but he didn't show it.

"Well, I'm glad that it is you and not another stranger that I must get to know," said Talon.

Talon, in full understanding, sat down at the small table.

"I didn't recognize you. You gave me quite a scare."

"I do sometimes have that effect on people," said Cypress as she reached for another sip of her drink.

"Do you usually associate with such a lively crowd?"

"Some people say that it is the best part of me, but I would beg to differ," Cypress said as she caressed the top of her glass.

She could feel the cold glass on her fingers as it perspired causing chills to run up her arm.

"Why did you get out of the carriage?" asked Talon.

Cypress was still concentrating on the way the glass of spirits made her feel when he asked the question.

"I could not be seen by the guards at the gate," she said as she stared off into the endless depths of her drink.

"Are you in some kind of trouble?" asked Talon.

"Yes, I am."

Talon felt a certain sort of determination to help her, and it was clearly shown in his face.

He turned and called for the bartender to bring him his ale. He knew that he would need it if he was going to be able to withstand the explanation that he had hoped he was going to get from Cypress.

"Am I correct in assuming that we will not be staying here tonight?" asked Talon.

"What would make you say a thing like that? I have already paid for you to stay the night here," said Cypress.

"I suspect that you didn't pay at all, that all of the people in this place know you and love you. Thus, they are trying to keep you safe from people like me, people that they don't know. And knowing the kind of woman that you really are, you would not stay the night in a place like this because it would be too dangerous for you. So, I suspect that you are putting me up to throw me off the track. However, there is one thing that I am missing in all of this. Why did you get into the carriage? Why did you trust me? And why have you made yourself known to me tonight in this very pub? You could have gone on about your business without interference from me, without me ever knowing who you were. You didn't need to pay for my lodging, you knew that I could have done that myself quite easily, and yet you persisted. You persisted to give me vital information that would easily have unmasked who you were."

"Should I have?"

"I wouldn't do it again if I were you."

"Because you know so much about me, it seems that you are going to be required to come with me."

Moments after Cypress said this, two men in black cloaks came from a table not too far from where they were sitting and stood shoulder to shoulder with Talon.

"Do not be afraid. They are here to escort you to your place of lodging. You will leave your belongings here, and they will be returned to you shortly. After we have searched them. Have I made myself clear?" asked Cypress.

"Yes, very clear."

"These are only precautionary actions as you so eloquently pointed out."

Talon was finally wondering what kind of trouble he had gotten himself in.

"Please come with us, sir," the two men said as they took a bow and grabbed his arms to escort him to the back room.

Talon didn't struggle because he knew that Cypress was not the kind of person that would kill or torture him. He, however, had not realized the fact that she was not the one who was taking him into custody. At the thought of this, he became agitated. He began to imagine what kind of machine they would use on him, how they would try to get information that he did not have. He began to sweat at the thought that this may be the last day that he would be alive. The two men had a loose grip on him as they led him past the hotel rooms and down into the wine cellar. They walked down the steps into the darkness. Talon could see a small ceiling lamp that hung at the point where the cellar ended. The two men brought him under the ceiling lamp and stood there facing the wall as if they were waiting. All three men stared at the wall for a few moments when Talon asked,

"What are we standing here for?"

The men didn't answer his question. They just stood there like human statues. Talon spoke again,

"I fail to see the meaning of us simply standing here."

"Be quiet," said the man on his left.

Talon could hear the people having a good time in the pub. At this point, he was becoming envious of them, wishing that he had never come to this place. He began to picture the meal that he could be eating by himself in peace.

"Tonight, I think that I would have asked for more butter, I like butter," Talon said to himself out loud unscrupulously.

Talon smiled at the wall as if it were a person whose spirit needed uplifting. He could smell the clean sheets of his soft bed and could feel his head sink into them. His stature began to be compromised as his legs weakened due to his overzealous longing to be at home in Fable. One of the escort statues grabbed hold of him firmly, and suddenly, Talon was aware of his surroundings again.

Talon looked down at the escort's arm. He had noticed that he was holding his cane in a sword sheath. It was barely showing from beneath the man's cloak.

Talon's vision was beginning to blur, and it was continually becoming more difficult for him to speak. He still didn't quite understand what was going on.

"Maaaay I agggsk a quueeston?" Talon asked as his head began to wobble.

The men said nothing.

"Whyyy arrr I still stannng herrre?"

Talon's feet were no longer touching the ground when suddenly the light above them began to flicker. The two men looked up and quickly held Talon more firmly. Talon was now completely unconscious.

The wine racks began to move away from the wall as the light began to flicker and move. The stone wall that lay directly in front of them began to turn, and with it, Talon and his two escorts.

The men dragged him through a hallway of purple stone and marble to a large doorway with a very large door that had a gold knob and a gold sign in the center of it that had nothing written on it.

The cellar door began to close as the men dragged Mr. Barrett down an exceedingly long bridge that was cut out of the stone. There was no railing of any kind, only a long stretch of earth down to a very magnificent castle entrance, and sudden death if you fell off the side. The men put him in a wheelbarrow that was set aside near the cellar door. They began wheeling him to the entrance of the castle. It would be clear to any onlooker that they were entering a hollowed-out space of the mountain of Pastel. Talon was in no position to see any of this; however, Cypress had made quite sure of that.

The two men, now at the entrance of the castle knocked, much like a stranger. The knock echoed heavily in the large cave. You could see for what seemed to be miles to the top. The architecture of the castle was absolutely breathtaking. An entrance cut directly out of the stone of the mountain. It was ingenious. The men stood there again like human statues, except there was no one asking why and there was no bothering of the silence, simply the soft and gentle breathing of Mr. Barrett. It was not long before the door to the castle was opened. An older man stepped out to greet them.

"Yes, what is it?" the old man asked.

"Very sorry to disturb you, Professor Galen, but we have been instructed by Ms. Yayls to deliver this man to you," said one of the guards.

"Deliver him to me?" asked Galen. "And just what am I supposed to do with him?"

"Ms. Yayls instructed us to inform you that he will need secure lodging over the night and perhaps something that will help with the pain."

"Always time to meet your friends, Cypress," Galen said under his breath. "Well, come on then. Let's bring him in. I should be able to find him a place for the night that would seem to be secure. We will put him in the third tower. There he will get some light when it shows itself in the morning," Galen said as the men wheeled Mr. Barrett alongside him.

"Have you any idea from where he came?" asked Galen.

"I believe he came from the city of Fable or something or other," said one of the guards.

"Well, he is here now, and we shall have to find something to do with him for the time being, or at least until Cypress decides to stop playing for the night. Wouldn't you say, my boy?" said Galen to the guard that had responded to him.

"Yes, I suppose we should."

"Wouldn't want to make her angry now, would we?"

"No, I suppose not."

The three of them went on walking through the hall, through the common room, and into the kitchen. The guards halted in the kitchen, and one of them went to wake up Ms. Phosit as Galen had instructed. Ms. Phosit was the cook; however, she knew much about herbs and things such as these. She was a bit on the heavy side, and her hair was red, but she always kept it in a knitted hat, and her hair was not long. She would often display herself as a woman that did not allow stupidity around her, however in her heart she was loving, kind, and relenting.

Galen didn't want Mr. Barrett to be asleep while the guards attempted to haul him up the stairs to the room in the tower. Besides, it seemed that the young man was going to need something to get rid of the headache that he would soon be experiencing.

Galen sat down at the large cutting table that rested directly in the center of the kitchen and pulled out a pipe. He looked at it longingly as he stuffed the dry leaves into the center of the small wooden bowl, lit a match, and began to puff away at it. He closed his eyes and listened to the loneliness of the castle, the great home that he had loved for so long. It was moments like these when he was up late at night with nothing to do but puff away at his pipe and listen to the crackling of the fire or the nothingness that was so loudly portrayed by the mountain of Pastel, that he enjoyed so much. It was a gentle atmosphere, and he could feel the wood from the table beneath him. *Gentle in here, harsh out there*, he thought to himself. He sat there enjoying his bliss when he was interrupted by the screeching sound of Ms. Phosit coming down the halls, upset because she had been woken up so that she could look after a vagrant, as she put it. She came whipping around the corner in her nightgown like a mother with a mission.

"Let me see him," she said as she put her hands on Mr. Barrett's face, laying his head back. "What did you do to him?" asked Ms. Phosit.

"He's only been put to sleep, Mary," said Galen.

"What did you use to put him to sleep?" asked Ms. Phosit.

"How should I know? It was Cypress who did it," said Galen as he took another puff of his pipe.

"And I thought I told you to never smoke in my kitchen. Run along, and I'll find something that will fix him up right quick," said Mary

Galen lifted himself off the bench as Ms. Mary Phosit's arms waved him out through the swinging doors of the castle kitchen.

"I suppose that I will be headed off to bed then. I shall see you all in the morning. Good night," said Galen through the swinging kitchen doors.

"Yes, yes, good night, Gumly," shouted Mary as Galen sauntered off, puffing on his pipe through the halls to his bedchamber.

Mary let the two guards go to their chambers. She could tell that Talon was no threat to them,

"Besides," she told them, "he won't be awake till morning."

Ms. Phosit opened about five different cabinets with fifty different spices and herbs, each one for its own purpose and taste. She, however, was going to make Mr. Barrett a special concoction that would wake him out of any sleep, subtract that of the sleep caused by death. She was also going to give him something for the pain that he would feel in the morning. Four minutes later and she was force-feeding the concoction into his numb face. Talon began to wake as she gently shoved the soup into his mouth.

"There, there," she said to him in a soft and gentle tone.

"You'll be up and about in no time," she said as she lifted him to a sitting position. Talon moaned and groaned but was still not coherent enough to realize where he was.

Ms. Phosit went over to the cooling room to get a glass of milk. She brought it to him and began pouring it down his throat.

"This will help the herbs go down," she said as she looked at his face and smiled.

Talon was a man with a gentle face, blue-green eyes, and black hair. He was quite handsome too though he would never have the attitude that would inform him of it.

"We don't want to wake you up completely, just enough to get the pain from your head when you wake up in the morning," said Mary.

Talon was not in the condition to understand what she was telling him though.

Mary heard the door from the kitchen swing open slowly.

"Have you got it, Mary?" asked Cypress.

"Oh hello, dear, yes, I do think that he will be fine in the morning. However, he will need a place to sleep that is nearby because I won't be able to carry him."

"Help me move him to the living room. He can sleep on one of the sofas," said Cypress.

"We should give him a little more time though," Mary said as she looked at Cypress with questioning eyes.

Cypress and Mary sat down on the benches that surrounded the cutting table.

"So, who is he, Cypress?"

"He is the man that gave me a ride to the city."

Mary looked at Cypress as if she had imaginary glasses to look over.

"I know what you are thinking, Mary, but he doesn't know who I am. I gave him no information," said Cypress as she looked away so that Mary would not see the lie.

"So, what did you talk about when you were being driven to the city?"

"Oh, he went on and on about the things that he owned, I think he mentioned a house in Fable and the fact that he would be going back there once he was finished taking me to the mountain. I suspected that he wanted something else. I was curious," said Cypress with a guilty expression on her face.

"You know"—Mary paused for a moment with one eyebrow lifted—"I once met a man who stopped to give me a ride in a carriage. The sight was not a pretty one when everything was said and done. Do you remember James? I ended up marrying him." She paused again to let her words sink into the young Cypress. "I heard that there was quite the storm out tonight, how was it?"

"Oh, it was very beautiful. I came into it after I left the Ministry," said Cypress.

"I was going to watch it from the tower, but I fell asleep in my chair, waiting for James to come back from town. When I woke, there was a mighty ugly guard staring down at me as if I were something pitiful or something. It was quite startling," said Mary. They both giggled, which inadvertently caused Talon to whimper.

"I'm still not clear on the reason that he is here. You said that you gave him no information," said Mary.

"Yes, but he thinks that I unknowingly divulged some to him. Really, I think I did it so that I could see what he would have done if he had had any real motive. I think that he will be sorry that he ever met me. He seemed like he was quite naive. We should probably get him to the common room before he falls," said Cypress.

"Yes, we probably should," said Mary

Both of them grabbed hold of Talon and struggled to get him through the swinging doors that led to the common room. They gently laid him on the sofa that was facing the fire.

"Well, good night," said Mary as she shuffled off to her chamber.

Cypress looked down at the young man's face and bowed low to kiss him.

"Good night, beautiful, foolish man."

She ran her hands through his soft black hair and left him to sleep.

5   A LIE OR TRUTH

TALON OPENED HIS EYES and for a moment thought that he had been sleeping in his own bed in Fable. After looking around for just a short time, however, he was stunned to be in a place that he didn't recognize. What was even more stunning were the three little girls that huddled around his head, apparently waiting for him to wake.

"Good morning," said the oldest of the bunch.

"Good morning," said Talon.

"My name's Asp Maleen," said the oldest.

"And my name's Petunia Maleen," interrupted the second.

"It is very good to meet you," Talon said with a smirk on his face.

The youngest didn't say anything, however, she just giggled here and there. Talon looked around some more to see whether he could recognize where he was.

Perhaps I'm in my house in Fable, in a room I have not seen before. But then, what would explain the three children? He thought to himself.

The girls were still studying him as his eyes roamed about searching the room. Talon stopped looking for familiarities in the area and turned his head to look at the youngest.

"And who might you be?" he asked smiling gently. "Are you the youngest of the Maleen?" Talon asked as he tried to lift himself up.

The little girl stood there with her hand clenched to a small stuffed animal and said nothing.

"Oh her? she's not a Maleen. She's my cousin Jenny Bricks. Her mother and father are dead, and she was sent to live with us," said Asp, quite profoundly offended. "We're just visiting the castle this week. Soon we'll be going home."

Suddenly and quite unexpectedly, Jenny whipped herself around and started calling out to the room down the hall.

"Aunt Cypress, he's awake, he's awake, he's awake!" she chanted as she ran through the open doors to the other room.

"She's not really your aunt." Asp yelled.

The two other girls quickly followed their cousin.

The small girls all had the same color of hair, that of a bright red, however their eyes were much different from each other. Jenny had the deep blue-green eyes that were much like Cypress's. That was what had made her stand out to Talon the most. To Talon, they were beautiful and for a moment he felt as if he were part of an exceptionally large family though he didn't know whose family it was, but he was glad that Cypress was there to tell him what had happened to him. Though he had no children, he thought that he would like his children to look as the three little girls did. They were comforting to him.

Talon was still too tired to get up and out of the couch, and he didn't quite know why. He couldn't remember anything that happened the night before, past the point of seeing the strange man in the corner of the bar and was absolutely mystified by the conclusion that he knew nothing of his own whereabouts. He did, however, very much enjoy the architecture of the room in which he lay. He could tell that the building was incredibly old and that it was not of a conventional design. There were no supports where there should have been. The room seemed to have a different personality than that of any human design that he had seen in both his history classes and with his own eyes. The marvel was not enough though to take his mind off the present situation that he was in. When he realized that he didn't have enough strength to get up from the sofa, he reasoned that he had possibly been injured and that someone had taken him in so that he could regain his strength. He lifted the quilt off him so he could look at his legs. Everything looked intact. Finally, he gave a sigh and rested his hands on his chest as he clenched the quilt.

He could hear the footfalls of people coming near him, both adults and children. *Or were they simply going to pass by his room?* He thought to himself. Talon was really quite anxious to hear someone tell him what had happened and what he was doing in this strange place.

Jenny burst through the open door, running to the head of the sofa that Talon was laying on. Moments later her cousins entered the room. The three girls wanted to come and see what it was that Cypress was going to do to the strange man that had stayed the night. The three girls fidgeted in expectation as they stood near Talon. Cypress slowly entered the room in a graceful manner and kneeled to inspect him.

"How did you sleep?" Cypress asked unsympathetically.

Talon paid the question no mind.

"How did I get here?" asked Talon.

"I poisoned your drink and had you brought here,"

She smirked at him.

"Why on earth did you do that?"

He pushed away her hand from his face.

"Don't be alarmed. I had to make sure you were not a Ministry spy,"

She inspected his face further.

"What is a Ministry spy?" He asked.

"Never mind that. You're here now, and in no position to escape. You should have the sense to not even try such a foolish thing," Cypress said while pushing back Jenny as she moved in to see what Cypress was doing to Talon's face.

"What do you mean 'escape?'" He asked frantically.

"Well, you surely didn't think that I was going to allow you to run around like a free man with all that you had come to know about me. Good god, man, I thought you were intelligent. Besides, I think that it will be a good change to have another face here that I don't have a hard time looking at." She smiled. "A person my age would be good too. I'm sick of feeling like I am a child, or at least being treated like one."

"Well, isn't that perfectly selfish," said Talon under his breath, just enough for her to barely hear him.

"You shouldn't sulk, you know. It makes you look tired,"

She bandaged up a small cut that was probably given to him when he was shoved into the wheelbarrow.

"I am tired, but I have no intention of staying here on this couch so that you can dress me up." He tried to lift himself up.

"You will be up and about in just a few minutes, so lie here and rest. I will come and get you when your lunch is ready,"

She lovingly caressed his cheek and gently smiled. The affectionate gesture that she made toward him surprised him, so he did not protest. The three girls were still staring at him with childish intrigue.

"Come along, girls," said Cypress as she exited through the doorway.

All three girls saw the warmth that was shown by Cypress to the stranger, which in effect gave them a reason to believe that he was not a stranger at all, but that he was in fact to be treated as one of the family. In instantaneously coming to this conclusion, the girls all gave him a kiss on the cheek before they obeyed.

Every surge of pain through his head reminded Talon that he had been defeated. He was feeling quite inadequate even for his taste. He thought about the carriage ride and the storm and realized that he was not all that uncomfortable being taken care of by Cypress even though she was the cause of his temporary lapse of knowledge and his headache. He couldn't ignore her beauty. He found himself wondering why he was glad that he had been abducted and wondered if he would ever see his house in Fable again. He looked around the room once more to admire the artistic manner in which it was designed and found himself wishing that this was his home. *It is much more interesting.*

Talon could feel his strength coming back, so he pulled himself up into the sitting position. He could see a set of slippers on the floor next to the fireplace and realized that his shoes had been taken off. He had decided to sit down in one of the two lounge chairs in front of the fireplace and watch the fire. Talon was finally comfortable. He stared into the fire and daydreamed. His thoughts concentrated on the night he and Cypress rode in the carriage together. There was not a night that he had ever experienced that was as wonderfully artistic. It caused so many memories to spring up in his mind. He could smell the cinnamon from the pub. However, there suddenly was an unusual smell that was invading his vivid recollection of that night, which caused him to look for it in reality. Talon turned his head to look around for it when he noticed a rather tall old man with a pipe standing in the doorway, watching him intently. Talon was not startled, however; he had had enough surprises for the day. Talon could see that he was a man of wisdom. His long white beard and the way that he stood displayed a portion of that wisdom as old age often does. But there was more with Galen than met the eye. His long wine-colored outer cloak draped heavily around his once strong shoulders and reached low to the stone floor. He wore a white inner cloak which wrapped his waist and reached down to his boots.

"My name is Galen Alester Gumly. You say that you came from the city Fable?"

"Yes, my mother lives there, I also have a house in Fable. I was going back to spend the winter there."

"I once had a grandfather that lived there for quite some time," He said as he puffed gently on his pipe. "He was ninety-five when he died. I took it quite hard. You see, I loved him very much. He treated me much better than my father did, but I suppose that those times were not the best to raise a child in. What, with the Requiem running loose and all." Galen paused and took another puff on his pipe. "I could always tell when the pressures of the world were coming down on him. My father was never a good performer. It didn't help him when I would be disobedient at times either. My grandfather was always a good escape from reality. He would tell me about all his wonderful and quite dangerous adventures that he had when he was a young man. I, for a long time, wondered what it would be like on my own adventures. They aren't so glamorous when you are experiencing the sensation that your life is moments away from being snuffed out." He paused again to take another puff of his pipe.

Talon took the opportunity of silence to interrupt.

"Where am I?"

Galen raised one eyebrow to the question and answered,

"Safe, my boy, safe."

Talon was almost tired of listening to himself ask the question at this point, and it was now perfectly clear that he was not going to get a useful answer out of anyone. Just when he was about to spit out another question, he was interrupted by a purring sound that seemed to be coming from beneath his chair. Talon froze, then a large black panther came from beneath it. The panther forcefully and quite gently brushed against his legs and then playfully rolled onto its back and wiggled with its paws in the air much like a dog would do. Talon was terrified.

"I see you've already met Davina. She seems to like you," said Galen. "Cypress saved her from being eaten by some Fondland."

The panther had planted herself in front of the fireplace and was watching Galen take a puff of his pipe.

"Oh, she's quite harmless," said Galen.

Talon had a hard time believing it though.

"Noon meal is ready," Cypress said from the doorway.

"Oh, I didn't know that you were standing there," said Galen as he stretched his head to look at Cypress. "I suppose that we should be on our way to the dining room then," he roused himself from the chair. "C'mon then, Davina," said Galen to the panther lying down in front of the fireplace.

She quickly got up and followed Galen into the dining room. Talon got up to follow Galen also.

The dining room was exceptionally large. Candle chandeliers hung down from the marble ceiling and a long table sat in the center. There were four doors on both sides of the table. The room was full of people. There was not a chair that was not occupied excluding the one that was reserved for Talon, right beside Galen's. Everyone had already taken their places and were waiting for the meal.

Before Talon had a chance to sit down, Galen had taken hold of his empty glass and was tapping on it with a butter knife. Once everyone heard the ringing from the glass, they stopped talking and gave their undivided attention to Galen.

"I would like everyone to meet our newest member of the Order," Galen said with a loud voice. "Mr. Talon Barrett. He has come to us from the city of Fable. I think I speak for everyone when I say that we are all glad to meet a new member and that we all wish the best of days to you."

After Galen spoke, everyone clapped their hands together to welcome the new member of the Order.

Talon was confused but seeing that he had no option but to surrender to their hospitality, he reluctantly sat down in his seat next to Galen. There were six adult people sitting at the table. Cypress sat on the left side of Galen and occasionally smiled at Talon.

"I heard that you own a house in Fable, Mr. Barrett," said a man at the far end of the table.

"Yes, it is near my mother's. I was going there to visit her when I met Cypress on the road," said Talon as he cringed at the idea that he would probably never see her again.

When Talon said this, the room fell instantaneously quiet, and Mary having just walked in with the food platter almost tipped it to the floor.

"Do you mean that you are expected to be there?" asked the man with panic on his face.

"Yes, she was expecting me last night," said Talon.

The man now stood up angry as he shot a piercing look at Cypress.

"And when she finds out that you are not there, will she call the authorities to look for you?" the man asked in a sarcastic tone.

"I suppose that she would," said Talon, looking more perplexed than earlier.

"I will not stand for this, Galen," the man shouted after quickly turning his attention to Galen. "She has jeopardized all that we have worked for. Twenty years for nothing? You give her too much slack. What will happen when they come looking for the boy? Who knows how much evidence has been left?" the man shouted again.

"Now let's not get all heated up, James. I'm sure Cypress took all of the precautionary measures in bringing him here," said Galen as he raised his hand to gesture for James to settle down.

James was a man in his middle age and had grown up near a town in the Fondland. He never saw the wars that raged on during Galen's time, he was born just after the wars of man had ceased. He was a man with a large build, and was very tall, and there were many gray hairs that had begun to infiltrate his dark brown hair. He had green eyes that were piercing and bright to the onlooker, however he at many times displayed the inept ability to show a sense of stupidity, or a lack of sensitivity for the feelings of the others of the Order.

"She didn't take into account that his dear old mother would be looking for him, did she, Galen?" said James while frantically waving his hand in the air.

"I hadn't told her that I was going there to visit my mother. It didn't really occur to me that I would be abducted by a woman that I was giving a kind gesture to. I'm sorry," shouted Talon, now breathing hard and feeling a surge of anger toward the man that was attacking Cypress.

"Oh, this is fantastic. He could be a Ministry spy," shouted James.

"I will have order at my table," shouted Galen as he sprang to his feet.

James stopped breathing for a moment and sat down as if he had been scolded by his father. Mary was still standing there, shaking with the platter of food in her hand.

"This is not at all an insurmountable problem to solve," said Galen in a gentle voice as he sat himself back into his chair. "I believe that we have resolved more difficult mysteries in our time,"

Mary began to pass the food around.

"Let's not make this an unpleasant meal," said Galen as he pulled out his pipe to take a puff.

Mary gently slapped his hand as she walked to the kitchen to get the rest of their meal.

"I thought I told you not to smoke in here," she said while leaving the room.

"Oh yes, quite right, I'm sorry, Mary," said Galen as he shamefully shoved the pipe back into his cloak. Cypress knew that she would not have to defend herself around Galen but was pleasantly surprised to see Talon come to her aid.

The food looked very tasty, or at least tasty enough to make Talon's mouth water. He was feeling very hungry because of missing his dinner from the night before and his breakfast from that morning. He was, however, not in the mood to eat very much with such hostilities at the table. James remained absolutely quiet the whole time, and he ate with a scowl on his face. Talon didn't have to eat very much though because of all the questions he was being asked by Mr. Potts, Ms. McFadden, Ms. Alester, Mr. Dolan, and Ms. Foster. They were a motley crew but there was something that they all had in common, and that was the truth that had been revealed to them. They believed in that truth and it was that which brought them together though they would have many disagreements at times, and it was that truth that they knew very well. They were not amateurs, but skilled men and women that had dedicated themselves over an exceedingly long period of time to get to the point that they were in now. Mary was the only one that believed; however, she was lazy in her practice.

Mr. Potts was tall, skinny, and funny looking. He always wore a different color of hair for that particular week of activity because he had lost all of his natural hair, and he often mumbled to himself in deep thought about philosophy and things such as these.

Ms. McFadden was a woman who wanted no man; she would not tolerate their foolishness. She had the look of an old widow though she had never had a husband, with her black dress and her black hair raised in an ungodly sized bun that rested on the top of her head.

Ms. Alester, Mr. Dolan, and Ms. Foster were related by marriage and they had all at one time lived in a large castle in Fable, however they had long since lost their families to the wars that had raged on, and because their castle had been taken as the property of the Ministry for a distribution center of their troops. They were confronted by Galen and they joined the Order out of homelessness. They could not, however, forget the truth that was given them, and they were neither stupid nor lazy to their cause. They were all exactly the same age and they all had the same hair and eye color. Galen did think that it was quite strange the first time that he had seen them, but he was now used to it, and in their older years he was able to tell them apart. They had black hair and blue eyes, were thirty-five, and they were attractive. They were brave and they loved to gamble.

Mary didn't ask very many questions though; she knew that she would get the answers to her questions from Cypress. *Cypress will tell the juicy stuff once she is good and ready*, she thought to herself while taking another sip of tea.

"So, were you born in Fable?" asked one.

"Did you like it there?" asked another.

"Do you have any brothers or sisters?" asked Mr. Dolan.

"No, I'm an only child," said Talon with a bored expression on his face.

"What's this Order you were talking about, Galen?" asked Talon. The question silenced the room. "I mean, what is all of the hiding about? What are you trying to accomplish?"

"The Order is a noble organization that seeks to separate the truth from the lie," said Galen.

"We have been keeping the peace for twelve generations," said James with a rather prideful tone.

"But the Ministry already accomplishes that, and they don't have to go into hiding," said Talon with a confused look.

"The Ministry has done nothing. They are a smoke screen of lies organized to mislead the masses into thinking that there will not be another war," said Cypress. "They have allowed humanity to be threatened by extinction because of their obscuring certain truths about our ancestral history. They do not teach people the ways of those ancestors, and they try to eradicate any knowledge of their existence. We are the peacekeepers. We are the ones that would rather accomplish truth and hide from the world than to stretch out our hands over the crowds from the towers while spewing lies that are self-destructive and cowardly. The Ministry does not have peace treaties with our vicious neighboring lands. The Ministry does not post guards other than the guards that are placed in the confines of their own castle walls," She said with an aggravated expression on her face.

"I don't understand. What would they have to gain by lying to us? It doesn't make any sense," said Talon.

"If you doubt me, why don't you try to take another sip from your drink," she smiled.

"Take a sip from my drink, what does drinking have to do with anything?"

"Just try it."

Talon was more confused than he had ever been in his life. Seeing, however, that not everything was what it seemed, he would entertain the notion even though he didn't know why the suggestion was implied. Talon looked at the crystal glass that he had been drinking from for the past few minutes. This time he was looking for something extraordinary in it. *Will it be the glass or the drink that would deceive me this time?* He thought to himself. He had already suffered defeat from the drink and yet was not deprived of curiosity enough to not take another sip of it. He slowly inched his hand toward the glass as if it were going to reach out and bite him. Everyone in the room was without interruption. Eyes intently fixed on the glass. Talon mustered up the courage and quickly grabbed hold of it. To his surprise, nothing extraordinary happened. He then began to attempt to raise the glass to his mouth. The glass did nothing. He tried and tried but was unsuccessful. Finally, he attempted to lift the glass with so much force that his hand slipped from it. With as much force that he used the crystal should have shattered. His hand jetted toward the chandelier as he tried to keep himself from falling backward out of his chair. Talon looked at Cypress in complete confusion.

"No bother, let me do it for you," she said as she lifted her hand from beneath the table. The glass began to float perfectly still in the air and up to his mouth. Talon, in absolute amazement, found himself impulsively reaching for the glass to take a drink.

"As I stated before, there is knowledge that you do not even know about your own race, and it's the Ministry that is keeping it from you," Cypress said as she smiled and relinquished the glass.

He didn't know what to say to her. He felt ashamed to have even questioned her.

"There are many things that you do not know about yourself, and that is why we are here to take you on a path of truth, a path of knowledge," said Galen. "What was your life before you came to this place? Was it more interesting, more thrilling than what you just experienced in this room?"

Talon said nothing. He was still in shock from Cypress's amazing display of power. Galen was looking into his eyes now, searching for the answer to his question.

"It is as I thought," said Galen as he turned his attention away from Talon. "Your life was boring, without meaning. You were a man deprived of passion, and before this point, you were a man destined to live out his days in a dreary existence, and after some time, you or your children would be subject to the powers of a world that you had no knowledge of," Galen scrolled his eyes across the whole room, reminding everyone of their lives before the Order. "When Cypress speaks about the war that is to come, she is not talking about the Requiem, or the Colossus. These are docile foes that we have been able to control for quite some time now. It is the growing threat that every kingdom on our Earth today is terrified of, so much so, that they would rather live in a dream world, a fantasy world that has no danger, no problems. They would rather become slaves. It is quite sad. But you have learned enough for now, we must leave something for him to learn tomorrow."

Everyone laughed at the small joke.

"I suppose that you will have to make some time to visit your mother, young man, however, for now she will have to be satisfied with a letter. Make sure you put in it that you're alright and that you have just been delayed in your visit, I'm sure that she will be worrying about you," he continued as he patted Talon on the shoulder.

"So how was the meal?" asked Mary.

"Oh, very good, yes, yes, very fine," said most everyone in the room as Mary began to collect the dirty plates.

"I especially enjoyed the peas," said Galen as Mary passed by him on the way to the kitchen.

Cypress stood up out of her chair and gestured for Talon to follow her.

"It was very good to meet you, Mr. Gumly," said Talon as he got up to follow Cypress.

"I think that we will become very good friends, my boy," said Galen as he pulled out his pipe and put it into his mouth, "very good, friends indeed."

Cypress was down the hall waiting for Talon when he caught up with her.

"I think that we should take a walk in the gardens, yes?" she asked Talon as she grabbed hold of his hand gently.

"I suppose that wouldn't do any harm."

Both of them walked together to the gardens, which were near the east wing of the castle. There were very tall windows on each side of the entrance to the castle from the gardens, and before they reached the doors, Talon broke hands with Cypress to open the door for her. She smiled politely as they entered the gardens together.

"It seems that I am out of my element," said Talon as he joined hands with her again.

"You won't be for long," she looked up into the sky. "We have learned to become a part of our environment, not a partaker of it," she scrolled her eyes around the garden campus. "Do you see those trees over there?" she pointed to the small house up in these two exceptionally large trees that had a rope bridge which connected the two. "The house that was constructed there was constructed to keep the trees from falling down. It acts as a support not simply for the trees but also for the groundskeeper. We have learned to work together with this planet so that there can be an interchange of dependency. We did not say, 'Oh, those trees are too big and too old. Tear them down and put a house there.' We used the opportunity to honor the trees while at the same time honoring ourselves."

Talon looked at her and smiled.

"Where do you get your powers from?" asked Talon.

"The same source that any human gets his or her powers from," she stared into the bright blue sky and watched the clouds slowly passing by.

"What do you mean any human?"

"Well, every human possesses that power. They're just not taught how to use it," she turned her attention to Talon and smiled. "Everything in the universe has a certain frequency of energetic vibration. It goes past the subatomic level. That includes the trees, the wind, the energy that is expelled by our mind to our extremities, and the power that is focused through our mind. We can learn to control objects, animals, gasses at that level because we are not a part of this particular universe. We as humans work on a different universal frequency, thus making it possible to manipulate matter in ways that we would ordinarily not be able to in the universe that we are indigenous to."

"I don't think that I quite understand."

"What I am simply trying to say is that in time, you will also have this power and quite possibly be better at using it than me."

"Why do you think that I will be more skilled than you?"

"You have a better imagination than I," she smiled, "Remember, not all people are alike. Some are more skilled at certain things, like art or reading or having compassion or love for one another. This is no different a subject. Whatever the case, a person must have an incredibly good imagination. It is the window to the mind."

The two had reached the other end of the garden and were beginning to circle the grounds.

"Where is this place?" asked Talon.

"That is a question that I cannot tell you just yet. But in the meantime, you can trust me and enjoy your stay here. Soon you will have to go back to the real world to see your mother. I want to make sure that you will come back to us before we let you go. Do you want to live a lie, Talon? Do you want to be subject to an imminent death, or do you want to have a life here with nothing surrounding you but truth?" She paused for a moment to let the questions set in. "Some wouldn't have such an easy time choosing as it will be for you. Some people love the lie and don't want to change their way of life simply because they are too afraid or indolent."

Cypress had been leading Talon to the two trees she had mentioned earlier.

"I want you to meet another friend of mine. He has been like a grandfather to me. I love him very much. His name is Bristle Wax Steward. He helped raise me when I was a child. He is the groundskeeper," she said as they slowly closed in on the house in the tree.

The tree house had a wooden staircase that led up to it. There were four and a half levels, and the house had tall wooden beams that were supporting it. Talon could see the smoke from the chimney as they approached the house's steps. There was a bell at the bottom of the staircase and a little sign that read,

"Please ring before entering."

Cypress took the first step as she rang the bell.

"By the way, might I ask you what you did with my cane?" asked Talon as they were going up the steps.

"Good day, good day," the old man called out to them from the entrance to the house all the way at the first floor. Not a long time, and yet not a short time either and they had climbed the steps leading up to the door. "I see you've brought me a new friend, Cypress," he said with an intense smile. "Come, come, come," said Bristle, waving for them to come in.

Bristle was an old man that was very strong in all that he applied himself to. His hair was white, and he was a short man with a kind face. His eyes were a dark blue and his body frail, however he could move very well. He worked hard and he saw much of the good fruits of his labor. Now that there was no war to be fought at this time, Bristle had dedicated himself to the working of his hands. He was the founder of the Order through his research in archeology. When he came upon the remnants of an old settlement, he linked the history to their ancestors and learned some of their secrets that they had taught in their time. He did further research and was led to the entrance of Pastel. It was from there that Bristle had rebuilt the Order, which had once been the peacekeeper of old. Since then, he had accumulated much knowledge on their ancestors and how they lived. Galen was the first of his order and there were many that had come after him, however there were several that had been lost to the fighting that had occurred against the Ministry. Bristle now kept mostly to himself and to his studies, out of everyone else's business. Once though he had helped raise a girl, now women, who appreciated him very much, and that was a task that he never neglected. Cypress always demanded much of Bristle's time, but he was happy to spend that precious time with her.

Talon by this time was very much tired of meeting new friends.

"Now let me have a look at him," said Bristle as he put his hands to Talon's face to inspect him closely. "It seems you've caught yourself a fine one, Nelly," he said, still bothering Talon's face.

"Nelly?" asked Talon without getting a response to his question.

"So, to what do I owe the pleasure of this visit? The ground's not looking tip-top shape this year, eh," Bristle said with a smirk on his face.

Talon and Cypress sat on a large couch that lay directly in front of the fire.

"I just wanted you to meet my friend and maybe teach him a thing or two," said Cypress with a smile.

"Yes, yes, yes, I can do that," said Bristle as he rolled himself in his office chair over to Talon. Bristle was sitting directly in front of Talon when he locked the wooden wheels so that the chair wouldn't slide around as they talked.

"So where have you come from, my boy?" asked Bristle with an interested look. But before Talon could answer, "Never mind that," Bristle blurted out quickly. "If I had judged anyone by what had happened to them in the past, I suppose that there would not be an Order, would there?" he said, still looking contemplated. "Why have you come to us is a better question, wouldn't you say, boy?"

"To tell you the truth, I don't really know," said Talon, sort of perplexed.

"Well, I suppose that that is as good as any answer. Besides, I would be worried if you knew. It would mean that we weren't doing our job then, wouldn't it, Nelly?" Bristle said with a pleased tone of voice. "I want to show you something, boy. Come look at this," he said, as he stood up out of his chair and walked to another room in the back of the house. Talon followed, wondering what was going to happen to him next.

"Come, come, come," said Bristle as he turned on the light to his very full literature room. He pulled one of the smallest books off the shelf. "This is the oldest book that I have in my library," said Bristle as he opened it slowly.

He pulled out a small sheet of paper that had been folded over many times. Bristle took the parchment and gently opened it. The parchment was so big that once he had finished opening it, it covered the whole table that sat in the middle of the room.

"Now look here," said Bristle as he brushed his finger across the parchment. "Do you see all of these lines?"

"Yes, but what do they mean?" asked Talon, completely fascinated by the parchment.

"Is it a map?"

Bristle was occupied with pulling an old clock off the wall.

"It will all become clearer to you in just a moment," he began to meticulously take apart the clock. He laid parts of the clock on to the table in an orderly fashion.

"Take a look at the parts of the clock," said Bristle as he stepped back to let Talon take a look. "What do you see in the parts of the clock? Do you see a pattern?"

Talon kneeled to examine the gears and complex parts of the inner workings of the clock.

"There are very small etched lines that are not usually present in a clock," he said, looking at one of the larger gears from the clock on the wall.

"Very, very good. How did you know that there was not supposed to be any markings there?" Bristle was quite amazed.

"My grandfather was a watchmaker. I used to watch him put the little rubies and diamonds inside of them when I was a little boy."

"That is absolutely fabulous," said Bristle with a very satisfied expression.

"Now do you see anything similar to the parchment from these gear sizes and markings?" He asked, excited.

"I don't think—" Talon paused for a moment and then realized a pattern in the paper on the table. "Wait, the lines are the same," said Talon, perplexed and filled with more questions than he could have imagined.

"If you'll notice, this little bunch of ink dots here in this corner, right here," he ran his finger across the folds of the paper to the left-hand corner. "This is our galaxy. This is where we exist, and the rest of the parchment is a portion of the vast universe," Bristle explained and then paused to let the overwhelming explanation set in. "And these lines, as you so most efficiently pointed out, are contour rotations of the space-time continuum. This clock is only one of many that were designed by your grandfather if I'm not mistaken."

"My grandfather?"

"Well yes. You did say you were a Barrett, didn't you?" said the old man somewhat surprised.

"As a matter of fact, I didn't, not to you at least," he said snappishly, feeling quite invaded.

"Well, I think Nelly said it enough times for me to remember," said Bristle, hoping to defuse the apparently distraught Talon. "As you can see here, the timeline distortion converges at this point," Bristle said quickly to take Talon's mind off the invasion of his family's history. "What do you think that denotes?"

Talon looked intently at the small dots of ink that represented the universe that was a home to Earth.

"I suppose that it would mean that at one time or another, there is, or was, a conversion distortion of the space-time continuum."

"And what do you think would be the effects of such a time distortion?" asked Bristle with expectation in his eyes.

"Well, it's possible that there would be severe gravimetric distortions in the atmosphere that could cause alternative realities to overlap and occupy the same space and time," Talon was surprised by his own words.

"And what would you say if I told you that there were only two universes that exist in our galaxy and that, being a human, you do not belong in this space and time, the one that you are standing in now?"

"I would say that you've gone yuppie. But considering the circumstances and the proof that you have given, I would have to say it's a good start at me believing you."

Cypress was standing in the doorway of the library, listening to Bristle and Talon talking. She was smiling and remembering the time when Bristle had explained all of this to her when she was just a little child. It was the most exciting memory from her childhood.

"This clock was designed to track the orbital pattern of time which is portrayed on this map. It tells us that there will soon be a converging of the parallel universes very soon now," explained Bristle. There is nothing that we can do to stop it, and in just a small matter of years, there will be a global war," he laid his hand on Talon's shoulder.

"Why will there be a war?" asked Talon.

"There will be a war as there has always been. The peace that we are experiencing is a precursor to that reality. The Requiem and the Colossus are preparing for the worst, and we must also."

Bristle folded the parchment together again and placed it back into the book. He took the parts of the clock and placed them in the wood casing and put the clock back onto the wall as Talon watched him intently.

"You're going to have to sit down for this one, my boy," said Bristle as he directed him back into the living room. Talon sat on the large old couch, and Bristle seated himself in his wooden office chair.

"As I said earlier, we humans do not originally come from this universal time. The world that we lived in was a horrible world. There were creatures that were so dangerous and what would seem to us today to be strange and uncanny beings. In the past, we have warded off the schemes of the creatures, and there are rules of war. But it has been so long that we have rejected our ways and will be completely unprepared for the fight that we will be forced to endure in the near future. As humans, we knew that we could not survive in such a dangerous environment, so instead of turning to our physical strength, something that was useless in a world like that, we turned to the knowledge that we had accumulated over the millennia of time. When the converging of the parallel universes began, we realized that there was a way to stay in this universe and not return to the universe that we originated from. We knew that it would be our only way to survive. Over the millennia, we have survived this way. However, the universe does not change, and when it is time for us to live in unison with the other universe, it will mean war, a war that we cannot escape from. We have, however, had the advantage for many thousands of years because we had learned to use the powers that were given to us by this universe. The parallels do not have that advantage. They have limited knowledge and are not efficient. Some races have no abilities at all. However, they are still extremely dangerous. Now that humans are oblivious to having the Legacy here though, we will be defenseless. We will be like cattle to them, and when they find out that we are in this condition, they will pay no mind to the laws of war, and there will be pandemonium."

Bristle turned toward Cypress and smiled.

"Yes, I do believe that you have caught a fine specimen, Nelly," said Bristle as he returned his attention to Talon. "I do say though, I must get back to the work that I was so happy to be distracted from. It was very good to meet you, my boy." He unlocked the wooden wheels on his chair and rolled himself over to his desk. "It was a very enjoyable visit. Do come again sometime."

Cypress gently grabbed hold of Talon's arm and gestured for him to get up and leave with her. Talon raised himself from the couch and said,

"It was very good to meet you as well, Mr. Steward."

Then Talon followed Cypress out of the house and on to the porch.

"Why don't you warn me when you think I'm going to have to learn something new?" asked Talon as he and Cypress slowly walked down the wooden steps of the tree house.

"If I had warned you, would it have been so exciting to you?" She locked her arm gently in Talon's. Talon said nothing.

"And besides, there is not much that can prepare someone for the knowledge that Bristle is always giving," said Cypress with a smile.

6 A SHADOW IN THE DARK

TALON AND CYPRESS walked back through the garden and up to the tower where Talon would be sleeping for the night. The sun was beginning to set, and they watched the occurrence together.

"Isn't it wonderful how there can be such beauty after such destruction?" asked Cypress.

"What do you mean?"

"The storm and how after it, the next day there is so much calm and beauty,"

"Oh yes, it is wonderful,"

Talon wasn't thinking about the storm or the sunset though. He was the kind of person that always fretted when he had to stay in class for too long or that sort of thing. He had never encountered such a phenomenal scope of problems as those that were revealed to him at Bristle's, and he didn't know if he would be able to cope with them. He could feel the cool wind rushing through the window of the tower and felt fear come over him. His world as he knew it was at an end. This wasn't some sort of trick; it was really going to happen. All the evidence was there in the little house in the trees, and the amazing demonstration of power by Cypress. Talon was not the sort to cry, and yet he found himself surprised by the ice-cold touch of a tear running down his cheek. Before he could turn away to hide his feelings though, Cypress's hand was at his face to wipe away the tear.

"Thank you," said Talon as he turned to look at Cypress.

"For what?" asked Cypress very empathetically as she repeatedly stroked his cheek with her thumb and gazed into his eyes.

"Thank you for saving my life," he seemed to look straight into her heart.

"You're very welcome," she said passionately as she turned her attention back to the failing light of the sun. "I was afraid at first too, but you will learn to be more courageous than I ever will."

The sun had gone down, and the stars and moon were coming out into the night sky. Talon could see the moonlight shining down on Cypress's face. *The moonlight makes her look even more beautiful,* he thought to himself. There had never been a woman that had treated Talon this way. For once, someone was returning the same kindness that he had shown with a much greater magnitude. For a moment, he felt as if he were in some kind of heaven.

"Yes, the calm after the storm is quite pleasant," Talon said as he turned his attention from Cypress to the night sky.

"Would you like to have some tea before you go to bed tonight?"

"Oh yes, that would be very kind of you."

"I'll have Mary come bring you some before you go to sleep tonight. Something that will help you to rest," she laid her hand on his shoulder.

"You have had a hard day. Why don't you come to the living room and keep me company until you get tired enough to sleep?" asked Cypress as she gently pulled at his black hair. "I promise to give you your cane back," she said, trying to convince him.

"I suppose I could manage to stay awake, considering that I spent half of the day sleeping," he said with a smile.

"I had your luggage brought up to your room. I think that they put it in the closet, so you can unpack your things later if you like," she said, smiling at the thought of the trouble that she had put him through the night before. "So, when you're ready, you can make yourself at home. I'm going down to the common room to visit with the others. I really would like it if you came down with me and got to know my family a little better," she tugged on his arm trying to get him to come with her.

Before he could answer her, he was startled by Davina pressing her head against his legs. "Ah," he shouted, looking down at the exceptionally large panther nudging him.

"Why does she do that?" asked Talon as he laughed and followed Cypress down the steps of the tower.

Talon could hear laughter coming from the living room as they approached. As they entered, Talon could see James and Galen playing chess near the fire. Mr. Potts, Ms. McFadden, Ms. Alester, Mr. Dolan, and Ms. Foster were playing cards on a table that they had temporarily set up for the night.

"Ah, good to see you two are still up and around," said Mary as she pulled up a chair to play cards with the others. James took a quick glance over at Talon and Cypress and reached down to make a move. Galen quickly grabbed Talon's cane to hit James's hand.

"It's my turn, old fool," said Galen as he turned his attention back to the pieces on the board.

"Well, if you wouldn't take so long, I might remember it," said James as he took another quick look at Talon and Cypress entering the room.

"You would think that with all the time that I have given you, you would remember," he mumbled with his hand resting on his chin.

Galen hadn't realized that Talon and Cypress had entered the room until they walked up to him. He was too concerned about the game, only because he was winning though.

"I see you are already putting my cane to good use," said Talon as he smiled. Galen looked up and realized who it was.

"Oh, my boy, come sit here, sit beside me and help me destroy James," said Galen as he reached up to grab hold of Talon. Talon and Cypress sat on the brick of the fireplace and watched the two men go at it.

"You can hit him with this if he tries to cheat," said Galen quite seriously. "I've already caught him twice."

Talon looked at Cypress and smiled as Galen forced the cane into Talon's hand.

James sneered at Galen at the notion that he was a cheater but said nothing.

"Don't forget, boy, you need to write that letter to your mother tonight," said Galen, taking his attention off the game for just a moment.

"Ah yes, it had slipped my mind," said Talon, remembering the conversation at the lunch table.

"I will get him what he needs," said Cypress as she got up from the fireplace.

"There is a place over there next to the window for you to write," said Galen as he pointed to the writing desk against the wall just beneath the window. Talon was getting up when he saw James go for another try. Talon quickly made good use of his cane.

"Ah!" said James as the bud of the cane tapped his hand.

"That'll teach him to cheat, won't it boy?" said Galen as he finally made his move.

"Yes, sir, it will," said Talon as he headed over to the desk with a grin.

"I was only anticipating!" said James quickly in his defense.

"Lies won't help you now," said Galen.

Talon stood his cane against the writing table and sat down.

"You will be there to see her tomorrow," said Galen as Cypress walked over to Talon to give him paper and a quill.

Cypress put a chair next to the table so that she could be next to Talon. Mary had gotten up to get Cypress some tea, and the others were going about their game, oblivious to their surroundings. Every now and then, one of them would shout out an "Aha" or an "Eat that for dinner." However, it did not distract Talon. He had learned to ignore sounds when studying or writing. However, it seemed to Talon that Cypress was giving him another demonstration because he was unable to write anything. The quill just lay there in his hand, resting on the paper in anticipation of a glimmer of educated thought to be transferred through it. But it continued to do nothing, nonetheless.

"What shall I say?" asked Talon, turning his attention to Cypress for guidance.

"Just say that you have been delayed for some time and that you will be there on Thursday. Reassure her that you are all right and that you will be there in the afternoon," said Cypress.

"All right, that seems good enough," he began to write the words on the paper.

Dear Ms. Barrett,

Mother, it is Talon, and I have been delayed for some time.

I am in good health and will be arriving in Fable on Thursday afternoon.

Hoping you are well.

Your loving son,

Talon Barrett

"That wasn't so bad, was it?" said Cypress as she took another sip from her tea.

"Glad I had your help," he said with a smile.

Cypress quickly put down her tea to seal Talon's letter.

"Where shall we send it?" asked Cypress as she melted the tip of a red candle.

"To 1926 Emerald Place, Fable Stone," said Talon as he pressed the hot wax with his seal embossed ring.

"Haven't you finished over there yet?" shouted Galen with a smile.

"Yes, we are quite finished," said Talon as he got up.

Talon walked over to James, who was unaware that Talon was addressing him, and gave James the letter.

"It is hard for any sane man to want to go back to a life of lies, you should understand that, shouldn't you, my friend?" said Talon as he gently lay the letter on James's lap.

Cypress was still sitting by the desk, drinking her tea. Davina was at her feet, purring.

"Checkmate!" shouted Galen as he made the final move on the board.

Talon was walking back to the table where Cypress sat so that he could keep her company. Mary walked up to Talon with a cup of tea in her hand.

"Would you like some tea, Talon?" she asked politely.

"Yes, thank you," he reached for the cup and plate.

"Cypress tells me that you were kind enough to give her a ride to the city. That was very gentlemanly of you," she said, smiling.

Davina had migrated over to Talon's feet and was gently pawing at his legs. Talon paid it no mind though; he was used to her unexpected presence. Besides, he always did like large cats; he had just not seen one so close before.

"It was raining quite hard, and I could not let her stay in the storm with nothing to shelter her. I think that she would have done the same, stranger or not," he took a sip of his tea.

"Nonetheless, it was a very kind gesture, and I think we all appreciated it," still smiling.

Galen had called one of the guards.

"Come here and take this letter to be sent," he ordered the young man.

The guard took the letter from James's hand and was off to have it sent.

Talon was just finishing his tea when he said,

"I think I'm going to turn in for the night."

He looked at Cypress as he got up from the desk and smiled. As he did, he took hold of her hand and gently kissed it.

"Good night," he let go of her hand. "And good night to you as well," he said while bending down to pet Davina with a smirk. She just purred on and on and pushed her head against his legs with more force than usual, acknowledging that she knew that her new favorite friend was addressing her.

"Good night," said Cypress as she took another sip of her tea. Talon headed up to his room for the night.

The next morning, Talon awoke from the light of the rising sun. He had forgotten to pull the drapes closed before he went to sleep.

"I needed to get up early," said Talon as he yawned and stretched his arms.

It was a beautiful morning, and Talon had felt more rested than he had in an awfully long time. He was grateful that his kindness had finally accomplished something good in his life, and he was going to enjoy every bit of it. He got up from his bed, looked at the sunrise for a short time, and then went to the wardrobe to get dressed. When he exited the tower room, there were two guards at the entrance. Talon was putting on his coat when he noticed them lingering in the hall.

"Are you ready to disembark?" asked the guard on his right.

"Yes, I am quite ready," said Talon.

"We have secured your carriage, and it is waiting. Please come with us, sir," said the guard on the left.

"Right then, let's get a move on," said Talon as he buttoned up his coat.

The men led him along stairs that turned from stone to marble and then to granite. When they had reached the top of the staircase, they emerged from a stone face to a courtyard. There were walls and a gate that surrounded the courtyard. The large gate led to a road that spiraled down the mountain of Pastel and into the city.

The carriage sat there waiting for him. One of the attendants ran to unfold the small set of steps connected to the carriage, and Talon began to get in. To his surprise, he noticed Cypress in the side seat.

"Come to keep track of me?" asked Talon as he entered the carriage.

"Yes," she smiled.

"Well, it is good to know that you're intelligent."

"I thought that I might like to meet your mother," she tugged on her velvet glove. "What is she like?"

"I don't think that she would like you," he looked at her truthfully.

"Why do you say that?" she said, stunned by the thought of someone not liking her.

"I just know my mother, and she is very particular about the people that she chooses to drink tea with. She is quite stiff with anyone other than me. I think that it would be more though that you would not like her," said Talon.

"Hmm, I see, well I'm not here on a visit, you make sure that she knows that before I get to her door," she said, feeling perturbed.

The ride down the mountain was pleasant to Talon, and he enjoyed the company of Cypress. He, however, dreaded the visit to his mother's and the reason that he was being forced to report to her. Talon knew that the presence of Cypress would be disruptive and enjoyed the thought of seeing his mother losing control of his life. It was not that his mother would dislike

Cypress as a person. It was what she represented that would probably drive his mother mad.

The carriage strolled down the mountain and into the city.

"We are going to need to take the road through the forest," said Talon. "Or would you rather go around it?"

"I don't see any reason why we would need to go around. We'll be fine if we go through the forest. So, is she going to attack me when I walk into her house?" asked Cypress sarcastically.

"No, but I wouldn't be surprised if she told one of her servants to do so," he said, with a smile. "You'll be fine. She just won't be very pleasant."

"I fail to see the reason that she would be so hostile to me. Is it the way that I am dressed?" she picked at her dress.

"I don't suppose that that would be an issue unless you were dressed in rags. Besides, you look beautiful."

The carriage had now left the gate of Pastel and the sign of Welcome in three different languages. The carriage turned and took the path that led them across the river and through the Ministry forest and across the mountains of Myth. They could see the valley of Paradoxtom as the carriage approached the city gates of Fable, a large city. A wall surrounded it to keep invaders from entering. The city was constructed completely of white stone and was a marvel to look at. You did not own a house in the city and not be known for it. It was one of the richest cities in the land, and you had to be so to gain any approval. Talon only had to say his name at the gate, and he was welcomed with fear and respect. The gate guards did not dare to ask who it was in the carriage with him, and they did not dare to look. Talon simply held out his hand from the window, and the guard kissed the ring in respect.

Everything in the city was white. White chairs, white tables, white carriages, and white streets. The only things that were not white were the clothes on the people that eloquently pranced on the stone streets. The signs were white with black lettering, and the shops were clean and neat. Cypress couldn't remember ever being in the city of Fable. She disliked the look of it. Violins and fancy balls, they were just not her taste. The diplomacy of it all disgusted her, but she didn't make any showing of her distaste for the city. She kept telling herself that she would be on her best behavior. *I have dressed the part at least*, she thought to herself.

"I think you were right," Cypress said to Talon as she shrank back from the window. "These people frighten me," she looked at Talon with a confused look on her face. "They don't seem real, like they were manufactured in a doll store. It's quite uncanny," she said with her eyes fixed on the people walking by.

"They certainly are not harmless."

The carriage passed through the inner part of the city and was heading toward the more prestigious parts still inside the confines of the city walls. They rode up to an exceptionally large house that had a garden and a water fountain that surrounded it. Great pillars marked the entrance to the house, which could be seen from afar. The carriage rode through the gardens and across the court to the entrance. There were two large statues that sat at the base of the pillars leading to the entrance of the house: one, a horse, and the other, a tiger. Cypress was staring at the statue of the tiger when the carriage stopped. Two of the house aides came out to greet Talon and Cypress as they exited the carriage.

"The mistress would like very much to see that you are in good health and would like to invite you to an afternoon meal in the gardens," said one of the aides while taking a bow. The other was busy taking the luggage from the top of the carriage.

"Yes, I would like that very much," said Talon as he bowed in response.

"The mistress would also like to know how long you are planning to stay," said the aide as he walked over to escort Cypress.

"It won't be a long visit, I trust. Only in answer to the mistress's ordinance," said Talon.

"I do see and would the mistress's son like separate accommodations for the madam accompanying him?" asked the aide.

"No! That will be all. I can find the madam to her quarters, thank you," said Talon, quite perturbed by the term "the mistress's son."

"The madam Yayls will be accompanying me to the mistress's invitation," said Talon to his aide. "Please inform the mistress of my decision. Thank you."

The two aides led Talon and Cypress to the guest room. Talon did not unpack the luggage. He laid it in the corner next to the bed and ordered the aides to leave the room. The two men took bows and respectfully left the room to wait outside.

"I do not want to stay the night, Cypress," said Talon the moment he heard the doors to the room close.

"Why not?" she asked with a confused look. "I thought that you wanted to see your mother."

"My mother is not the same person that she was when I was a child. In my opinion, she has allowed herself to be consumed by the world around her. I am simply a commodity. Something of value, but not of very much, not very much without certain attachments, that is."

"I don't understand," She looked concerned.

"You will see. I have a sneaky suspicion that she is up to something. I'm glad that you came with me. It will throw her off the tracks for a little bit. I have half a mind to enjoy watching her face contort when she finds out that I have invited you to the setting. She doesn't like it when she doesn't have complete control of a situation."

"Why have you come here then?"

"I don't know really. I probably shouldn't have responded to her summons though. So, I would like to make this visit short and sweet, which, however, is a very difficult thing to accomplish. It is nearly noon," he glanced at the clock on the wall. "We should get moving."

Talon opened the large doors to the room.

"Are you ready to be introduced?" asked the aide as the room doors were being opened.

"Yes, we are ready to be introduced," said Talon in response.

"Very good then," said the aide.

The walk through the hall was a lonely one for Talon. He could hear nothing but the stiff sound of their feet clashing against the white marble floor; and Talon, in his loneliness, remembered the only other time in which he walked to the gardens from a hallway with Cypress. He found himself imagining that he was walking to the gardens in the mountain of Pastel. The steps were too loud and consistent though, and he couldn't keep his concentration on that day. This frustrated him, making him even more determined to leave sooner than expected.

"I want you to walk in front of me when we reach the entrance to the garden," Talon said to Cypress, whispering.

"What for?" she whispered back at him.

"Just trust me and don't ask any questions."

Cypress did not think Talon to have a mischievous side, so she quickly walked ahead of him, thinking that it was some kind of custom. She could see Talon's mother and company sitting in white wooden chairs, talking over a white wooden table in the middle of the garden.

"Ms. Cypress Yayls!" announced the aide in a very loud voice.

"And Mr. Talon Barrett," announced the other.

Talon knew that the fact that he was not announced first would confuse his mother all day long, and so he enjoyed every step over to the little table in the middle of the garden. He stiffened his arm in an open position and placed Cypress arm in his interlocking them. They both slowly walked across the garden with smiles, wondering what it was that they were going to have to deal with.

There were two chairs that were unoccupied when they reached the small party, and there were two aides to offer the chairs to them.

"Madam Cypress Yayls, meet Headmistress Morastah Barrett," said one of the aides quietly as he pulled the chair out from under the table.

"It is very good to meet you, Ms. Barrett," said Cypress as she properly sat down in her chair.

"Mr. Talon Barrett," said the other aide as he too offered the chair. Talon sat down.

"It is good to see you, Mother," said Talon with a smile.

"And I you, my dear," acknowledged Ms. Barrett.

"Did you get my letter, Mother?" asked Talon.

"Yes, I did. It was quite short though, you would think that after so much time that has passed, you would have more to say, at least in a letter when you have time to rehearse."

"Yes, Mother, indeed."

"It does look as though you are well though. That is good news. And who is this beautiful young woman that you have brought? Is she a friend or is she something more?" she asked with a smile.

Talon was surprised by his mother's composure. Ms. Barrett would usually be sneering at his friend by now. The non-sarcastic compliment was the most surprising to Talon, however. Talon had seldom seen her treat anyone with such respect.

She is up to something, he thought to himself, *something that I am not completely aware of.* He would ordinarily be able to see what his mother was scheming in just the first few moments, but he was at a loss this time.

"I would like you to meet a good friend of mine. She has been quite useful in my efforts to create competitive paintings. It is what I have been doing with my spare time, you see," said Ms. Barrett as she pointed to the young woman sitting next to her. "She is quite a good teacher. I thought that you two might come to appreciate each other seeing that you have much of the same interests," she smiled at Talon. "She is also quite an accomplished pianist. You do like pianists, don't you, Talon?"

"Ms. Anah Derval, meet Mr. Talon Barrett," said one of the aides. "It is very good to meet you, Mr. Barrett," said Anah with a smile. "The pleasure is mine," said Talon.

This was by far the most pleasant atmosphere that Talon had experienced in his mother's company in quite some time, but he was not going to be fooled, he thought to himself.

"Madam Yayls, may I ask where it is that you have come from?" asked Ms. Barrett.

"I was born here in Fable. However, I have spent most of my life living in the valleys of Marlon. It was a very peaceful place. I often do think back to the house that my parents had there."

One of the aides was bringing the meal as she was speaking.

"Well, I should tell you that it is a good thing that you are making the right friends in the right places," said Ms. Barrett, looking a little mischievous. "Talon will take you in the direction you wish to go, won't you, my dear?" she continued as she turned her attention toward Talon.

Talon was not going to answer such a well-thought-out question though. He was too busy trying to find out what his mother meant by it.

"Oh dear, I'm afraid that I am going to have to talk to you later in private, if you don't mind," said Ms. Barrett as she reached across the table and gently grabbed hold of Talon's hand.

"Yes, Mother."

"Well, I'm feeling quite tired. I think that I am going to have to rest for a bit in my room. Do not disperse on my account," she said as she lifted herself out of her chair. Everyone stood up to pay their respects as she walked across the green grass of the gardens.

"So where did you study the piano?" asked Cypress.

"I studied at home. There was a teacher that would come to the house every week," said Anah as she reached to take another sip of her tea.

"And you, why did your parents decide to leave Fable? I can't see any reason that they would," said Anah.

"There was a growing threat from the Lock, and he didn't want to take the risk that he would be captured."

"I had never heard of any such threat," said Anah quite smugly.

"The threat had been neutralized after we left, and my parents began to get used to it in Heris, so he decided to stay there."

"I don't mean to interrupt, however, I have some important business that needs to be taken care of, so this visit cannot be very long," said Talon. "I don't mean to be rude, but I think it will be best that I speak with my mother privately immediately," said Talon as he raised himself out of his chair. "Please follow me, Madam Yayls,"

"Indeed," said Cypress.

"Good day, Madam Derval," said Talon as he lifted Cypress out of her chair by her hand.

"Why the rush?" asked Cypress as they walked across the garden and up the steps to the hallway entrance.

"I am sick of it here, and I am sick of my mother's games that she loves to play with me. Meet me in the room shortly. I am going to get to the bottom of this,"

They sped through the hallway. Talon quickly parted with Cypress as he walked toward his mother's room. There were two guards at the entrance to the door to her room. Talon quickly announced himself to them, and one of them opened the door.

"What is it, Mother? Why have you summoned me? I am a terribly busy man," said Talon as he sat down on the couch in front of her bed. Ms. Barrett was sitting at her powder dresser when Talon walked in the room.

"Oh, don't be so selfish, my dear, I am doing this for you."

"Just what exactly are you doing for me, Mother? I want to hear it now!" Talon demanded.

"I am dying, and before I leave this place, I would like you to be a part of a good family. I want you to have a good wife, and because it seems that you have not had much success in the subject of marriage, I have chosen for you. There will be no debate, do you understand?"

The thought was too much for him to stomach. He had hoped that he would see his mother become a civilized person again before he would have to part with her in death. Talon had not clearly heard the second part of her statement because he was too grieved at the thought that he was soon going to lose his mother in sleep.

"What is the matter with you?" asked Talon as he grabbed hold of her shoulders firmly. "Do you not have the decency to tell me the way a normal person would? Do you think that I am more concerned about a trivial marriage when I know that it was spawned by your imminent death?" He stared intently into her eyes. "I love you, and I am more concerned about you than some prestigious family that you would like for me to inherit. You should have told me in the letter," he held firmly.

"I didn't want you to concern yourself with it. After all, it is my life that is ending, not yours."

Talon relinquished her from his hands and sat back down on the couch in shock.

"Are you sick?" he asked with an expression of despair.

"Yes, and I'm not going to get better," she continued to brush her hair. "You're going to marry Anah, and that is that."

"You would be so selfish, wouldn't you, Mother?" He was angry. "You would be so selfish as to try to control my life even from the grave. How can you expect me to allow this?" he raised himself from the couch. "I kept on waiting for you to go back to the way you were when you used to show genuine love for me as a child. You have changed, and I fear that I will never be able to see the woman that you were before you die. You are not my mother; my mother was a completely different woman than the woman who I see standing in front of me now. You are an impostor."

"Think what you will about me, but be sure to do as I say, boy."

"I am no mere boy. I stand here as a man, and you shall realize that by the end of this day," he said firmly.

"I have given you everything. You threaten yourself, not me," said Ms. Barrett, now with wicked disappointment in her eyes. "You dare to stand up to me when your future is in my hand? I question your competence, and I am trying to create a future for you. I want nothing but the best for you, and if that means forcing you to marry, then so be it."

"I will not be forced into anything, is that clear?" said Talon.

"Well then, what is it that you are going to do? Are you going to walk the streets, begging for your next meal? Where will you live without a penny? Will you be so brave to withstand such things, or will you better yourself with a beautiful woman, an offspring to the name, and a secure foundation of friends to ensure your continued existence?" said Ms. Barrett with a smile, thinking that her foolish son was going to surrender to her demands.

Talon began to calm when he thought of the idea of no longer being a slave to his mother's every whim. He knew that there was no getting out of the Order, and the thought was soothing to him. The fact that his mother was completely unaware of his abduction and conversion was comforting to him as well. Thinking of the control that his mother had lost in one night calmed him. He was, however, sad to think that he would never feel the touch of his mother's hand through his hair in the morning as he so vividly remembered as a child; he would never feel the warmth of love shown in her young face and would never feel the safety of her arms. His mother had died long before she had ever gotten sick, long before his father died, and long before he had even realized it. Talon felt so alone in the world at just that moment even though he had made so many friends the night before. He was so alone, he kept thinking to himself. All that he had ever known, had ever loved was lost to the world's desires and wickedness. It had finally dawned on him. He would not have been able to endure the pain of this moment if he had not stopped on the road that night, had not shown that one act of kindness. He would not have been able to withstand the loss of one hope unless it had been replaced with another. He would be relying on the Order now. *That isn't that distasteful of a thing*, he thought to himself. His mother had been in the dark for so long that it had covered over her like a shadow in a dark room. She was one of those kinds of people that Cypress had been talking about the night before, and Talon could not even stomach the look of her. Talon took one last look at his mother in the hopes that she would recover from herself; that she would show compassion for her son once in what seemed like forever.

"Why have you done this, Mother? Why have you made such trouble for yourself?" he asked in a gentle tone. Ms. Barrett said nothing, surprised that Talon was so collected. Talon stood there, tall, and resolute.

"I truly do love you; do you not see that? And knowing this, you choose to defy me. Do you not trust my judgment? I remember to a time when both you and I had nothing of great value. We did not stand behind the walls that other people erected. We did not pride ourselves with mundane things because they were glamorous and pleasant to our senses. We, you, and I, lived in a small place, barely able to survive. And it may have been hard for you as a mother, but I knew that. I was not a foolish boy. I understood everything that you tried to protect me from, and I loved you for your strength of morals and character. I loved you for the love that you showed me. These things I do not forget. Why do you insist on torturing me, making me see you the way you are now? You prance around like a god, and if anyone gets in the way of your feet, you tread on them. Do not be misled into thinking that you will be able to tread on me. I would not think that you could use me for one of your twisted little games if I were you. I will not marry this woman, and you will have to accept that fact, and if you truly are dying, how dare you think that you can manipulate me like one of your servants? This will be the last time that you see me, Mother," he said with a cold heart and a cold expression.

"It appears that I have birthed a fool. You will forever regret this decision to defy me," said Ms. Barrett, now also standing in defiance. "You are a stubborn man, and you will suffer for this. What do you think that I was toiling for all those years? When your father died, there was nothing left for us. I had nothing handed to me. I was a foolish and naive young woman, and many times it almost cost both of our lives, but eventually, I learned how the world worked. I learned that certain sacrifices must be made in order for survival. You have not realized this fact. However, you will soon. It seems that you are going to learn how to be a man at a noticeably young age. I can only wish that you will continue well," she said with an arrogant countenance.

"I am no fool. I can see that you are hiding the love that you once had, behind a mask of lies and deceit. I can tell you that it is not for my benefit that you are giving this woman to me. You are scheming something evil, and I will have no part in it. Have I made myself clear?" He began to head toward the door.

"Very clear," said Ms. Barrett with a smile. "And you shall have nothing of mine while you continue with this disobedience."

Talon was walking down the hall when he heard his mother shouting at the aide to do something for her. He was never going to see his mother again, but it did not bother him too much in realizing that the person that he once knew to be his mother had been long dead and that he had not been with his mother, that he had lived with something else for too long and that he had been released from his once-consuming bondage.

7 A LEGACY IN THE NIGHT

THE NIGHT AIR was cold outside, and Talon could feel the uneasiness of Cypress when she looked at him. She didn't like the idea of traveling at night, and she wondered why Talon had left so suddenly from his mother's. He would not tell her anything that went on in Fable only a few hours ago. But she could feel that something unnerving had occurred, and she was worried about him.

"I wish you would tell me what happened. Perhaps I could help," said Cypress as she put her hand on his shoulder.

Talon just looked outside the carriage, deep in thought. Cypress shrunk back in her compassion to the fact of Talon's nonresponsive attitude. *He is very troubled*, she thought to herself as she removed her hand from his shoulder.

"I'm sorry that I caused you grief," said Cypress, trying to extract a response from Talon.

"Don't be foolish, there is nothing that you did that could make me feel this way," he said still looking out the window of the cab.

Cypress was glad that she had gotten something out of him; she was getting bored of her own company.

"She was not at all concerned about you being there. I, for the life of me, could not figure out what she was planning, which is an unusual occurrence for me. This time, however, she was plotting something that was so selfish, so evil that she masked it behind her love for me. I had never seen that woman before. It was a new kind of wickedness that I was completely unprepared for," he sat there clenching his cane in anger.

"Did she tell you what she was planning?" she returned her hand to his shoulder.

"No, but I was not going to stay any longer to find out," he held his cane tightly. "She did want me to marry that young girl that was sitting at the table with us, and I suspect that the girl was part of a very well-thought-out plan for my mother to gain more power or wealth or maybe both. This time she will have to find a different way to get what she wants. She will no longer be able to control me," he said now looking intently into Cypress's eyes.

"Well, I was happy to break the umbilical," she said, smiling with pride for her newfound friend.

"I suspect that I was quite fortunate to have been abducted by you. Otherwise, I would have no place to go to at this very moment, and I would have possibly succumbed to the notion of being married to a beautiful young woman," he said, with a mischievous look in his eyes.

Cypress showed herself unpleased with the playful tone in Talon's voice. Talon smiled and turned to look out the window of the carriage door when he noticed something near the road leading into the forest. Talon was unsure of the figure, but it seemed to look like the figure of a tall man in a gray cloak. Cypress had seen the change in Talon's attitude.

"What's the matter?" asked Cypress, now trying to get a look through the door's widow on Talon's side of the cab.

"There is a man standing out in the middle of the road," he said, with a concerned look on his face.

Cypress could see nothing from where she was sitting, so she began to climb over him so that she could take a look. Talon turned his attention off the man so that he could move over so Cypress could find out what he was talking about. They had all but changed seats before she could be in a position to see the road.

"I don't see anything," she said in disappointment. "Besides, there is nothing to worry about a man walking on a road, you're just being paranoid," she continued as she returned herself to her side of the cab.

"I saw a man with a lamp in his hand, and he was not walking on the road. He was standing there in the middle of it, it was quite strange," said Talon as he examined the blackness of the night through the carriage window.

"But he's not there now, is he?" said Cypress, annoyed with the trivial disturbance.

"No, I suppose not, he must have gone underneath the bridge to the river."

He squinted his eyes trying to get a clearer view of what he thought he had seen in the black night.

"You were probably hallucinating from the stress of the visit to your mother's," said Cypress, still upset that he had bothered her with nothing.

Cypress had begun to wish that she had not come with Talon when suddenly, there was a bright light that burst through all the windows of the cab, and the carriage jolted to a harsh stop. Both Talon and Cypress didn't waste time asking each other what had happened. Talon quickly opened the carriage door and got out, so had Cypress. The light was a blinding one, and it was coming from what looked like a horse in the middle of the road. At the sight of it, Talon gasped and looked down at the carriage master who had been thrown over the six horses of the carriage to the feet of the radiant creature. Cypress had reached to pick up the man when the glowing animal slowly kneeled to rest its head gently on her shoulder. Talon, still stunned by the appearance of the glowing horse, found himself slowly moving closer to the creature with an outstretched hand. The animal raised its head quickly, gave a forceful snort, and brushed a hoof against the ground, kicking dust into the air. *Seems gentle enough*, thought Talon as he slowly approached. The carriage driver moaned and groaned as Cypress slowly lifted him off the ground and to his feet.

"What is that?" asked Talon, still approaching the animal slowly, distracted from the man who needed assistance.

"Are you all right?" Cypress asked the man as he rested his hand on one of the horses pulling the carriage.

"I'll be alright, but I'm going to be bruised in the morning," said the man as he climbed back into the driver's seat. He had landed in just the right position. If there had been any difference in the way that he had fallen, he would not have been alive.

The light from the creature was now beginning to fade, and the darkness of the night had begun to overcome them again.

"What is it?" asked Talon a second time, still mesmerized by the creature's beauty.

The creature had now stopped glowing and was standing there in the middle of the road, kneeling to eat some grass that had found its way up through the gravel.

"The horns of a male deer on a stallion-like creature, and the ability to shed light," mumbled Talon as he reached for the mane of the animal.

"It is a Cyclicorn, and it shouldn't be here," said Cypress as she grabbed hold of Talon's hand before it could touch the Cyclicorn. "And they don't like to be touched, or so I was told," she continued.

"How is it able to glow like that?" asked Talon with his eyes fixed on the dark figure in the light of the moon.

"It's able to do it the same way that I was able to move your glass, except animals display power by instinct, often for protection. If the Cyclicorn had not shown itself, it would have been hit by the carriage. But there has not been any record of an animal passing through the barrier," said Cypress with confusion in her voice.

"We should take it with us. It won't be safe when someone sees it," said Talon, now reaching into the back of the carriage for a harness to put around its neck.

"I don't think that that is a good idea," there was worry in her voice.

"Oh, it seems tame enough to get it to follow the carriage," he unraveled a long spool of rope and tied it to the back of the carriage.

"And how do you suppose you are going to get that rope around its neck?" asked Cypress in a sarcastic tone of voice.

"By gently laying it across his neck first," he removed a rope from the compartment in the rear of the carriage.

Talon, with one end of the rope, gently tossed it over and around the Cyclicorn's neck. The animal did nothing but chomp away at the little bushel of grass in the middle of the road. Talon gave it a slight pull, and the Cyclicorn slowly walked toward him as Cypress watched from a distance.

"I don't think that this is a good idea, Talon. I've heard a lot of really bad stories about Cyclicorns," repeated Cypress as she stepped back and raised her hand in front of her ready to defend herself with the Legacy. Talon clicked his tongue and gently tugged as the animal followed him to the back of the carriage.

"You see; there was nothing to worry about. I could see that he was a gentle one by the look in his eyes," said Talon with a smile on his face. "I think that we can get underway again, wouldn't you say so?" asked Talon to the carriage master as he tapped the top of the cab with his hand.

"Yes, sir," said the carriage driver while rubbing the back of his neck.

"Right then, let's do so," said Talon as he got into the cab.

Cypress lowered her hand and shook her head in disapproval as she walked over to the carriage and got in. Talon was lighting the candle inside the lamp in the cab when the carriage began to roll again. He could hear the heavy hooves of the Cyclicorn following the carriage, and he noticed that the carriage was moving slower. It didn't matter how fast the carriage moved to Talon though; he had had enough excitement for the night and wanted things to slow down a little bit anyway. Cypress, however, was not at all her usual self. She had begun to act much like Talon in that she was not sure of what was going to happen next. The reality of the thought that something must have recently come through the barrier was unsettling to her.

The ride of the carriage became gentler as it entered the Myth forest. The ground was soft, and the moonlight barely shown through the tops of the tall trees. Talon was enjoying the night because it had taken his mind off the horrible visit to his mother's. The forest was deep, and it would be a long ride through it, which made Cypress all the more uncomfortable. This was something that she had not planned to encounter, and she was anxious to tell Galen about it.

"I suspect that you were not expecting to find one of those roaming about, did you? I thought that only humans were able to come through the barrier," Talon said as he looked in Cypress's eyes questioningly.

"Someone must have come through recently, but that would mean that either the map is wrong, and we have already reached the time of convergence or someone has learned to manipulate the barrier, which is not a good thing. That would mean that there is a hostile that could still be in the area and we should not be traveling on the road," Cypress said with a worried look.

"I doubt that the map could be wrong, it wouldn't be consistent," said Talon, now looking out the window of the cab. He had begun to feel fear approaching, but before he could respond, another flash of light erupted from behind the carriage, and Talon felt the snapping of the rope with a tough jolt. Talon and Cypress both looked back through the carriage window and could see the glowing Cyclicorn running off through the forest.

"Something's wrong," said Cypress quickly, but before Talon could ask what she was talking about, Cypress had opened the door of the cab and was jumping out onto the forest floor.

Talon quickly responded to a red flash of light that came from the left side of the road with a startled look, but before he could realize that they were under attack, he felt what seemed like a powerful gust of wind throwing him out of the carriage many feet away and onto the forest floor. He lay on his back in pain. The agony, however, didn't stop him from looking back at the carriage that was engulfed in flames. Talon felt hands grabbing him as he struggled to his feet.

"Get up, we need to hide!" said Cypress as she pulled him to run alongside her. "Hurry up!" she said, gasping for air.

Talon kept looking behind him to see what had happened. The driver had been taken by the flames and was lying on the ground dead and on fire. Three men emerged from within the forest and approached the burning carriage. One of the cloaked men turned his head in the direction that Talon and Cypress were running and gestured for the other men to follow.

Talon, seeing that the men were giving to the chase, no longer looked behind and began to run as fast as he could up the hills and through the trees. Cypress was still dragging him behind when he decided to run, once he began running for his life it was not long when Talon began to overtake her. Seeing that Cypress was not nearly as fast as him, he grabbed hold of her and swung her around and onto his back like a piece of luggage that needed a quick transport. With both of her legs locked in his arms, he sprinted, darting through the trees like a strong stag. Cypress could hear the cracks of trees falling and could see flashes of light accompanied by thunder that shook the ground Talon ran on. She clenched his chest like she would the neck of a horse. Cypress had never before been so frightened, and she began to shrink back to former feelings of helplessness when she was a little girl. Talon could hear and see nothing but the large thick trees that passed as a blur in the moonlight. Suddenly he was thrown off his feet as a bolt of lightning struck the tree directly in front of him. Both Talon and Cypress quickly tumbled to a stop in the ferns of the forest. Talon could barely breathe while trying to muster up the strength to get himself to his feet and reach Cypress, who had been thrown some thirty feet away. Talon got to his knees and called out to Cypress, but she didn't respond. Flashes of lightning struck the trees that surrounded them, and Talon could see the three men approaching through the trees.

"no!" shouted Talon as he covered his ears with his hands, trying to block out the deafening sound of the thunder.

Talon knew that this was the last few moments that he would stand alive, and in all that was happening, he could not think of anything but

Cypress and what would happen to her if he were to be killed. He was too weak and too powerless to even protect his most precious friend. Talon raised himself to his feet in a calm sense of the inevitability of his death as lightning repeatedly struck the ground around him. He could hear and see the bolts narrowing in on him as the three men approached with outstretched arms. He stood there, proud to face such a death, but could feel the tears that had begun to run down his cheeks. He knew that Cypress was unconscious, and he felt glad that she would not have to see him die.

He began to focus his sight on the three men and stood ready to fight in every way he knew how when he noticed the figure of the man in the gray cloak with the lamp standing some distance behind the three men. Talon failed to see how the man with the lamp fit into all that was happening until he saw the man reach out his hand at the three men. Talon was now focused on the man with the lamp and could feel a strong wind coming from all sides of the forest. The wind began to spin as the dust and leaves of the forest around and above the men began to accumulate. He could feel the current begin to pull him toward the stratocirrus of debris, dust, and water; and before the three men could look up, the funnel became an explosion of lightning and wind that instantly struck at the heart of them. There was nothing remaining of the three men, but a cloud of dust left to settle in the cool night air of the forest.

Talon stood there in shock of the sheer power that he had seen and knew that he would never be the same. The man with the lamp was nowhere to be seen when Talon began to look through the dust cloud left by the destructive force. He was no longer facing his death and was surprised at the quandary. Where had the man come from? For that fact, where did the other men come from, and why had they attacked them? Talon was facing an overwhelming flood of questions that raced through his mind until he realized that he needed to find Cypress and tell her what had happened, if she didn't already know.

The night air was brisk; and the night had, surprisingly to Talon, adapted all too easily from horror to harmony as if the occurrence had not even taken place. He, however, could not feel comfortable simply calling out to Cypress because he was afraid that something else horrible would hear him, and he would find himself in another predicament that he had no power to escape from. So, he quietly searched the forest floor for Cypress. He brushed through tall ferns, small bushes, and the occasional small creature that would find its way in his path. Finally, he found Cypress unconscious and lying at the foot of a fallen tree. He slowly kneeled and gently brushed his dirty hand across her cheek.

"Cypress," whispered Talon.

She gave a soft moan, and Talon lifted her up into the sitting position.

"Cypress," he whispered again as he pulled the hair out of her mouth and off her face.

She opened her eyes and gasped as she violently tried to lift herself up to continue running for her life.

"Shhh, everything is alright. You're going to be fine," Talon said as he firmly restrained her, settling her.

When she realized that she was no longer in danger, she quickly looked around for clues to what had happened while she had been unconscious.

"What happened?" she asked while clenching her hands tightly around Talon's arms.

"It was amazing. I thought that we were dead, but the man that I told you I saw earlier on the road appeared from the trees and just vaporized the three men." Talon paused for a moment to gather his thoughts. "He's gone now though. He just vanished from sight within seconds," said Talon, amazed at what he was describing. "The man was so powerful; I couldn't believe what I was seeing. It seemed like a dream," he reached to pick Cypress up on her feet.

The whole night seemed like a really bad dream to Talon when he thought about it.

"We're going to have to find the horses to the carriage if we are going to make it to Pastel," Cypress said as she shook the leaves and dirt off her cloak.

"I don't think we'll be able to, in all of this, they're long gone by now," said Talon pessimistically. "We would have better odds of finding shelter here for the night," he continued.

"You might be right," said Cypress with the look of defeat in her eyes.

"Besides, I'm exhausted. Quite frankly, I wouldn't mind it if we just stay here for the night," said Talon, now planting himself on the fallen tree to rest. "Who were those men?"

"I don't know, but I think we have a bigger problem on our hands than we thought," she too leaned on the tree to rest.

"I saw the commotion from the top of the mountain, do you need any help?" asked a voice from the darkness of the forest.

Talon and Cypress, startled by the unfamiliar voice, quickly looked around; but they could see no one. A four-foot-tall man in a dirty white cloak emerged into sight from behind a large tree. His cloak was ripped in some places at the base where Talon could tell that the man had fashioned a tall man's cloak into one more suited to his size. He carried a small walking stick and was fiddling with a bug on the ground.

"My friends call me the Musician." The small man paused for a moment to allow for a response from either Talon or Cypress, but there was none. "I have a dwelling not too far from this place, so if you are in need of a place to stay, I will be happy to help," he lifted the bug to his face to inspect it.

"Where is the lamp you were carrying?" asked Talon.

"Oh, I was not the one who saved you, boy. She was a much larger person than I," said the man.

"She?" asked Talon as he tried to remember more clearly.

"Yes, it seemed to me that it had the figure of a woman, though I was much closer to her than you were. She was quite powerful, wasn't she? I was surprised to see something like that happen in the forest of Myth, it is usually quite docile here," said the small man, struggling to sit on the fallen tree next to Cypress.

"I thought it was a man myself," said Talon in disbelief.

"Yes, I do believe that it would be hard for a man to admit that there might be a woman in the world that was stronger than he," said the Musician with a mischievous smile.

Talon said nothing but reasoned with himself that that could not be the case with him; he was quite comfortable knowing that Cypress was more powerful than him.

"Come, we shall make a pleasant night of it yet," said the Musician as he hopped off the dead tree and gestured for them to follow. Talon looked at Cypress, and they both followed the small man through the trees.

"It's not far, we shall be there in a few moments," said the Musician as he hobbled through the brush and over the large roots of the tall trees.

They came to a spot in the hill where it unnaturally curved; and the Musician began to clear away dead brush, trees, and ferns that he had put there to conceal the stone entrance. When he had finished clearing the passage, they came to a solid stone wall. The Musician reached out his hand, and the door began to regress, opening into a hallway of purple stone and marble.

"Do you know where the woman went after she saved us?" Talon asked the Musician as they passed through the corridor.

"No, she immediately evaporated out of sight," said the Musician as they approached a door with a gold knob and a gold sign that said nothing.

Talon was oblivious to his surroundings because of his preoccupation with the stranger that showed up out of nowhere and disappeared just as quickly. Cypress, however, closely examined the walls and the stone steps; she realized that the design was much like that of Pastel. She had not heard of any other place that had been constructed in this way, and she was curious as to where they were being taken.

The door opened to a small cave that led to a small door that had been carved out of the hillside. The small man opened the door and entered the stone house. He set his cane to the side of the entryway and went into the kitchen.

"There is a creek that runs underground through the hills. If you need cover to go where it is that you are going, then that is a good passage to take," said the Musician as he shuffled through the kitchen cabinets for some tea.

"Would you like some tea?" he asked while reaching for the wooden cups he kept in a drawer underneath the sink.

"Yes, that would be quite nice, thank you," said Talon as he walked over to the chair that was sitting in front of the fire. Cypress was still examining the house when she sat down next to Talon. The little man brought a little table over and placed it in between Cypress and Talon and then returned to the kitchen to get the tea.

"I have some cookies too if you would like them," said the little man, still shuffling around in the kitchen for goodies to eat with his tea.

"Yes, thank you," Talon responded as he stared into the fire and tried to remember anything that he might have missed on the road. Cypress was now staring into the fire also, but she was concerned about who those men were and was trying to formulate a reason that they would have had to want to kill Talon and her. The Order had many enemies, but none of them knew how to use their powers. This must have been an ancient evil, something that she had not heard about, something that possibly Galen hadn't known about either. The thought that there was something going on that the Order had no knowledge of made her hands sweat and shake. *Who knows what will happen next?* She thought to herself.

The Musician walked into the living room with a plate of long cookies, three cups of tea, and he set them on the small table that he had put between Talon and Cypress. Now that he had no cloak to conceal him, they could see that he was a middle-aged man with dark skin like those from the southlands. His hair was black and short, and it was clear that it was unkept. His eyes were brown with a hint of a honey color.

The Musician went into the closet and pulled out a small rocking chair and slid it across the stone floor and up to the little table that he had brought out of the kitchen.

"Why do your friends call you the Musician?" asked Talon as he brought the cup of tea to his mouth.

"At an early age, I found that I could make sounds come from the wind with my mind. I later used the ability to make music, just for the fun of it though. When I began to hone my abilities, I realized that I could do other things like retrieving objects from across the room without having to get up out of my chair. There were many people that began to shun me, and I ran away to the forest and came upon this little house. People didn't like the fact that I was short too, they figured I was some aberration. But there were some people who were always kind to me, and they didn't mind the fact that I could do the things that I could do. That state of peaceful mind led me to find other people like me, but there are very few. That is what led me to you. The first thing that I saw was the bright light from that odd-looking horse and the bolt of lightning that struck the ground. The fact that your young lady friend used her mind to throw you out of the carriage was also a key factor of my curiosity," he smiled.

"If you were there from the beginning, why didn't you help us earlier?" asked Cypress in an aggravated tone of voice.

"I didn't know whether you were hostile or not," he mumbled through the crumbs of his half-eaten cookie. "And after the young man tossed you onto his back and began to run, there was no way I could help, I am too slow, and I don't know how to transport myself. Evaporating makes me queasy anyways. I'm doing what I can to help the both of you," said the little man in an aggravated tone.

"And we are very grateful for your help," said Talon as he looked into the dwarf's eyes with conviction.

"So, are you going to stay here the night?" asked the Musician as he slapped his knees with his hands in excitement.

"I don't think that we can stay. We are expected, and they will begin to worry," said Cypress.

"As they should, considering the night you two just experienced," said the Musician with raised eyebrows. "Right then, I shall need to show you where the tunnels to the lake are, and then you can get to where you are going."

The Musician led them to the entrance of the tunnels that connected to the rear of the stone house.

"You shall need a guide. There are many ways in which someone can get lost. Wait here, and I will get my cane and cloak, it's quite cold down in these tunnels," he shuffled off through the stone corridors to the stone house.

Talon and Cypress were standing at the entrance to the underground river and could see the small wooden bridge that ran across it. They were waiting patiently when suddenly, there was a loud sound like cracking fireworks, or a large tree being broken in two by the hands of a giant. The air expanded and contracted around a tall figure that had just appeared out of nothing. The cloaked woman stood facing the river with her back to Talon and Cypress. Cypress reacted with a quick wave of her hand, but the woman was much too fast for Cypress. Cypress stood there helpless, locked in the grasp of the strange woman's mind.

"Do not be frightened. I will not harm you," the woman said as she clenched the hand lantern. The woman dropped her hand and relinquished Cypress. "You cannot trust the Musician," the woman said calmly and forcefully.

"And why can we trust you?" asked Talon quickly.

"You have no choice, and I was the one who saved you not him," the woman said with disgust in her voice. "I can transport you to a safe place where he will not find you," said the woman as she raised her hand again. "Go east, and you will find your way. There is no time," she said, and before either of them could respond, the air began to compress around them.

Talon could feel a great weight pressing down upon him from all directions, and then suddenly the pressure was gone, and he was in a different place. He quickly looked around and could see Cypress right next to him. They were still in the underground tunnels; however, there was a door that was right next to them.

"She said to go east, right?" asked Talon.

"Yes, and this door would lead us straight there," responded Cypress.

Talon quickly opened the door that led them to another stone hallway. Cypress moved the stone door away from the entrance and caught a glimpse of lights not too far through the trees.

"The city of Pastel!" whispered Talon as Cypress and he exited the tunnels. "How did you get in undetected before?"

"I have friends that will let us in through another entrance."

They both crouched and walked from bush to bush and tree to tree as they slowly began to approach the gates to the city. Talon could see the main entrance through the trees as they circled the city slowly.

"Come on," whispered Cypress as she grabbed hold of his arm, and they quickly ran across the train tracks that led to the central station near the rear of the mountain and up a steep path of stone steps. Talon practically hugged the mountain while going up the steps with Cypress; he wasn't too fond of steep heights. The steps led to a small shack that had been made to conceal another entrance to the castle of Pastel. The passage had been made to look like an old, abandoned mineshaft. They both ran through the dirt tunnels and over the fallen beams of wood. Cypress stopped beside another tunnel that had been boarded up. She stretched out her hand, and the boards folded up, revealing a passage of stone.

"Be careful, these passageways are guarded," whispered Cypress with her hand still extended.

Talon said nothing; he was not about to question her any longer. He had now learned to completely trust Cypress's instincts and judgment. Cypress slowed her advancement to a near stop and only took a few steps past the stone threshold. She was expecting something to happen, something dangerous and deadly like all the other times before, but nothing happened.

"Someone has been here recently, and they have defused the traps," said Cypress as she lowered her hand, taking her guard down. We must hurry. Someone might have infiltrated the castle. Otherwise, they would have reset the traps," she said while reaching for the door that lay directly in front of her. The stone folded back, and she sped out into the library of the castle. Talon could see the book rack return to its normal position as the door slowly closed behind them. As he was walking, he noticed that there was blood on the ground.

"Stop!" said Talon as he quickly halted and kneeled to make sure that what he was looking at was really blood. He touched it with the tips of his fingers and brought the red substance to his nose. It had a metallic smell and was too thin to be anything other than blood.

"There is blood on the ground." The moment that Talon said this, Cypress stopped in her tracks. There was a trail of blood that ran from behind the door that they had just entered through, and it continued through the corridors. Cypress began to follow the trail of blood through the halls to the common room, and Talon was right behind her.

The trail stopped at the couch for a moment where there was a larger concentration of blood, and then continued through to the kitchen. Talon and Cypress could hear many people in the kitchen rustling around. There were whispers and some knocking over of glass onto the floor. Cypress swung the doors to the kitchen open and could see a man in a read tunic lying on the kitchen cutting table. He was clearly severely wounded, and Mary was trying to save his life. The man moaned and groaned on the solid wooden slab, and there was blood everywhere. Galen was looking into the eyes of the man and whispering things to him. Talon could not make out what it was that Galen was saying, but it seemed to him that Galen knew the man and was trying to comfort him. Cypress, at the sight of the man, ran over to the head of the table and began to shed tears.

"You should not be seeing this, my dear," whispered Galen as he lifted his head to address her. Cypress grabbed hold of the man's hand as she brought herself closer to say something in his ear.

"It's Nelly Jack—Jack I'm here, don't be afraid," she whispered in his ear.

At hearing this, the man clenched her hand tighter to let her know that he could hear her and was listening to her.

"I—I," said the man on the table, trying to say something to her.

"Shhh, don't speak. Everything is going to be alright. You're just going to have to take some time to get better," whispered Cypress, still holding his hand.

Cypress looked at Mary as she was compacting something into his wound. Mary looked back with a worried expression, and Cypress understood.

"Who did this to you?" asked Galen with his hand firmly placed on the wound for pressure.

"They, they," said Jack while gasping for breath.

"I think I know who did this," said Cypress to Galen with a vicious look. "They were probably the ones who came after Talon and me," she continued.

Galen's attention was now not on the man and realizing that Cypress was saying that they had been attacked, he looked at her tattered and filthy face with shock.

"What do you mean the same ones that attacked you?" asked Galen, now angry and shouting.

Galen was losing control. No one knew about the Order other than those in the Order and the ministry, but they did not know where they were, and that would mean that there was either a spy or someone in the Ministry who had been gathering information. Galen looked away and threw his pipe to the floor.

"These were no ordinary humans either, Galen. They were able to manipulate their powers," said Talon from the doorway. "We barely escaped with our lives."

Galen had nothing to say; he stood there angry and worried.

"Something has gone wrong. The Ministry would not have known where you two were tonight, and I can tell you that I am certain that they did not know. There is something else here at work. Jack being attacked I can understand and possibly link to the Ministry. However, the fact that the two of you were attacked does not make any sense. I don't understand it," said Galen as he wiped the sweat from his forehead.

"There's something else. There was a woman that saved our lives. We would not be here if it weren't for her. She showed that she was immensely powerful, and she killed the three men that were coming after us," said Talon, looking for hope that Galen would figure something out.

"He will be all right. I got most of the splinters out, and he should be well enough to tell us exactly what happened to him in about an hour or two," said Mary as she wiped the blood from her hands with a towel.

"Who's the man on the table?" asked Talon.

"He is a spy for the Order, a spy that, until he was attacked, had an especially important message for us. It seems that we are going to have to wait for it though," said Galen, still frustrated from recent events. "Did you find out who the woman was?" asked Galen.

"She was too mysterious, and she never revealed her face," said Cypress quickly.

"At first I couldn't tell whether she was a man or a woman. She was too far away. She saved our lives though, and that was enough for me to trust her. The odd thing was that she carried an encased hand lamp. I don't know why, but that struck me as very odd. We first saw her on the road. She was just standing there in the middle of it. It was sort of like she was waiting for us. She also transported us to the city, and I am incredibly grateful for that as well," said Talon.

"There is one other thing. We met a man that helped us to get to an underground lake that leads from his stone house. Galen, the house was constructed almost exactly the way Pastel was. It was amazing. It must have been constructed by the same people, and there was a door that led from the tunnels to the city which was constructed the same way also. I think that there were more than just the Order that came through the barrier, and I think that they left the Legacy with others. For instance, the strange woman, she was more powerful than any of us could ever think to be. She must have been trained and trained well. We can only reason that there may be hostiles that have been planning this for some time," Cypress said, looking intently into Galen's eyes.

"That wouldn't be consistent, Cypress," said Talon as he moved closer so he wouldn't need to raise his voice.

"You're forgetting the animal," he continued.

Cypress had forgotten about the Cyclicorn. Many of the moments of that night had evaded her, and realizing that Talon was right, she stopped talking and leaned on the table where the wounded man lay asleep and in pain.

"What animal?" asked Galen with curiosity in his voice.

"There was a Cyclicorn in the middle of the road. We almost hit it," said Talon, wondering what Galen was going to tell him next.

Galen raised his hand to his chin and looked as if he was pondering something. All his anger and fear were of no importance to him now. There was a much larger mystery that needed solving if they were to expect to survive. Galen stood there looking into oblivion and preoccupied with his thoughts.

"It had to have come through the barrier, Galen," said Cypress, interrupting his thought.

"Yes, that would be the appropriate assumption, Cypress," Galen mumbled through his hand. "But the question is how? There is no mention of anyone passing through the field except when the convergence takes place, and I don't recall the mention of any humans being left behind. I don't see how it is that they could have survived in the other world as it is," continued Galen, raising his eyebrows in curiosity.

"I need to rest and think. Call for me when Jack wakes up," said Galen as he walked through the kitchen door into the common room to sit near the fire. Cypress quickly followed him and sat in the second chair next to the fire.

"I fear the worst is not at our door yet," said Galen as she sat down in the chair.

"I thought that we were not going to survive the night, but Talon surprised me," said Cypress, with her face looking depressed.

"How did he surprise you?"

"He probably doesn't know it yet, but he began to use his powers tonight. He became strong and amazingly fast. I had never before been so frightened," she said while wiping the tears that had begun to fall. "Talon's right, you know. We would not have survived the attack of those three men without the help of that strange woman with the lamp. It's her most of all that proves that there are others that have realized their powers. However, she was no meager amateur. I suspect she carries that lamp around for a reason that doesn't involve her simply needing the light," Cypress said, now staring into the fire.

"She must have difficulty manipulating light. It is not something that everyone can do," said Galen questioningly.

"He's awake now, and he can talk," said Mary, now entering the room from the swinging doors of the kitchen. "I'm going to have him put on a cot and brought in here so he can rest," she continued.

"Yes, thank you. That would be exceedingly kind," said Galen as he waved his hand, gesturing for Mary to proceed.

Moments later Mary, Talon, and Mr. Dolan were carrying Jack through the doors of the kitchen to the common room. They gently laid the man down on four stilts that were connected to the wooden bed in front of the fire.

"Do you remember anything that happened to you, Jack?" asked Galen, holding his hand to comfort him.

"I was riding on my horse through the forest, and suddenly, a tree was struck by lightning right in front of me. My horse got the brunt of the attack. I was only grazed by the wood that went flying from the explosion. I knew that it was an attack, so I took a chance and laid on the ground, playing dead. Three men emerged from deep inside the forest and walked up to me. They had presumed that I was dead because neither my horse nor I were moving or breathing, and they went back into the forest. I have no enemies at the Ministry, Galen. They must have been waiting there to ambush someone else. When the three men walked farther down the road, I crawled to my feet and hid behind the tree. When they were out of sight, I began to walk to Pastel. I passed out a few times along the way until I reached the shack," Jack said, lying down, breathing hard.

Galen was now leaning over him listening to every word that came out of his mouth.

"Galen, the Ministry judge that Cypress talked to, he signed the agreement, but something happened that we did not expect," Jack said as he grabbed hold of Galen's cloak.

Galen stood there and said nothing but closely listened.

"The Ministry saw fit to throw him in prison for his judgment, and he is there now. They nullified his judgment and released him to the authorities on the grounds of treason. He will not live out but for another five days until he faces execution. We were foolish to think that the Ministry would stay out of our affairs, but since the war may be upon us sooner than we anticipated, all we can do is hope," Jack said with a tear in his eye. Galen, in shock from the report of Jack, sat back down in his chair. Talon was sitting next to Jack on the brick floor of the fireplace.

"We need to break him out of prison," said Cypress quickly.

"Yes, we do, and I think that both you and Talon would be perfect for the job," said Galen with a smile on his face.

8 AUZGOOL

CYPRIS BEGAN TO JAB at the map of the Ministry castle grounds with her finger, telling Talon that they could enter from this direction or from that direction. Talon couldn't make heads or tails of the map though; it was too intricately written. He stared at the candles as they flickered, shedding light on the beautifully made chair in the library sitting lounge. He could see the night air beginning to fog just outside the window and began to ponder on one of the moments at home when he was a little child still being tucked into bed by his father. Talon didn't know much about his father, just the occasional memory that would spring up during a time of discomfort or boredom and what he had heard from his loving mother. He thought him to be a good man though, not by anything that his mother said, but by the look in his father's face whenever Talon saw fit to daydream about him. He was noticeably young at that time though and it was hard to remember his father. The setting of the fireplace and the tall walls reminded him of those comfortable moments. Tattered old books accompanied by gleaming new volumes and the gentle dark colors that would reflect from them. The candlelight made them visible, and the fire made everything so clear and wonderful to Talon. The maroon carpets with their many designs of flowers and people from ancient times made it easier to think. Talon was, however, not in the mood to think about anything, let alone help Cypress plan a raid into one of the most fortified castle grounds and dungeons of all time. Cypress's words of planning fell upon deaf ears as she continued to speak on and on with her calculations of distance per ratio to power of force applied from all different distances. Talon was not a quantum physicist. And though Cypress wasn't either, Talon didn't know it, and he wasn't about to start learning any time soon. So, he drifted and drifted into his mind further and further as she spoke until Cypress stopped talking and addressed Talon with a question, and he didn't respond. Upon hearing nothing for some time, Talon turned his head on his hand that he had been resting on for some time just to find out why it was that she had stopped talking. Cypress glared at him in disappointment and slapped the palm of her hand on the center of the map in anger.

"concentrate," she shouted. Talon, almost falling out of his seat, wasn't about to disobey a command such as this; he knew he would pay for it later. She looked at him and began to start at the beginning without the calculations.

"We will enter the Ministry castle here," said Cypress as she opened a map of the Ministry castle wider so that Talon could see it more clearly. "They have guards here and here," she said as she pointed to the entrance of the Ministry on the map.

"Where is the prisoner being held?" asked Talon with confusion as he stared at the map.

"They are most likely holding him in the east wing of the dungeons. That is the building over to the right," She scrolled her finger across the map. "It is not connected to the Ministry except for this one passageway which is underground. We will have to stun the five guards that are stationed in that corridor. We could either do that or we could come from above and blast a hole in the side of the dungeon wall. That would take them by surprise, but we will have to deal with a lot of guards, and some of them may know how to use their powers," she looked into Talon's eyes to see if he was taking it all in. "What do you think?" she asked, still staring at him.

"I think that it is going to be an almost-impossible task, and I'm not sure that I want to be involved with it," he said with a small smile.

"Well, it doesn't seem to be that you will have a choice either way, and you're just going to have to learn to survive. You didn't do that bad of a job for your first time when we were being attacked," she said with a smirk. "I told you that you would be more powerful than me. You simply need to have a little faith in yourself," she continued.

"I stood there like an idiot, helpless and powerless to save myself let alone you, and if that woman hadn't been there, we would not be alive right now. So, it is pointless to tell me that I need to have faith in myself when I already know my limitations," Talon said, now becoming aggravated at the subject of conversation.

"You do not know your limitations, you are setting your limitations, but what you haven't realized is that you have already tapped into your powers, and it is that which gave us the time and distance to survive tonight."

"What do you mean I have already used my powers?"

"No normal man would be able to run near as fast as you were, especially if he were carrying a woman on his back. You were using your powers in an instinctual way much like the Cyclicorn did that night. It's not something that I can do, and you did it. Those three men had to transport themselves to catch up with you, and when they did, they were still behind. It was quite extraordinary even for a person who knows how to use their powers."

"So, you're saying that I am already starting to use my powers?"

"Yes, that is exactly what I am saying. That and the fact that you almost saved our lives. You are going to be an immensely powerful person, Talon.

You need to understand that fact and have more faith in yourself. If not for yourself, do it for me," she placed her hand on his.

"You two said that there was a man in the forest that helped you. Do you know his name?" asked Galen as he entered the common room from the stairs of the castle tower. The entrance of Galen was very interruptive, and Cypress quickly pulled her hand from Talon's.

"Yes, we did find out what his name was. Why do you ask?" asked Cypress.

"I want to know more about the place from which he came. You said that he knew how to use his powers?" asked Galen.

"Yes, he did," responded Talon.

"Well, I am going to have to find out more about him. It might be possible that he was once a part of the Order," said Galen as he rubbed his chin in deep thought.

"I don't think that he was. He didn't mention any knowledge of the Order. Otherwise, I'm sure that he would have asked how it was and would have been prepared to take us to Pastel himself. He was only going to take us through the tunnels and up to land," said Cypress.

"But the woman knew where the castle was because she transported us to the city," said Talon.

"Yes, that would be a good assumption. This is something that we must get to the bottom of. We cannot leave it be. I will go to the forest and try to find the man. What was his name?" asked Galen, still rubbing his chin.

"He said that his friends called him the Musician," Cypress said, looking up at Galen standing in front of the table where the map had been laid.

"I will be going alone. You two can stay here and get a good night's sleep so you'll be strong in the morning to break into Auzgool."

Talon was not going to argue with Galen; he wanted to get a good night's sleep. It was the thought of the next morning that he didn't enjoy. Cypress was ready to go to bed also; but Davina, however, had been sleeping almost the whole day since Cypress wasn't at Pastel to keep her company. And naturally, Davina wanted to spend more time with her. Davina was purring under the table when Cypress called her to bed with her, and Talon had already sped off to his room in the tower.

Galen had already passed the entrance of the door of Pastel and was heading toward the stables to get his horse. He loved his horse, and he would have no other if it had died unless maybe if the horse looked the same, acted the same, and felt the same way as Ebon. Galen knew that was something that would not be likely to happen; he knew that there was no other horse that could come close to Ebon. Galen was fixing the horse for the ride to the forest as he thought about her. He gently brushed his hand along the coarse hair of her mane. There was nothing better than a good ride through the forest when there is no one trying to kill you, but Galen figured that the attack on Cypress and Talon was an isolated incident. He really did not know that to be the truth though. Possibly, he was becoming a naive old fool. Whatever the case, he had to get to the bottom of the mystery. *Besides, I can handle myself,* he thought as he mounted Ebon. Galen was dressed for a cold night, and he knew that he was not going to get any sleep that night. But he was not the type to procrastinate. When something needed to be done, he would not hesitate to do it.

Ebon rode hard on the path to the forest; the warm air from her rushed in and out of her lungs with every leap. Galen knew that if there was going to be any danger, he would have to move fast. His route through the forest was not straight. He weaved in and out of trees at great speeds as if he were already being pursued. When he reached the middle of the forest, he pulled hard on the reins, and Ebon came to a skidding stop. Her breath was still strong and rapid as she inhaled and exhaled the cold night air. Galen, concealed by his cloak, stood tall on his horse as he scrolled his sight along the surrounding areas. He stood there silent for a moment and listened to the forest. He could hear the cracking and screeching of the growing trees and the condensation that would collect on the leaves and fall to the ground with a soft sound in the dirt. The hooves of Ebon were loud thumps in the dirt as she fidgeted on the forest floor. Galen came to a slow breath and whispered into the wind, "Musician." Ebon kicked and shuffled the dirt under her hooves as Galen held the reins firm. A small figure emerged from behind a tree only a few feet from where Galen and his horse stood. Galen could see the shimmer of the necklace that hung around the dwarf's neck from the light of the moon that shone through the trees. The small man had his walking cane and his tattered old white cloak.

"What is it that you wish from me?" asked the Musician.

"I wish to pay my respects to a new friend of mine. A man who did me an exceptionally good deed, a man they call the Musician. Are you this man?" asked Galen, still sitting high on his horse.

"And what was this great deed that the Musician had done for you?" asked the dwarf.

"He came to the aid of two people that are of the most importance to me, and I wish to know the man behind the name," he held the reins of the horse firmly.

Ebon was becoming uncomfortable due to the small man being in such close proximity. She slowly sidestepped away from the Musician in disobedience to Galen.

"I am the man you speak of," said the Musician as he pulled back the hood of his cloak and smiled. Galen immediately relaxed and dismounted.

"My name is Galen Gumly. I am pleased to meet you," he outstretched his hand.

"And I you. Why don't you come to my house, and we can talk."

"I would much appreciate it," Galen grabbed the reins of Ebon and began to walk alongside the Musician.

"We aren't far from my house. It's right here," said the Musician as he pointed to the stone entrance. He waved his hand, and the door opened. Galen followed the little man through the door, through the cave, and through the entrance of the stone house without anything to say to him. The Musician leaned his cane against the side of the entrance and went into the kitchen.

"Would you like some tea?" asked the Musician.

"No, thank you. I don't wish to take up too much of your time," said Galen as he sat down in the chair in front of the fire. "I just have a few questions for you that I'm hoping that you will be able to answer," Galen looked at him with a serious expression.

"I will do my best to provide," the Musician said as he poured himself some tea from the piping hot porcelain in the kitchen and walked to sit in the chair next to Galen.

"I understand that you know how to use the Legacy," said Galen as he looked keenly into the dwarf's eyes.

"Yes, I do, but only in a limited fashion."

"How did you learn to use it?" Galen paid close attention to his answer.

"I taught myself. It didn't come easily, you know," he looked at Galen as if he were a little child in trouble with his father.

"I do have an unusual question though. You see, I am part of a group of people that had no knowledge of any others that were able to use their perceptive powers, and fools were made of us by you and your friend, the woman with the lamp. Are there others that have done as you have done?"

"Why, absolutely there are, and by the way, I never laid eyes on that woman till tonight. I had never seen such a display of power either by both the pursuers of your friends or the woman. I don't know where she came from either. She was quite skilled though."

Galen was pondering on how there were men and women who could use their powers without training when he noticed that the dwarf's necklace was not a necklace at all but a large key that had a gold chain connected to it. He began to stare at the key when the dwarf quickly shoved it underneath his shirt. Galen, from what he had seen, remembered a symbol that was in the library of Pastel, which was exactly the symbol on the key lying covered on the Musician's chest.

"Well, I think that I have overstayed my welcome. I'll be going now," said Galen as he quickly got up out of his chair.

"Well, it was nice having you in my home. I hope you will come again," said the Musician.

Galen would have stayed longer; however, the symbol on the key around the Musician's neck was enough information for him because he already knew where to look for the answers. The symbol must be the clue, and he wasn't going to waste time in the forest when the answers were over in the castle of Pastel.

Galen quickly exited the house and mounted Ebon. Ebon broke into a hard ride immediately, and he was on his way back to Pastel. He anticipated no danger and dashed a straight shot the long way out of the forest and through the hills and up the side of Pastel Mountain to the entrance to the stables. This took some time. He quickly dismounted and put away his steed. He went practically running down the halls to the library. Everyone was asleep, and Galen didn't care if he had woken any of them up anyway. He was going to find something great he could feel it, something that had not been seen for thousands of years, and it was possible that the dwarf had the key.

Shuffling through books and peering closely at shelves, he tried to remember where it was that he had seen the symbol on the key before. He searched for hours, pulling books off the shelf, and looking for secret passageways that might be hidden in the walls but had so far found nothing. Galen was now too tired to continue his search through the library and decided that he was going to sit down and rest. After all, it had been an awfully long night. He walked over to sit on a chair that was built into the side of the shelf; all the chairs folded back into the shelves, and when someone wanted to sit for a quick read, they would be easily accessible. He pulled out one of the wooden shelf chairs and sat down, breathing hard with his hands to his face. The night had begun to get the better of him, and he began dozing off. He was staring into the nothingness of a doze when he saw it through the blurry tears of exhaustion. He saw the symbol etched into one of the chairs all the way at the back of the library.

He slumped off the wooden chair and crawled to the chair in the back. He pulled the stool out, but nothing happened. Galen looked at the symbol closer and could see that it was not in its right position, and he quickly assumed that the symbol was pointing to something. He looked to the left as the symbol was turned to the left and found an old wooden book that he had not seen before. The cover was solid wood, and it had the symbol etched into it. The book did not open like a regular parchment. Galen pulled the papers out of the book to read them, but there was nothing to read. Galen looked at it from all angles as he spun it around, looking for something to read, but there was nothing there. Then he saw the symbol facing up, etched into the wood shelf where the book had been taken out. He looked at the symbol closely and knew that he was remarkably close to whatever it was that he was going to find. He thought to be more careful of where he put his hands now that the mystery was becoming more real.

Galen took an even closer look at the surrounding areas of the empty spot in the shelf where he had retrieved the book. There was nothing but the upright symbol etched into the shelf wall. Galen stood back and reached out his hand in front of him. First, he thought to gently push on the entire shelf wall with his mind, but nothing happened when he tried. So, he narrowed the force to the surrounding area of the place where the book had been. Suddenly the segment of shelving began to gently slide back into the wall. The wall made a sharp clicking sound, and another segment of shelving began to retreat into the large stone wall. Finally, the whole wall shelf began to slide open, revealing another entrance of stone.

"Aha, success at last!" shouted Galen as he stepped through the open doorway.

It was dark and cold in the doorway, not like the other parts of the castle. It exuded a sinister feeling from Galen. Cobwebs lay like blankets along the walls, and there was no light besides that which crept in from the entrance. Galen walked slowly, and as he walked; he could feel something queer in the flow of wind that had begun to whip around him. He was extremely uncomfortable almost to the point of fear; however, his mind was centered on his curiosity, not his fear. The hall of stone and web had been designed to focus universal energy through the one entering, and Galen could feel the flow of energy surrounding him and slowly being drawn through him. The purpose for the design eluded Galen until he saw torches begin to light all around him and he could no longer see the light from the entrance of the doorway. Galen knew that he had emerged into another chamber when torches burst into flames using his collected power, and as soon as they had been lit, he no longer felt fear from the weird usage of his body. He entered the chamber with caution and noticed twelve doors that surrounded a round room. There was only one that was much larger compared to the others, and they each had a separate symbol etched into the stone tablets in the center of each door. The doors were solid stone, and they had stone keyholes that were cut out directly in the center of them. There were some that did not have keyholes at all though. Galen could see the light from the torches flicker on the twelve doors that surrounded him. He slowly moved his body toward the door with the symbol that he recognized from the book. He examined the door to find a way to open it, but there was none other than that of the keyhole that stared back at him through the blanket of cobwebs and dust. Galen moved closer and looked into the large hole but saw nothing in the darkness. *What could be behind the mysterious doors?* thought Galen as he peered through the keyhole, seeing nothing but black. He stepped back in frustration and reached out his hand to the keyhole. Cobwebs inverted through the hole as Galen tried to form a key with his mind that would open the door. His hand clenched and oscillated as he concentrated on picking the lock, but nothing happened. In frustration, he opened his eyes and ran to a safe distance and reached out his hand again to blast a hole in the stone.

Now using both hands to concentrate, he burst out in a cry of strain as he tried to relinquish a deadly blow at the door, but the force dispersed into the wind and the stone torches flared feeding on the exertion of energy. The door was untouched. Galen stood there now exhausted, breathing hard. He began to realize that the only way that he was going to get through the door was to find a way to retrieve the key from the Musician.

Galen collected himself and quickly exited the chamber. As he left, the torches snuffed themselves out, and the chamber sealed behind him. He was not sure what to think about his new discovery, and his nerves were not doing so well at this point. He emerged into the library still out of breath and wondering what it was that he was trying to protect all these years. What were his beliefs and his values that he had held for so long telling him about the things that he had just seen? Had he been wrong or was there simply another piece to the puzzle that he didn't know that he needed? Had he been deliberately deceived or had the truth been hidden from him? He was going to find out one way or another, and he expected most of the secrets would be revealed in the library. *It is a good place to start*, he thought to himself as he began searching the hundreds of thousands of books that lay shelf by shelf in front of him, and if he did not discover the answers in the shelves, he would start by paying another visit to the Musician and never stop till he had the complete answer.

It was morning by the time that Galen had finished his strenuous research only to find nothing that could help reveal secrets to the twelve doors or a reason that they had been built. He stood looking at the last book when the sun revealed itself through a window, shining brightly on Galen's wrinkled face. His face changed quickly when the light hit it, but the light from the sun was not the cause. It was a thought that had begun to race through his mind, something that he had not thought of earlier, a thought that would take a lot of explanation for Galen himself to understand. *What is the meaning of it?* he pondered in the morning light. It was more like a doubt, as one might put it into words for Galen, a doubt in all that he had learned and studied, a fact that would make the books on the shelves obsolete and useless. Galen stood in the middle of the library unaware of his surroundings and living only in his mind. He stared blankly into the sunrise, realizing that the books on the shelves were not from the same time that the castle of Pastel had been built in. It was a point of fact that had eluded him for many years. Years it was that he had stared at the books without reading the bulk of the library. He, however, could not understand how it all fit together. There was simply not enough information. Hundreds of books both large and small lay on the floor, some soaking in the spattered pools of blood from hours earlier. Galen couldn't help but feel angry about the things that he had discovered; they would make every peaceful endeavor much harder to accomplish than before.

Cypress awoke in her bed as Davina pawed at her and purred with contentment. The morning had shown itself through the tall windows of the castle room. Cypress loved the mornings with their cool atmosphere. The cool air combated by her warm quilts and the loving personality of Davina made the mornings, to Cypress, almost heaven. However, the mood was normally disturbed by what she knew she would have to be accomplishing for that day; and today, she thought, would be one of the hardest to get through if she and Talon did not thoroughly prepare themselves. It would have to be a swift and fast extraction if they were going to have any chance of surviving the raid. She was nervously content with the way she had planned the attack and confident that Talon would be of some use.

All we must do is to get in and get out, with the court official though, she thought to herself. She was too ready to do this and was not happy that she would have to wait till it was dark. She flung her quilts off her in frustration and quickly lifted herself into the sitting position. Cypress did have the ability to be patient on occasion, but she rarely used the talent. She was still young and trivial at times, but the morning air was not something that could contribute to her uneasiness. She would often decide to step out of the tower and onto the wall and stare at the morning sun as it would slowly reveal itself from beneath the horizon, as she did this morning. The soft breeze caressed her hair, and the stone of the castle wall was cool beneath her bare feet. She looked down into the trees of the forest that surrounded the city of Myth and at the city of Pastel just over the edge of the mountain, which concealed her home, and took a deep breath. She could smell the wind from the coast many miles away and imagined a place where there were no troubles, nothing to fight for, and nothing to die for. She, however, knew that would be a life with no excitement; she was a person that needed challenges to overcome. Birds perched on the tower and sang as she stared off into the valley and pondered.

Flashes of light erupted, and pieces of wood flew through the air as Cypress, now a little girl, sat huddled in the darkness of a small shack. The night air was freezing, and she was only wearing a white nightdress when her father burst through the door to her room. Cypress could see large men as tall as the trees around them, picking people up off the ground as they tried to run for their lives. She could hear screams of people being torn away from the ones that they loved and could smell the smoke of burning hay and flesh. The moon was just in view as her father reached out to grab hold of her when suddenly, large fingers came grasping her father. A few moments more and he was whisked away by the large hand. Cypress could hear her father screaming for the hand to release him as large thumping sounds shook the ground around the small shack. The crackling and whistling of the burning houses became louder when the screaming and stomping of the large men had stopped. She sat there on her knees in the middle of the only shack that had been neglected by the fire and stared into the night air, unable to blink; she could hear the footsteps of a man and two other people. They were whispering to each other as they walked along the ground of Heris. A man appeared in the doorway, and when he saw Cypress, he called for the others to come and blanket her up. Cypress stood on her knees motionless, staring into the night. A light in the forest was barely visible to Cypress from behind Galen's open arms and she could see a dark figure of a woman standing, holding a lamp in her hand far off in the distance. A hand rested on her shoulder before Galen could grab hold of her.

"Nelly," whispered Galen as he patted his hand on her shoulder and began to lift her up off the ground of the Pastel castle wall. "Did you experience another memory?" he asked as he held her hand ever so gently.

"Yes, but I remembered much more this time," she said, leaning on the stone and looking into the valley again.

"I am going to have to teach you to be prepared when memories resurface with such force," said Galen as he looked into her eyes.

Cypress, however, was not concerned with Galen standing there and showing compassion toward her. She was too concerned with the new addition to her memory.

"The woman with the lamp," Cypress said with complete confusion. "The woman with the lamp was there when my mother and father were killed," she continued.

Galen looked confused also, and he was wondering if she had inadvertently interjected the sight of the woman into the dream. He was beginning to worry about her health, and Cypress could see it in his face when he looked at her.

"I'm not going crazy if that is what you are thinking," Cypress said as she turned away from Galen in anger.

"I wasn't thinking that at all," said Galen as he turned her toward him by the shoulders to look at her in the face.

Cypress stood there with her head to the ground, and she was breathing hard.

"I could never think that of you, and you know that. I have always thought that you were made for a very great future, and I have already seen that. You are a good woman and a powerful friend. I will always look at you as if you were my own daughter, because I love you," said Galen, now holding her to his chest and in his arms.

Cypress could not resist Galen's acts of kindness, but this time she was not crying. There was still someone alive that knew exactly what had happened to her parents and why the Requiem had invaded. The determination in her eyes revealed that she was going to find out.

The afternoon was eventless for Talon except for Cypress's changes to her plan to enter the prison dungeons. Talon looked into the fireplace and tried to drown out what seemed to him an endlessness of background noise that was continually coming from Cypress's lips as she thought to herself. Partial words accompanied with partial thoughts whispered from Cypress until she was ready to tell Talon exactly which route they were going to take to the Ministry castle. Talon almost wished that he had a pipe to puff on; it would give him something to do. He hadn't gotten to the point of becoming envious of Galen sitting in the chair opposite to him though; it was Galen's unknown interest in a wooden book with nothing written in it that Talon was jealous of. Talon figured he was waiting for Cypress to tell him exactly which way he was going to get killed; it seemed the inevitability of his situation. He tried to keep his optimism, but her plan was so dangerous he didn't see how he was going to survive. So, he secretly tried to formulate an escape route in his mind so that Cypress wouldn't get mad at him and so that he would not be shown the fool. Talon was naturally an optimist though; it was only that her plans seemed to be impractical. All that changed when she called Talon over to her to take another look at the map though. In explaining that they were going to take a boat across the lake from the woods that surrounded the Ministry castle up to the edge of the prison, blast a hole, grab the Ministry official, and take the boat back across the lake to the woods; Cypress had finally gotten it right, or at least according to Talon. Talon thought that that wasn't that thick of an idea. Everything was so simple and sweet; they would get in and get out in a flash; no one would ever have an opportunity to attack them at all.

Both Cypress and Talon trotted through the forest toward the Ministry castle with two horses and a small wooden carriage that had a small wooden boat inside it. The sun had just fallen past the horizon, and the air was now getting very cold. Talon could see the island that was home to Auzgool but didn't feel at all nervous about their little venture. In fact, he had now become very confident, not only that they were going to survive, but also that they were going to succeed. Stars flickered in the night sky, and the moon cast a blue through the trees and onto the forest floor. Though her plan was amazingly simple and very good, Cypress was not going to think that there would not be any real danger. She would not have the same attitude as Talon no matter what the plan was; she had seen too many of her closest friends get killed on peaceful nights like this one, and she was not going to let her guard down, not even for one moment. The carriage hopped and bounced over the rocks and brush of the forest floor, making heavy tracks in the dirt and mud. Sandbags dangled at each corner of the carriage as the horses trotted alongside Cypress and Talon as they walked slowly through the forest to the edge of the lake. Water splashed up and down to and fro up against the bedrock that made a steep drop into the lake. Cypress led the horses backward, allowing the carriage to roll off the rocks and into the lake. The horses stood there nervous from the new sensation of the carriage now not having much weight and its incessant rocking back and forth in the water. Talon got in the boat and pushed off the carriage, and Cypress disconnected the small wooden carriage from the horses. The carriage began to sink very quickly, and Talon brought the boat up to the small ledge of rock for Cypress to get in.

"There aren't any guards on this side of the dungeons. I think it's because they don't think that anyone can get out on this side, there is a lot of water," said Cypress as she reached out her hand to get into the boat.

"Either that or they have neglected it. Either way, this is going to be easier than I thought," Talon said as he moved the paddles to the boat out of the way so that Cypress could sit down.

The gentle rocking of the boat made the experience very pleasant for Talon as he pushed the water beneath it one stroke at a time. Cypress was, however, not so relaxed like Talon; she wanted the danger to be over as quickly as possible. The moon reflected on the lake as it shone down from the heavens, and the wind gently blew through the trees of the forest. When they had reached the edge of the island of Auzgool, Cypress stood up in the boat and quietly called to the man inside the dungeon. It was the easiest way to locate him, she thought to herself while looking intently through the bars set into the stone wall. Talon froze when she called for the man; he hadn't quite realized that there was going to be anything so vocal about their presence and was now afraid that they would be discovered.

"Sol. Are you in there?" whispered Cypress as she cupped her hands around her mouth.

Talon was now wishing that they had taken the Musician along instead of Cypress; at least he could do the job effectively.

"Sit down, you're making too much of a racket," Talon angrily begged as he pulled on her cloak.

Cypress quickly slapped his hand away and gave him a very unpleasant look and then stopped calling so that she would be able to hear Sol if he was too weak to call out loudly.

A long pause fell before it was interrupted by an old man's voice that came from inside the dungeon.

"I am here," said the voice.

"Ah, good," said Cypress as she stepped up closer to the barred hole at the side of the stone wall. "Get back. I'm going to blast my way in," she said as she quickly reached out both of her hands. "Move the boat back a little bit," instructed Cypress, still standing tall in the boat.

Talon eased the boat away from the wall of the prison, and moments later, a loud crash erupted as pieces of stone and metal went flying through the air and into the lake around them with many splashes. Talon quickly positioned the boat at the entrance to the large hole in the wall, and an old man jumped out into the boat, still chained to whatever was left of the wall. Cypress grabbed hold of the old man and broke the chains off him.

Talon was rowing hard and fast now, trying to get to the horses on the other side of the lake. Sweat began to roll down his back and down his face in the freezing night air. He was sure that they were going to be caught now that they had made so much noise. Fear began to grip Talon with each thrust of the oar into the water. *There is going to be someone waiting for us*, he thought to himself in panic.

Fortunately for Talon though, he performed well when he panicked, and so he could be confident that he would not pass out and be more trouble for the group. He would fight the urge to do anything stupid and would think more clearly than usual; *that is one of my good traits*, he thought to himself as he forcefully rowed on. Cypress began to calm as the edge of the forest eased closer and closer. Sol lay in the boat, breathing hard from the excitement. Cypress could tell that Sol had been treated badly; he had been beaten, and she could see that they had not fed him. His skinny, rankled legs shivered in the night air along with his skinny arms that were huddled to his chest. Sol's white beard had been dirtied from the dungeons, and he stared into the night sky as a man broken in spirit. Cypress stood looking over the lay of the land for foes when the boat came to a jolting stop at the edge of the rock face of the forest.

Sol had not seen Talon's face until he stopped rowing and turned to help the man up. Sol's face grew pale when he saw Talon, and he began to fight to keep Talon from grasping hold of him. The old man began crying out for help as Talon struggled to restrain him. Cypress had already gotten out of the boat when she saw Talon grabbing hold of the screaming and kicking old man. Talon lifted him up and out of the boat onto the ground of the forest. Finally, Sol broke free and burst into a frantic run through the forest, but before he could go too far, Cypress reached out her hand. Sol was lifted off the ground into midair; he fought and groped at the air as he spun round and round. Cypress clenched her hand when she realized that Sol was going to be trouble. Sol stopped thrashing the air and had begun to grasp at his throat as if someone were choking him.

"Be silent," whispered Cypress as she walked closer to Sol with her hand stretched out in front of her, using her mind to keep hold of the man. Anger had come over her because of the man's stupidity, and she stood in front of Sol as he clawed at his own neck, trying to pry apart the hands that were binding him.

"Tell me you will shut up when I release you," she said, now staring directly into Sol's bloodshot eyes.

The old man whimpered and nodded his head in agreement.

"That's enough," screamed Talon, now running to Cypress.

Cypress paid Talon no attention.

"Release him now," Talon screamed again as he stood there and clenched his fist.

The man fell to the ground with a quiet thump and lay there gasping for air. Cypress walked away with an angry look and mounted one of the horses that they had brought along. Talon walked up to the old man and picked him up gently off the ground. Sol had passed out by the time that they strapped him to the back of a horse.

"Why did you act so cruelly to him?" asked Talon, confused.

"He would have gotten us all killed if I hadn't," she said in a forceful tone of voice.

Talon looked at Cypress as if she were something that he had not seen before, and she could see the difference in his attitude toward her.

"It is a cruel world, Talon. Sometimes other people will not respond to anything other than cruelty. I'm sorry that you had to see me act this way. However, sometimes it is a necessity for the situation," Cypress said in a loving tone.

She didn't want Talon to think of her as a ruthless person, and she didn't want him to become afraid of her like most other people. She wanted him to see her as the person that she really was, not the person that the world had turned her into.

"Your mother," whispered Sol, strapped to the back of his brown, black—and-white speckled horse.

Talon and Cypress both turned and looked at Sol in confusion, but only Talon asked what it was that he was talking about.

"Talon, your mother was on the council that sent me to prison, and she has been looking for you. I'm sorry I thought that you were working with her. You're going to have to go into hiding now," said Sol with his mouth pressed up to the neck of his horse.

9 BEHIND THE DOOR OF BETRAYAL

SOL AWOKE INSIDE one of the castle quarters that were for guests. With sweaty hands, he reached to throw the quilts off him. He looked around but was too old to care where it was that Talon and Cypress had taken him. Nothing but an old Victorian chest lay at the foot of his bed on the ground and a set of new clothing that had been planted there so that he would have something decent to wear. Doors of solid four-inch-thick wood separated him from a world that he knew nothing about, and he was beginning to think that he was no better off there in the room of the tower than he was in Auzgool. He was too old for this, he thought to himself as he slowly rolled himself out of bed. Talon had left his cane for the man to use lying against a chair not too far from the head of his bed.

"Well, that was mighty kind of you," Sol mumbled as he reached for the clothes at the foot of his bed.

The morning light was a disturbance to Sol, and he raised his shriveled hand in front of his eyes so that he could look through his window at the beautiful garden that lay just outside. Sol slumped as he walked to the window so that he could take a sharper look and moaned with pain from the night before. There was a red bruise that ran from one ear to the other that made him look like he was a man that had broken free from his leash. Rings of red circled his wrists from the chains of Auzgool, and his fingers were black because of shuffling them through the dirt for days.

Morning light burst through the window as he got dressed for his day, and he could see the trees from the garden sway as the wind blew through them. Sol was glad that he had somehow escaped from death and was grateful that Cypress and the Order had thought to save his life. It was an unusual gesture even in the times that they were living in. He stared into the blinding light from the sun and smiled.

The top of the highest part of the castle wall was visible from the window. Sol took another look around the room and realized that he was in a much better place than before; here, these people would take care of him. He would not have to worry about them abandoning him or treating him badly. He had already been shown that his life here would be a good one, and he was becoming more and more confident of that fact as every minute passed.

Talon's eyes focused in and out rapidly as he paid his utmost attention to the chessboard that lay in front of Galen and him. Galen wasn't staring at the board though; he was staring at where Talon's eyes roamed so that he could see where it was that he would possibly move next. Talon was well unaware.

The fire cracked and spewed as they played next to it. Snow had begun to fall outside, and what was left of the season had died from the cold. The whistling of the wind could be heard through the fire flue, and Talon was bundled up next to Cypress as he played. Talon couldn't think of anything that he would rather be doing at that moment, and he couldn't think of anyone that he would rather be sharing his time with. His new family was that of something that you would hear about in books. Galen was now much like a grandfather to him, and Talon was used to the weird things that Galen would do—things like carrying around an old wooden cover to a book that Talon knew nothing about for over a month now and not letting anyone not even Cypress, into the library where he spent most of his time. Talon always got a fuzzy feeling when there was some truth that was kept secret from him. It made him feel loved. Everyone knew that Talon hated being schooled in a flash; he told them that it made him feel like he wasn't human or something like that. They did on occasion slam some necessary knowledge on him just to see him scratch his head in frustration. Everyone, though, was wondering what it was that Galen was doing in the library. It wasn't like him to be so secretive. They knew, however, that they would find out soon enough. Galen never revealed something to them unless he had an educated understanding of the whole situation. So, no one was worried about the temporary deception.

Talon was also very happy about the non-eventful weeks that had been taking place; they gave him a chance to acclimate to his new environment. He did, however, have a thought to go down to the city of Pastel so that he could have a little fun outside of the castle. *It is unhealthy for me to be locked up in this place*, he thought to himself. Talon often thought to call it Galen's Auzgool only for a small laugh. He was thinking of all that had taken place only a few weeks earlier and felt that it had been a dream. He looked around the room, taking his eyes off the chessboard, imagining that this place couldn't be home to the bravest people that he had ever known, they were just normal people with their squabbles and their complaints about the world. The only one that always reminded Talon that he lived in an amazing world was Galen and his secrets, but Talon wasn't concerned about those things. He was content to live a normal life with the others for the time being, and he was happy for the first time in months. Shadows were cast from Galen's hand as he reached for the wooden queen with a smile. Galen knew that if anyone knew what he had done and what he had discovered in the library, it would be devastating to many, so he had locked it up so no one could enter and discover it themselves. Galen's next move would be to revisit the Musician and convince him to relinquish the key into his possession. But he thought to give it some time. Perhaps he would find another clue in the library or another place in the castle. It had seemed for now that whatever had attacked Cypress and Talon on the road had gone away, and it was a peace that Galen was not going to neglect.

"I want to take Talon to the city. We really do need to get some fresh air, you know," said Sol as he rocked in his chair next to the fireplace.

Sol looked much better compared to how he had looked previously. He was only happy, and he was walking much better than he had in years. He was glad to be free of the bondage of the Ministry, as he so often put it in words. He felt as if he were a part of something powerfully influential to the world, and he didn't hold it against Cypress for being so hard on him at the onset of his unscrupulous escape, at least on his part. Cypress turned and looked at Galen; she was not comfortable with the idea of Talon and Sol going out alone on a cold night, and Galen knew what she was thinking just by the expression on her face.

"If you really think that you need to experience something fun"—he paused for a moment— "you will need an escort. I do think that Cypress and I could use a little bit of fun at this crucial junction. We will go with you and keep track," said Galen as he turned to look in Sol's direction.

James was sitting on the sofa, and he agreed to go too.

"We shall make a night of it," he said as he closed the book that he had been reading.

Sol hadn't forgotten the compassion that Talon had shown him the night that they broke him out of prison; it had created a very good relationship between the two. Thus, there were times when Sol would include Talon on some feeling that the two had that was mutual, such as them both wanting to get out for the night. Sol saw Talon much like a grandson; it was a feeling that he had not felt for some time, and he was enjoying every crucial moment. Much like a new father wouldn't take his eyes off his new son, he wouldn't want to miss his first steps.

Talon made another move on the board and looked at Galen with a smile as the fireplace continued to crackle and whistle.

Pastel shimmered in the light of the moon as the snow on the ground reflected the light from above. Talon saw the sight and gasped at the mountain's beauty; and he was now, more than ever, proud of his new home. He would forget that there were people that would like to take all that he had away, and he would enjoy himself and the people that he loved, his new family. The lights from the city masked the light of the moon from within the city, and the people of the bustling city masked the sounds of the forest and the creatures in it. He was in heaven.

Galen, Cypress, Sol, and James walked through the entrance of the pub as the people danced and swung their beers in song; women danced on the top of tables and men shouted and kissed their feet. Talon couldn't help but smile when he reached the bar of the pub when the spirits master looked at him with admiration; it made him remember the first night that he had been with Cypress and all the pain that came with it. He could laugh about it now though, now that he had realized that it was all for his own good; it made him proud of himself seeing that his kindness toward someone had finally paid off.

Galen puffed on his pipe and stood in the doorway, feeling not so much pity for the young men and women vomiting out by the side of the honorable establishment, or at least that is how James described it. James talked and talked to the spirits master, to the women that passed with ales on wooden platters, to the men and women with the instruments as they played. And Talon had, for the first time since Sol's rescue by Cypress, seen Sol move and thrash his hands in the air. Sol called it dancing.

"Not bad for eighty-five, huh?" said Cypress, leaning on the bar next to Talon, also in awe of how well Sol was moving.

"No, not bad at all," said Talon, smiling back at Cypress.

Snow covered the streets and the streetlamps; it stuck to the tops of the rod-iron fences that were planted here and there down the sidewalks of the city. People walked up and down the streets, clenching their clothes because of the cold. The Pastel wasn't the only bar in the city, and it wasn't the largest, but it was the only one that the Order could feel truly safe in. Galen could see the lights of other bars just down the street and could hear their music in the distance. Carriages rode by, and there were some men fighting only a few blocks away from the bar. It was too cold for Galen to stay outside the doorway though, so he sauntered back into the bar for a glass of wine or hard liquor; Galen wasn't too fond of beer.

"Some Canterian whisky please," said Galen as he sat at the bar with Talon.

"I really did need this excursion. Thank you, Galen," said Talon as he reached his hand to Galen's shoulder.

Galen just looked back at Talon and gently smiled.

"I think that I'm going to get some brisk night air in my lungs. What do you say, Galen, you want to come with me?"

"I just came from outside. I think that I would rather stay in here, but don't go far. I don't want you to get hurt. People in this town can get dangerous,"

"Don't worry, old man. I'll be fine," said Talon as he raised himself from the chair.

Talon was thankful that he was finally out of Pastel Mountain, but he was the kind of person that could only handle so much of crowds and loud noises; he liked an atmosphere that he could hear his own thoughts in. All he needed was a new setting, and the streets of Pastel did fine for the job. Talon leaned himself outside the bar on the rod-iron fence that was connected to a streetlamp and looked at the moon through the halo of the lamplight that came from the pub and wondered what it would be like to live somewhere else, a completely new world that would be very alien to him. Something without danger—he didn't really enjoy danger that much. He could go his whole life without a stitch of danger in it, he thought to himself as he pulled the ice-cold beer to his lips and took another swig. *Not one stitch*, he repeated in his mind. He looked back at the men in the street still fighting and the stores that were still open, the other pubs that were bustling and the people shouting in laughter and joy. Then he turned and looked at Galen in the Pastel Pub and Lodge talking to Cypress and laughing also, at James begging the most beautiful woman that played the violin to give him a chance to play, and at the old man Sol, now sitting on one of the benches that surrounded a table with a woman belly dancing. Sol was staring at the bell bracelets that hung around her feet like a cat tracing the path of a string and was breathing hard. Talon was also happy to see everyone having fun, and he was getting the peace that he so desperately needed.

Talon was still watching his friends when a deafening crack and two flashes of light sounded into the air. Two men in blue cloaks grabbed hold of Talon, one on each arm. He didn't have a chance to react before another cracking sound and bright light deafened his senses; then there was darkness and an extreme pressure on his chest. He could see the commotion in the pub come to an instantaneous halt along with everyone's heads turning in his direction. Cypress had begun to run through the people in the pub toward him as Talon's view distorted, then darkness again with nothing to hear. Just when he thought that he wouldn't be able to bear the pain in his chest as it now traveled through his whole body, light appeared along with new surroundings. Another cracking sound and he was falling about five feet from the ground onto stone tile. Talon crawled along the ground, gasping for air like a dying python. Eventually, the air came back into his lungs, and he was able to stand up. When he looked around, he saw torches lit only to make parts of the room visible; much of it was too dark to make anything out. Tile stone lay in a circular pattern in the center of what seemed to Talon, a court hall. Many people sat on the benches that lay theater style down to a long table and podium. There was not one seat that had not been filled with someone in dress uniform, all with brightly extravagant material.

"I'm sorry if we startled you, your evaporation was a difficult one, I presume?" said the middle-aged man sitting in the center of the table behind the podium.

The walls were tall, and there were many pillars that surrounded the round room. Talon said nothing; he was still trying to catch his breath.

"We have some disturbing evidence against you, Mr. Barrett," the man said as he watched the two trackers struggling to keep Talon on his feet.

"Where am I?" asked Talon, still breathing hard.

"You're in Ministry court hall number six. We cannot send someone to the dungeons without a customary trial now, can we?"

Talon was now beginning to realize that he was in a lot of trouble. He was now the one who was going to Auzgool. *For what reason?* Talon asked himself in his mind. He didn't care really, he thought again. Being a part of the Order gave them ample reason to hold him, and there was no reason for hope other than that of the Order coming to rescue him the same way he and Cypress rescued Sol. Either way, it would mean him staying in a dungeon cell with chains around his neck, wrists, and ankles for a few days. *How did I get in this position?* Talon asked himself, and *how did they know that I was in Pastel? This was wholly unfair,* Talon thought as the middle-aged man went through his charges of wrongdoing.

"Do you understand the seriousness of these charges?" asked the man at the podium.

"Yes," said Talon, still struggling to get free from the two men that were holding him.

"Would you like to say something before you are taken into custody?" asked the man as he turned to Morastah Barrett, sitting on the council bench next to the middle-aged man.

Talon saw his mother when the man turned to look at her, and his stomach turned in anger.

"Mr. Barrett, I feel that I should pay my condolences to your mother for having to track you down and send you to us, but according to her, it was a necessary step in preventing your further delinquency." The man turned aside and gave the platform to Morastah. Talon's mother stepped up to the podium and spoke.

"Mr. Talon Hanson Barrett, you are charged with aiding the escape of a known criminal of treason. Your sentence is to be carried out for a term of ten years in the dungeons of Auzgool until you await your execution, which will be carried out when your ten-year term has expired. Guards, take the prisoner away."

Talon had never felt anything like the feeling of one being betrayed, until now. He would never forget this, and if he did ever get out of Auzgool, his mother would pay for what she had done to him; he would make sure of it.

Cypress had reached the door by the time that the two men and Talon had disappeared with blinding brilliance. She was breathing hard in her panic. James stood there staring at the place where Talon had been, in shock of the effectiveness of the abduction. There was nothing that they could do for him. All they could do was stand there and look. Cypress was now outside, hoping that what she had seen was something in her imagination, her mind playing tricks on her. *He might just be down the street*, she thought to herself in denial of the truth of the matter. This would be a hard thing for her to handle. When her tears had begun to fall from her face into the cold ice on the streets, Galen was there to comfort her. She didn't resist him this time and sank into Galen's arms. The men outside had stopped fighting and were also standing and staring. People inside the pub stood there in confusion as to what had happened; some of them were fearful that it was an invasion from the Ministry and that they were all going to be picked off one by one. It was clear though that everyone's night had been spoiled by the clear injustice of the whole ordeal. They walked back to their homes, and the lights of the pub were shut off in respect for the Order's loss. Men and women held their heads down whether they felt the effects of what they had been drinking or not. It was, all in all, a very sad night for everyone.

Sol walked alongside Galen, Cypress, and James as they mounted their horses and rode through the streets of Pastel.

"I suppose that it was not a very good idea to go out tonight after all," said Sol, now walking alongside the others. "At least we know where he was taken, that's not a very hard mystery to solve, we'll have to find a way to break him out just like you did for me," Sol said optimistically.

"It's not that simple, Sol. We don't even really know where he is. Guessing at the matter isn't going to do us any good. We are going to have to find hard evidence," said Cypress, now looking into Sol's eyes sarcastically.

Sol knew what it was like in the dungeons of Auzgool; he knew that Talon would have a hard time coping with the harshness of it. Sol, however, knew that if Talon did survive the experience, he would walk away a new man, or at least a man that knew a lot more about what it was that the world that he lived in was capable of. He would learn endurance, he would learn humility, and he would learn to absolutely appreciate all of what it was that he had prior to his abduction.

Sol knew that the love of his family was not an issue nor the love for the Order, but he knew that it would enrich the experience of love in every way possible. He would also become a more passionate man than he had been. If Sol didn't dwell on the good things that would come from every experience in life, he knew that he would not be living at all. The pain of the world would be too much to manage. For the others though, it was not only a good night that had ended badly; it very well could have been a good friendship that had ended. No one of them though, was about to give up on the fact that they would find Talon alive.

Talon didn't resist the guards as they led him through the Ministry halls. He had reached a defeat that he had not anticipated. He had been instantaneously broken, like a fine horse that had been locked up for too long, and he was in no condition to bring himself out of his depression. Betrayal of the mother—he hadn't thought that the concept could even be brought to mind, not by even the cruelest man in the cruelest times. Obviously, he was wrong, however, and it left him near unconscious. The guards carried his limp body through the halls and down the stairs through the only entrance underground and to his cell. He could hear men and women wailing and the chains that bound them ringing on the stone floors; he did not dare to look at their pain. The guards hurled him through the air and onto the stone floor of his cell. Pain shot through his body after hitting the ground and wall. Talon lay there in shock of his situation. Blood trickled from his face and from his ears because of the Ministry's mistreatment. Talon curled into the fetal position and put his hands over his ears to drown out the cries of the others in the prison.

It was freezing in the dungeons; there were no stained-glass windows to block out some of the cold from outside, only the holes cut out of the stone with bars to keep the prisoners from escaping. Talon could not help but regret his neglect of gaining the knowledge that he could have used to break himself out. *If only I knew how to transport myself,* he thought to himself with his hands still to his ears. It was hard for him to think with all that racket. The pain of others would only amplify his own, and he didn't want to hear any of it. Ice sat on the base of the cell bars of the window and freezing water dripped down the wall to the ground. Rats scurried along the floors, stealing morsels of meal from each prisoner that was not paying close attention, and the smell was absolutely awful. Talon was curious as to what would happen next in his life; ever since he met Cypress, his life had changed so dramatically. At the very moment of being in such hardship, Talon had become stronger than he had ever hoped to be. Life for him was no longer an uninteresting episode. Every moment now was the greatest mystery and adventure. Now he would be intrigued at all that was happening to him. It was just another curious experience that would pass on in the long and exciting new life. The thought of this brought the most comfort to Talon. He lifted himself into the sitting position, leaning against the cell wall just under the window, and smiled. Perhaps he would be able to break himself out of prison after all.

Cypress heard deafening blasts as she ran through the halls of Pastel Mountain. Galen, James, Mary, and the others had escaped the initial attack in the city of Pastel; but they knew that they had been compromised and they were in grave danger. Once the Requiem would break through the mountain's defenses, they would be helpless. Cypress, Galen, and everyone but Sol was running through the east tower and breathing hard. The stables were only a few steps away when a huge beam of wood came crashing through the entrance from the stables, demolishing any stone that it encountered. Sol had been killed at the entrance and was lying dead in the middle of the courtyard. The giant that wielded the large tree swung it indiscriminately as he tried to get into the entrance for more destruction. No one needed instruction to head back the other way and try to find another exit.

The castle was surrounded, and the Order was trapped inside. Galen, panicking, ran to the library entrance and unlocked the door. He had hoped that they would be able to exit quietly through the secret door that led to the mine, but when they opened the exit, they could hear giants bashing their way through the mine as well. Cypress and the others didn't bother to ask why it was that all the books had been thrown from their shelves because no one noticed; that was until Galen closed the entrance to the library and ran to the back of it with both of his hands stretched out. There was not much that they could do against a giant, and there was a very good chance that they would not survive against forty or fifty of them even with the Legacy. The others quickly followed Galen up to the wall. Galen concentrated, and the shelves and wall began to open to the chamber with the twelve doors. This was the only chance that they had of survival, and it was a slim one at that. Galen and the others ran through the entrance to the chamber, and he sealed it behind them.

"Where are we?" asked James as they all quieted down in the hidden room.

"I don't know. I haven't figured it out yet," said Galen, still breathing hard from the sprint through the castle.

Cypress sat on the floor and waited for what she thought was the inevitable. She felt as if she was powerless to do anything for herself and the others of the Order. She was glad that they had sent the relatives away the day before otherwise it would have been exceedingly difficult to keep track of them during the attack. Cypress did not know if she would see them again, but she was glad that they were safe and not in Pastel with the rest of the Order. What would become of them now that they all were being torn apart? There was now nowhere for them to live peacefully, no place for them to accomplish what it was that they had set out to do from the very beginning; and though she was the optimistic type, she felt that she would never see Talon again.

That was the most painful thing of all. More painful than losing her home that she had known for twelve years, more than the death of Sol, and more than any pain that she would encounter in the future. *There is no way that we can save him now*, she thought to herself as she sat on the dirty stone of the floor of the chamber. She curled her knees to her chest and tried to drown out the thunderous sounds of the Requiem demolishing her home as the light from the torches shone brightly in the chamber.

Bristle was standing and staring at the symbols in the center of each door. He was probably the only person in that room that was not devastated by the thought of losing their precious home. He was too interested to think about that. He wasn't fond of Sol either, so there was nothing that could hinder his curiosity toward the room and the twelve doors. Mary made a short scream from the sound of a giant breaking his way through the entrance from the mine, and the others jumped—all except for Bristle. He was too busy fingering the marking on the head of the first door. They could hear the giant pounding about as it walked, smashing tables, chairs, book racks, windows, and other important things to the Order. It sounded now as if there were more than one: one in the kitchen, one in the common room, and obviously, one in the library. Mary had begun to cry when the sounds stopped, and everything seemed to go silent. When she realized that the thrashing had stopped, Mary got a hold of herself so that she could hear what it was that was going on just outside the secret door.

Silence fell upon everything. Bristle turned his attention away from the symbols, and there was the sound of only nervous breathing from everyone. Bristle heard distant steps of giants as they stomped away. Still silent, Bristle closed his eyes and concentrated on seeing what it was that was on the other side of the wall. If he concentrated enough, he would be able to form an image of what was in the next room. Terror filled Bristle's face for just a moment, and he quickly reached out his hand toward the others in the room. Not a moment too soon and he was throwing Cypress, James, Mary, and Galen against the other side of the chamber. Each one tumbled and fell and slid against the other wall of the round room. Large stones went flying in all directions when the large six-foot round beam burst through the wall that the Order had been close to. The tree crashed against the stone over and over again as the giant laughed. Moments later and the giant's feet were visible. Galen looked over where the first of the twelve doors once stood, but there was nothing but a narrow passageway that he could see extending for what seemed to be miles through the dust and rubble of the door that once stood hidden for centuries. Galen didn't hesitate for one second. He was up on his feet and through the narrow passage of stone and wood. When the others saw Galen run, they quickly got to their feet and followed. They ran into the darkness, not knowing where it was that they were heading. Cypress could hear the fast footfalls of Galen, but she could not see him at all. Sounds of the screaming giant were amplified through the passage of darkness, but it only made her run faster. Cypress could feel the disorienting feeling of the narrow taking a slight turn in the darkness, and every now and then her shoulders would make a brushing collision with the stone walls.

We have hope, Galen thought as he ran. Galen often thought of the castle of Pastel as having a personality of its own, but never could he have said before that it was the castle of Pastel that directly saved his life; that, however, was yet to be seen. It was not long when Galen heard the giant wailing in pain and screaming for help. Galen was surprised by this, and he came to a sliding stop in the darkness. Cypress didn't care what was happening to the giant; she kept running. Cypress hit something hard in the middle of her sprint and quickly fell to the ground. Galen picked her up off the ground after she collided with him and told her to be quiet. The giant wailed as if it was being tortured, and the others of the Order had stopped running also. Soon there was nothing, but the blood curdling screams that were now echoing through the narrow. There was what could have been the sound of an explosion accompanied by a burst of fast-moving wind that pushed itself through the tunnel, and then dead silence. No one moved an inch. James couldn't control himself, and he whispered into the darkness of the tunnel ahead of him

"Is it dead?" as if the others had seen and heard something that he had not.

No one answered him.

"We should keep moving," said Galen as he grabbed hold of Cypress in the dark. "We can seal the entrance later, once we know where it is that we are going."

Galen could hear rushing water in the distance as he and Cypress walked, but they never met the stream.

"The water is behind the walls," said Cypress in the darkness. "It must be the stream that Talon and I went across," she continued.

"That would be an appropriate assumption," Galen said as he held her hand slowly leading her. "I suspect that there is much more that we do not know about our own history even though we have been searching for the truth for so long. I do believe that we are closer to finding the whole truth though, and that should be comforting," he continued.

Cypress didn't respond; the darkness had begun to consume her sense of reality. They had been in the corridor, walking, for hours. *Who knows how much longer it will take for us to get to wherever it is that we are going*, she thought to herself. The darkness began to infiltrate her mind, and she began to slow. Cypress kept thinking that she would never see Talon again, and she was exhausting herself.

The tunnels continued for what seemed forever to Cypress until they reached another tunnel that crossed their path. Galen stepped down into the second tunnel, which was much larger, and crossed to the other side.

"This is where the tunnel ends. We need to choose which direction to go," Galen said as he petted the wall directly in front of him.

Cypress stepped down in the black and stumbled over something in the darkness. She bent down to investigate with her fingers when the others came walking into the larger tunnel.

"Train tracks," Cypress said as she searched with her hands the steel tracks that led into the nothingness.

"We should go left," said Galen, now heading in that direction.

Cypress could hear the footfalls of the Order in the dirt and gravel as they walked. Eventually, they came to the back of a train.

Cypress walked alongside the back section and called for James to come closer to her.

"Do you have a match?" asked Cypress as she felt for his arms and hands.

She felt through his pockets and felt for his shoulders and arms, but he did not help her look for the matches. There was only a strange breathing from him that she thought was peculiar. That was until she touched his hand and realized that he was not James at all. The figure in the dark clenched its rough claws around her hand, and she screamed in terror. The creature shrieked at the sound of the scream of Cypress and fled. Galen could only hear Cypress's frantic breathing and the sound of the creature shuffling its way through the tunnel far off into the distance. Cypress was shaking violently in fear when the sound of James opening a lantern and lighting it in the rear of the train echoed in the black. The others, all except for Bristle, were completely oblivious to the reason for Cypress's cry; they stood there in places that, before just a moment ago, had been completely black to the senses. James reached down to pick Cypress off the ground in between the tracks of the train.

"Are you all right, is there something the matter?" he asked obliviously.

Cypress squinted in the light of the lamp and frantically looked around for anything else that might be in the tunnel that she had not been aware of.

"Did you notice the creature that had been walking with us the entire time?" asked Cypress in a perturbed tone.

"Yes, I did, but I wasn't sure what its intentions were, so I didn't reveal my knowledge of its presence," said Bristle, patting Cypress on the shoulder, acknowledging that she was not hallucinating.

"I want you to light every lamp that you see," said Galen to James, pointing all the way down to the end of the train. James acknowledged with a nod and began to light the candles down to the last one in the cab of the train.

"There is still coal, and I think that there is water in the tank. The train should be able to move. It looks like it's in good condition. It hasn't been attacked or anything like that," James said as he returned to the cart in which everyone had settled.

"We can settle here for the night if you feel all right with it," Galen said as he leaned in one of the chairs of the train compartment.

"Have you gone mad? There is no way that I am staying here where anything can get to me while I'm sleeping. I would rather take my chances on wherever this train leads than wait for that thing to come back," Cypress said as she looked at Galen as if he had indeed gone mad, accompanied with a disappointed shake of the head.

"We can lock the doors if you're uncomfortable," James said with a smile.

"That thing was huge. I thought that it was you, James, and who knows where it came from," she said, still emphasizing her argument.

"I suppose that we will have to get this train running and hope that what awaits us on the other end of the tunnel isn't worse than what we have already encountered," said Galen as he looked around the train at everyone.

Cypress was in no mood to entertain game playing with the others of the Order, and she was perfectly willing to stay up all night if that was what it took to get out of these dark tunnels. Only Cypress and Bristle knew how queer the creature was, and Cypress was not going to wait around for it to bring its friends. So naturally, she was the first to volunteer shoveling the coal into the furnace, and Bristle was there to help her in any way he could. When the furnace was hot, they could hear the boiling water in the tank gain pressure, and Bristle regulated the pressure valves for optimum performance. It was not long when smoke began to billow out of the chimney of the train. Though it was a very old train, it worked very well. It had been preserved for, as Galen put it, possibly thousands of years or when the Ancients created the tunnel system.

Galen was, out of them all, the most curious about what it was that they might find on the other side of the tunnel. What kind of new knowledge would be revealed? This would be the find of a lifetime; there would be no one to share it with though, no one except the Order, and they were dull, Galen thought to himself as he pulled out his pipe and puffed. James sat in the seat across from Galen in the dinner trolley and had started laughing at the predicament that they were in. *It seems funny*, he thought to himself, *the fact that Talon is the cause of the Ministry's investigation and destruction of Pastel. Perhaps we have had this coming for some time though.* He didn't dare to smear that fact in the face of Galen though; it was just something that you didn't do to him, and fortunately for James, he knew it. For Mary though, the whole happening had taken its toll. She was not a young woman anymore, and when she had been, she was not active; she was in the Order only because of her husband, but she was a great asset to it, she had hoped. The running through the tunnels were the hardest for her; she had gotten used to having a good home away from all the lies of society, and it was hurting her most of all finally having the realization that the pleasant life that she had been living was now over. Now she was homeless, without a place to call her own. She had had a lot of friends that had died over the many years; they died horrible, violent deaths. She hoped that she would live to see the next day. The attack from the Ministry was too close for comfort, and she was tiring of the constant hiding.

"Why don't we destroy the Ministry castle, why don't we just kill them all? It would get them out of our way and out of our way for good," she said angrily.

"If you would like their blood on your hands, well then, I suggest that you do. But I for one will not take that responsibility. It is better for me to let them kill themselves. That, my dear, is something that they are doing as we speak. They will suffer their own annihilation while we stand back and let them be dominated permanently by death. When they cry out for our help, we will not be there to help them, and it is not far off," Galen said as he softly clenched his pipe and puffed his troubles away.

10 ASSCATAN

TALON STOOD STRONG, facing the cell wall of Auzgool. He reached his hand out in front of him and visualized the wall being reduced to rubble through the Legacy. He closed his eyes and strained with all his thinking power, all what he knew that he possessed, but nothing happened. Nothing could make him quit now that his life was on the line. He tried staring at the wall intently, but still nothing happened. Then he remembered what it was that Cypress had said the second night that he had seen her.

He concentrated on the subatomic and pictured the molecules of the wall jumping about more and more rapidly. Many in the cells beside him watched the crazy man that would stare at the wall; some laughed and jeered at him. He saw into the wall and concentrated on separating the electrons from the nucleolus. His hand began to quiver, and light began to erupt just in front of him, in the middle of the air. In the sudden shock of what he had caused to happen, he lost his concentration, and the light dispersed. There was one though that watched in amazement and said nothing. The young man stood on his knees at the entrance of his cell and clenched the bars of the cell door. His eyes were wide at the clear sight of the strange new addition to the dungeons when the wall of Talon's cell exploded out into the ice of the lake that surrounded Auzgool. This bore a striking resemblance to the escape of Sol, he thought to himself. Talon pondered on what it would be like to see Cypress and the others of the Order, but there was no one out in a boat to take him to the forest. In fact, there was no one at all that he could see, no one anywhere. He knew that he was not the one who had caused the explosion of the wall. It must have been someone from the Order; he was confident of it.

He could see the ice that covered the lake, which met at Auzgool from the forest, and he could hear the rustling of the trees and the dropping of snow off them. Talon could see his breath in the cold night air. He had begun to figure out how exactly he was going to get across the lake when his feet began to lift from off the stone floor. He was now floating in the air and slowly drifting across the lake. He looked around when a light in the distance caught his eye. As he looked closer, he could see the figure of a woman holding a lamp, she was inside the forest. Talon was now becoming afraid. *Why is this woman helping me? What is it that she is trying to get from me?* He thought to himself. In a noticeably short time, Talon had been brought to the floor of the forest gently and eloquently. He could no longer see the woman with the lamp, and it made him feel at ease knowing that he would not have to talk to her and ask her questions that she would not answer. *It will be a long journey on foot to get to the city of Pastel, but at least I am out of that terrible place*, he thought to himself as he pulled his clothes closer over his skin.

The wind blew across his face, making it numb from the cold. Each step was harder until he had the sudden thought to do what he had done in his cell, create light from nothing, or so it would seem to an onlooker who didn't know how to use the Legacy. As he walked, he concentrated on a ball of snow that he had formed, and slowly the snow changed into a light-sustaining point of fire, which in Talon's view, tumbled and tumbled in the palm of his hand. The ball of light began to emit heat, so Talon was much more comfortable now, than he had been earlier. It was now, more than ever, that Talon knew the power that knowledge could evoke. He would never again neglect his abilities, and he would fight against himself and his foolishness to learn the Legacy. He concentrated on the ball of light and thoughts of his home in Pastel, his family, and his friends. He thought of what it would be like to see Galen's old face again and didn't care if he won him at chess every now and then; Talon would be happy just to be there, sitting in the common room with the warm fireplace blazing and cracking. It would be like paradise.

The snow in the trees would melt and fall off the leaves and branches as Talon walked near them with the small globe of fire in the palm of his hand, and creatures roamed about in the trees. The snow under his feet turned to water and began to flow down the hills of the forest, cutting its way through other snowbanks. Talon didn't know exactly where it was that he was going even though he had traveled the same route before; it was much different in the snow. He enjoyed concentrating on something that was worth his time, and he loved the feeling of such power.

He had now only traveled a fifth of the distance to Pastel when he realized that there was something following him; Talon heard hooves crushing the snow and long breath strokes in the cold night air. He turned around quickly to find the Cyclicorn trotting in amongst the trees beside him. Talon stopped immediately. The horse stared at the orb of fire that Talon was holding in his hand, which made him conclude that it was the light that had attracted the animal. He held the orb out in front of him with his mind. The light from the sphere mesmerized the horse as it left Talon's hand and began floating through the air toward the Cyclicorn. Snow melted as the globe of fire passed through the trees toward the horse. Talon concentrated, and the point of light hovered just far enough from the horse's nose to make it snort and brush its hooves along the ground. The horse dropped its head with its large antlers and followed Talon's light as it began to move back over to him and into his hand again. Talon reached out toward the creature and ran his warm hand over and around the tips of its horns, down and along its forehead, and through its mane of long white hair.

"I shall call you Fire Horse, or just Fire, how does that sound?" he said to the horse as he ran his fingers through its hair.

Cypress shoveled the coal into the furnace as the train puffed on to its destination unknown. Bristle manned the control station; he could hear the screeching of the steel wheels on the tracks as the train sped through the tunnels. Cypress had shoveled all of what was left of the coal into the furnace and went to sit in the cab with the others. She didn't know if the train would reach its destination and at this point, she really didn't care. She was glad to have a rest. It had been many hours since they had found the train.

"IT MUST BE ABOUT MIDDAY NOW!" shouted Cypress as wind whipped through the tunnels and through the windows of the train trolley.

James had opened the sliding windows to get a bit of fresh air, as he put it. Galen was obviously upset from the flowing wind. Whatever it was that he was smoking in his pipe was burning too fast, and the non-politeness of James was evident to everyone else but James himself. Everyone was now getting colder from the icy water that came with the air through the trolley.

"Close the windows, you old fool!" Galen said to James just enough so that he could hear him.

"Yes, yes, perhaps you're right," said James as he lifted himself from his seat to shut the windows. One window at a time, the sound in the trolley died down, and with every click of each latch, the atmosphere became more comfortable. When the whistling had stopped and the last window was shut, James sat down near Galen again and apologized for the interruption of comfort.

Pillars of stone came in and out of view through the windows of the trolley as they passed through the tunnels. Mary could feel the train take quick turns through the tunnels as the trolley rocked in the opposite direction of the turn. She was not too excited at this point, but it was nice to have a bit of peace from the thought of being pulverized by a large tree that had been fashioned to destroy anything it encountered. Yes, she was quite happy to not have that kind of danger at the moment. She huddled herself into the corner of one of the long chairs that was connected to a table and fell asleep to the clinking and clanking of the wheels of the train. She lay there with her knitted scarf and her mother's dress under a heavy wool tunic. She hadn't quite had enough time to take off her apron when the Requiem came bursting through the entrance of Pastel, but fortunately for her, she was not dreaming of the nightmare of her life. In her dream she had just woken up from that horrible nightmare and was running through the halls of Pastel to each and every room to see if everyone was all right, and it was not long when a smile reached her lips from the depths of her emotions.

Galen began to doze off also with his pipe still in his mouth and his hand still at his side. Smoke would billow from his mouth and his nostrils as he snorted and spat into a full-blown snoring session, which made Cypress realize once again the reason she had picked the west tower of Pastel to sleep in every night; it was the farthest from Galen's. Not even stone walls and six-inch solid wood doors could keep that sound from passing through the halls at night. Cypress was willing to stay up this night, and it would seem that she would have to.

The light from the train's lanterns burned brightly in the dense darkness of the tunnels. Every now and then Cypress would see other passageways whiz by, and the irregularity in wind movement outside of the train would cause a suction that would rock the train into the direction of the passageway that passed. James was wide-awake and looking at Cypress as though she had caused all of this to happen. He knew full well though that it was only a matter of time till the Ministry found out where it was that the Order had been hiding; it was possible that they had known for many years but were too scared to attack. The Order was now taking drastic feats of accomplishment; and the Ministry, though in their current state of ignorance, was not about to let the Order take over their kingdom. The Ministry had used the Requiem before, and James didn't understand why they had thought that they would not use them for their benefit again. It was a foolish mistake on James's part, and it was harming him at this very moment in time. He looked down at his hand in his lap when the train began to slow. The moment that the train cleared the tunnel into a massive cave that spanned miles to the surface and miles from one end of it to the other, Bristle began ringing the bell and yelling back at the Order in the trolley to wake up and open their eyes to the truly magnificent sight. Galen immediately stopped snoring and was up out of his chair and onto his feet, looking out of one of the windows of the trolley.

"You were right," Galen said to Cypress as he looked out into the underground city. "It is about midday," he continued while gasping at the magnitude of the architectural masterpiece.

Daylight came from large crystal-like mirrors that were directing the light from far-off places linked together by small tunnels that surrounded the city from all angles. A large castle wall encircled the entire city. There were fortress towers, entrance gates, a moat, and many drawbridges that were left open. The train encircled the city and entered it through the wall at the far end. The course of the train gave a splendid view of the fruit trees and other plants that had been clearly planted by the previous tenants of the castle. Rows of trees came down from the slope of the base of the moat down to the expanse of the cave. There were pools of water that overflowed to other pools, having the eventuality of flowing through the tunnels that had been made for the water to escape through. It was the most beautiful thing that Cypress had ever seen—a true paradise. Cypress looked at Galen and smiled.

"I'm certain that you somehow led us to the right place," she said as she placed her hand on his shoulder. All Galen could do was smile back and turn his attention back to the beautiful sight.

The train came to a stop at a docking station that had many signs that read "Welcome to Asscatan" in twelve different dialects. Other signs directed people who didn't live in Asscatan to places where there would be lodging for the duration of their stay there. The signs were not placed in a form for a sort of tourist; it was more of an organizing of a secret society. There were groups that were numbered and groups that were placed by their tribe and tongue.

"This is absolutely fascinating," said Bristle as he ran his fingers along the letters of different dialects that he had never seen before.

The castle was not like the plants and animals that were still living; all they needed were the sunlight and the streams and pools of running water to survive. The castle, however, was old and overrun by plants and insects; it revealed itself as one subjected to the time that it had spent all alone with no one to take care of it.

Cypress emerged past the money changing booths at the entrance of the train station and began to walk through what seemed to be a marketplace. Spiders scurried across the ground on their webs that lay over and in between the stone crevasses and stone floor. Each step that she took rang through the castle grounds and into the darkness of the inner parts of the castle. She remembered what she had encountered in the train tunnel and wondered if its origin was there in Asscatan, so she was naturally inhibited in her curiosity that would usually cause her to enter the dark parts of the castle. There were no doors to the entrances of the outer chambers that led to many outside sections of the castle. These sections led to previously manned stationing posts that ran along the outer wall and some that led to what looked to Cypress as working stations for blacksmiths and sandal makers. She looked along the walls of the entrances that had strange lettering that went all the way around the entrances and exits; most had appeared to be deliberately chiseled off. Cypress could think of no reason why.

She began to look around at her surroundings, not paying attention to the markings on the walls or the separate chambers of the outside portion of the castle, when she was startled to realize that Bristle had been beside her the whole time, admiring the sight too. Cypress made a quick little jump in fright but said nothing.

"Isn't it absolutely brilliant?" asked Bristle, still staring at what lettering that could still be made out. "These are the same markings that were preserved on the doors in Pastel. They seem to be the remnants of an ancient race of"—he paused for a moment— "humans, but the tone and texture of the stone carving is much more eloquent than that which has been seen by human eyes before. The skill to do such carving would take centuries of one's life to achieve. Clearly, there is a big piece of the puzzle that we have not discovered about our ancestors. Will you accompany me into the chambers of the castle? I want to see if this was a kingdom, and if so, that means that there will be some extravagant accommodations that I would be most interested in. Wow, what a turn of events, wouldn't you say, Nelly?" Bristle said without even looking in her direction.

All of this was just too fascinating to him; he was like a child in a candy store.

Galen was at a far distance off, up in the towers that connected to the bordering wall; he was curious to see what weapons they used for defense. James and Mary were with Galen and were walking along the castle wall. Cypress took another look around right before she entered the inner parts of the castle and smiled. She had just realized that they had been given a new home. One that would be almost impossible to be found by the Ministry—a hope that excelled all hopes, a place where she could take Talon to safety. For Cypress, the whole world had just become a haven, a place of rejoicing. She opened her arms and looked to the ceiling of the cave and spun in circles with a smile that not even she had seen for many years. They had triumphed; they had won the war. This was all it would have taken for them to do what the Order had set out to do; this city would make all the difference in the world to their cause.

Bristle entered the chamber that led to the innermost part of the castle, possibly the part where the nobles had lived. It was better than Pastel in every fashion, a monument to humanity. Light burst into sight by flames from torches as they walked through the hallways to the chambers. Tall wooden doors separated the different rooms and chambers, and then they happened upon the library. Books filled hundreds of feet in one direction and hundreds of feet in the other. Tables and chairs were set up near massive fireplaces. The most fascinating thing though was when Bristle grabbed a book and sat down in one of the filthy old chairs, and suddenly, the fireplace burst into flames, crackling, and spewing gently and efficiently. Bristle looked back at Cypress when he had stopped marveling at the amazing sight of the fireplace and smiled.

"We'll never have to stoke the fire again," he said enthusiastically.

Cypress felt as if she had never left home, and she was ready to find the stores of coal so that they could get underway back to Pastel to break Talon out of prison. She was happy that whatever it was that had touched her hand wasn't anywhere near the castle, and she was enthusiastic about the job that would have to be done in support of the Order.

Galen was now out of the towers and making his way to the library where Bristle and Cypress were. Galen entered the library and was astonished. He could see large bones hanging from ropes that were shaped into creatures that he had never seen before or read about. There were diagrams and parchments and stone tablets that told about the strange creatures that were now extinct. The parchments talked about the creatures not originating from their world, but that was as far as they elaborated. Galen could see a distinct propagandized version of information being fed to the masses at that time and was fascinated by the efficiency of it. The writing was in the oldest tongue that Galen could remember, but no one now knew how to speak it. Once again Galen thought of this as the greatest find of the century for the Order, which meant something because it was only the Order that searched through archeological finds such as these; they were always looking for secrets to their ancestors and where it really was that they came from, always the truth and never the lie. *It is disappointing though*, thought Galen as he flipped through the pages of bound volumes, *disappointing that there was knowledge that was being held back even in the days of the city of Asscatan.* It would mean more searching and more digging, but it would be a great adventure, Galen thought as he took a closer look at the fossilized bones that were hanging from the ceilings.

Cypress walked up to Galen and requested that they go back for Talon. And to Galen, it seemed the most logical step to take, so he agreed. But he, however, would go alone this time. There were dangers that he could not anticipate, and he was not going to allow any other lives to be lost, and that was that. Galen pried Bristle from his book and called for James to help them find the coal. Cypress suggested that the location of the coal was near the station. "It had to be" was how she put it. It wasn't long when they located the coal and were hauling it up to the container behind the drivetrain and into the stove. Galen started the engine and was off back through the tunnel that they had just emerged from. As he backed the train up onto the turntable, he saw another set of tracks that led across a bridge to another tunnel continuing in the opposite direction that Galen was now heading. *I will investigate that further when I come back*, he thought to himself as he worked the levers and control valves that regulated the train's velocity and the pressure in the train's water tank. Meanwhile, the others would make good use of the time that they had to clean and restore the castle of Asscatan.

Talon's horse trotted through the forest gently and slowly; it was not used to the idea of having someone on its back and thought to take the journey to wherever he was leading it slowly. These of course were instinctual thoughts though. Talon didn't really mind taking the journey to Pastel slowly. He knew what it was that awaited him there, and he would cultivate patience, this time. He would relish the idea that he didn't have to walk home, that he didn't have to worry about anyone chasing him. The fact was that everyone would be so happy to see him when he walked through the doors of the pub that would lead him to the cellar door and into the castle of Pastel. They would ask him how he escaped. And he would tell them this extravagantly proportioned story that would make him out to be the lesser hero, and then he would tell the truth to Cypress, as he would hold her in his arms and tell her that while in prison, the only thing that he could think about was her and her beautiful face. He would even pet Davina for a longer duration and perhaps allow her to curl up next to him in bed as he rested from his devastatingly strenuous ordeal. He would expect Cypress to kiss him and tell him that she secretly loved him too and that she had been waiting for him to say something that would give her the courage to tell him, and they would both smile together. He even thought that Galen and James might get overprotective of Cypress and step in to prevent the union. Talon would have to explain his intentions and what he was going to do about his love for Cypress. But all his daydreaming on the back of the Cyclicorn would not change the fact that Pastel had been destroyed, that another home had been found, and that Sol had been killed and Davina had been lost.

Talon and Fire trotted to the place where the lights of the city should have been shining brightly; they passed through demolished doors and walls. The pub was totally destroyed, and there were bodies that lay on the stone streets. People were scattered about in the gutters and under fallen roofs. Men and women had been obviously thrown against, and through walls and windows—the sight was the most horrible thing that Talon had ever seen. Seeing this, he had the sudden thought that Cypress and the others were killed, and that was why the woman knew to come and break him out of prison. It was Cypress's dying wish, he thought to himself. He could no longer think; he could no longer feel anything in his extremities. His body had become numb to the idea that Cypress had been killed and the others of the Order. He would have nothing. Talon's stomach curled into a ball, causing him to vomit the disgusting food that had been given to him in Auzgool, and he fell off the horse to the hard stone streets of the city. He didn't care if he was dead or alive; to him, his life had already ended.

Talon was staring at his own vomit that he had fallen into when he heard footfalls quickly running toward him. He didn't care if it was another guard there to take him back to Auzgool; he didn't care about anything at all.

"Sir, are you OK?" asked a young voice from far off.

Talon was completely unresponsive. Small hands grabbed hold of Talon and rolled him onto his back.

"What's the matter with you?" asked the young boy as he stared into the eyes of the clearly disturbed Talon. "Are you drunk with the drink? This would not be a good place for you to wander in the state that you are in," the young boy said to him as Talon turned to spit out more vomit to the ground.

The boy looked at him with utter disgust and turned him back onto his stomach to allow for the purging of his nerves to continue.

"Wow, you're in a mighty sour mood, aren't you, mister?" the boy said.

Talon just whimpered and moaned as tears fell from his eyes.

"Why, you're not drunk at all, are you, mister?" He paused. "It's the state of the place that's got you upset, isn't it?"

Talon just moaned and whispered,

"Nelly."

"Well, we'll fix you right up once we're out of this place. That's a mighty queer-looking horse that you have there, mister. I suspect that it must be worth a lot," the boy said, now thinking out loud to Talon. "The name's Braum, Braum Barrett, and I can't be here long."

Talon immediately turned and looked at the boy in total shock. Braum had a small note in his hand, and he was shoving it into his jacket pocket as he looked at the Cyclicorn. Drool and disgust dripped from Talon's lips as he stared intently at the young man's face. The boy turned his attention back to Talon when he saw Talon's face.

"What really is the matter with you? You're a hard case."

Talon did nothing but stare at the boy. "Well, like I said, I can't stay long, but I thought that you should know that your friends have not been harmed except for Sol. He's dead, you will find them in through the doors of Pastel which you will reach through the entrance of the library."

Talon quickly pushed himself up to his feet.

"What was your name again?" asked Talon in his confusion.

"Never mind that now, I must go," the boy said as he pulled out what looked like a spherical pocket watch and lifted it with his mind, making it hover in the air in front of him.

The mechanism hovered and began to tick backward; lightning strikes began to emerge from the ground to the ticking object hovering in the air. The boy quickly grabbed hold of the object with his hand, and a loud cracking sound erupted from the focal point where Braum had grabbed hold of the ticking globe, and the boy was gone along with the orb that had caused the eruption in time. The only thing that was left was the little piece of paper that was once in the boy's pocket and now fluttering down through the air. *He had lost his little piece of paper* Talon thought to himself. It came to the ground like a dead leaf off a tree and rested on the cold icy stone that lay just in front of him.

Talon wasn't worried about the young man being familiar in his face; it was the name that really stumped him—the name of his grandfather. Everything was alien to him, like the globe that ticked backward; the evaporation didn't even look like a normal transport. There was something not right about all of what he had seen, and to his surprise, Fire hadn't run away. She just stood there as if nothing had happened, as if there was no startling explosion of power, and as if there was no boy that had come running toward them. It was all quite peculiar. Talon was no longer worried about his family though; he believed the young man more than he had ever believed anyone else that he had been introduced to in such a way. Now that he thought of it, he had never been introduced to anyone in such an amazing fashion. Talon shook his head like a dog shaking off water and reached for the piece of paper and looked at it; it read like this:

FIRST BLOOD Y567778789

Talon shoved the paper into his jacket and under his tunic. He quickly mounted the Cyclicorn and rode through the city to the top of the mountain of Pastel where the stables had been. He could see the stone pillars that once held the walls to the stables in place reduced to broken stones and dust, but it was when he saw Sol's old and broken body lying in the center of the courtyard that his heart had begun to ache. Talon had very much so wanted for the young man to be mistaken when it came to Sol's death; however, the reality of his death could not be escaped, not even by Talon. A tear began to fall for his old friend as Talon dismounted from his horse. When he reached the place where Sol had fallen, all he could do was stare down at the man that was closest to a father that he had ever had.

Talon looked around to see if his attacker was still in the vicinity, but there was no one there. He walked over to Fire and began to slowly walk her down the steps of what was left of the entrance to the stables. He walked her through the damaged halls of the tower and down to where the doors to the library had once been. He walked her across the demolished bookcases when he stopped. Something from the far end of the library had caught his eye.

"Stay here," he said to the Cyclicorn. "And be quiet," he continued.

Talon crept behind the fallen shelves and through the fallen walls and pillars of the library. It was cold, he could see the night sky through what used to be the sealing of the castle. Wind blew freely through the cracks and holes of the ruins of Pastel. Two very large feet were hanging out of what seemed to be another hole in the library, but the hole led to another chamber that Talon had not seen before; this little point of fact made the experience much more interesting to him. He crept toward the opening where the giant's feet extended from, but there was no action from the giant. And because it was not breathing, he assumed that it was dead.

Talon was climbing over the large man when he could hear what sounded like a train in the distance. It made no sense to him, so he decided to investigate how it was that the man had died. There were large claw marks and deep lacerations, wounds that were inflicted by a large sword. He had concluded that Cypress had slain the man in order for them to escape when he saw a figure of a tall man emerge from the darkness; he was breathing hard.

"Galen!" shouted Talon as he climbed over the dead man to get to Galen.

"Ah yes, boy, I was just coming to go help you escape," he said as he stepped over some rocks that had been demolished by the Requiem. "Come with me, you're not going to believe what it is that we have found,"

Galen paused for a moment to see Talon's response to his command, and then asked,

"Do you have a lamp? It gets very dark in there, and there are things that we do not understand," He looked at Talon and waited for him to respond, but Talon said nothing. "Well?" Galen asked again.

"I don't have a lamp, but I can do this," Talon said as he concentrated on the moisture in the air and used its power to create another ball of fire.

Galen stood there looking at the ball of fire in absolute astonishment. It was as if everything that he had been doing before had absolutely no importance at all; he just stood there looking at the globe of fire floating just above the palm of Talon's hand.

"By the Ancients!" was suddenly blurted out of Galen's mouth.

It was the most beautiful thing that he had ever seen, and it was coming from Talon.

"No one person has ever been able to create light from nothing, it is said that it can be manipulated perhaps, and even that task is the most difficult of them all, but you"—he paused for a moment— "you have made it come from nothing and hold it in the palm of your hand."

Galen began to reach for the globe of light in Talon's hand but hovered his hands around it as if he were trying to mold it much like a potter would mold clay.

"How did you—"?

Galen's question was interrupted by the cracking of the seal of the third door from the first; it gasped and sucked air as it opened, making an eerie hissing sound. The globe's energy was being drawn as four streams of fire slowly progressed to the four corners of the door.

"It's the light that you have created that has opened the door," said Galen in total shock.

At this point, Talon had stopped concentrating, and the sphere had disappeared. All that was left for light were the torches that were still burning from Talon's initial entrance into the chamber. Talon looked down into the doorway that had been opened but saw nothing in the darkness. He took the first step onto the stairs that led down in a spiral for as far as Talon could see, which were only a few feet in front of him. He paused for a moment and reached out his hand toward the center of the staircase, and light began to form in the middle of the air. More streams of light began to head down toward the bottom of the staircase as Talon headed down it. Galen followed Talon as he headed down the spiral staircase to the bottom of the chamber, and the orb of light slowly descended with them as they stepped down the steps. When they had reached the bottom of the stairs, the streams of fire began to enter into the center of another stone door that stood directly in front of the exit from the staircase. It was not long when that door opened too.

Galen had planned to return to the train after he freed Talon from prison, but he had not anticipated Talon's own release from prison. He had not questioned Talon about his escape because of the amazing things that he had learned in captivity. The fact that there were going to be new secrets that would be revealed was something that Galen could not pass up either. Even Talon didn't know what it was that they had found at the first door, but in seeing what it had taken to open this door, Galen knew that they would find something great—perhaps greater than before.

The door at the end of the staircase opened with a loud depressurization sound. Talon brought the sphere through the passageway ahead of them. It was dark and cold, and there were no overrun cobwebs that lay along the walls and floors. There were no weird sounds that echoed through the corridors—just silence. The chamber hallway was a steep slope down into the depths of the earth. Neither Talon nor Galen could really have a guess of where it was that they were headed. Talon was no longer afraid though. He was no longer the boy that pulled over to the side of the road to help a beautiful woman. He had felt the loss of his family, the loss of the woman that he secretly loved, the loss of both of his homes; and he had seen the most horrific things that one person could lay eyes on. He knew that he now had the power to truly help the Order, and he was now more confident than ever that the things that were to come would be of good challenge but nothing that he couldn't handle once he mastered the other forms of manipulation. These thoughts did cross his mind though:

What if he hadn't met the young man with the spherical clock? What would he have done if he had not found Galen? What would have transpired in his life if they had truly been killed? Questions like these raced through Talon's mind as he concentrated on the ball of fire that was now shedding light through the corridors of the mystery. He was asking these questions when the end of the passage shone in the light and led them to another chamber.

The orb had stopped emanating streams of fire while they were passing through the corridor, but when they reached the new chamber, something had begun to draw the energy from the water and fire again. The sphere was under Talon's control until they entered the round room where a peculiar archway extruded out of the rock face. The orb was ripped out of Talon's grasp and sucked into the arch of stone that stood cut out of the stone directly in front of them. The moment that the ball of fire reached the inner part of the archway, it dispersed into a loud cracking sound and then was gone. The room was immaculate, and the purple tile was smooth in the darkness. Talon tried to form another ball of fire, but there was no moisture in the air to alter the molecular structure of. Galen rested his hand on Talon's shoulder in the dark and asked him what had happened. Talon didn't answer him back. He felt Talon move toward the archway, and before Galen could respond again, a blinding light and a loud crack followed. Galen knew what had happened. He had seen Talon's figure in the middle of the archway when the light flashed, which gave him the impression that the archway had been designed to evaporate anyone who stepped through it. There was another light and crack, and the door to the chamber was closed; a moment later and Galen was no longer in the room.

*

Talon emerged on the other end of the stone archway in a calm and collected way. His stature had not been affected by the pain that he had grown accustomed to from evaporating, and moments later, Galen was emerging through the portal with a loud cracking sound and a blinding light also. Talon looked around the large chasm that the portal had taken him to. There was a tall tower that was surrounded by a large body of water. Light shone across the water like stars from a deep night sky. The water swayed and splashed as it flowed from one end of the cave to the other.

This cave, however, was not of a natural design. There were large spikes of stone, and water streamed down from the ceiling of the enormous cave. The tower was made of black stone and was not unkempt. Talon thought that after all the time that must have passed, the tower and wall would have shown signs of wear or disarray. It was, however, immaculate. There was not even dust that lay on the stones of the wall. The tower was obviously a corner tower; its two walls were extended into the side of the cave that could be seen from Talon's view. Light from mirrors in thousands of places in the cave's ceiling reflected light onto the tower's walls, onto the tower's gates, and onto the water that flowed all around the tower, creating a small lake and moat that extended right up to its walls.

"The rest of the castle must be hidden behind the stone wall. It must be only an entrance of some kind," said Galen as he stepped near Talon.

"You're probably right," Talon responded. "It's cold and dark though, I don't think that I would like to call this place my home," Talon said as he turned his attention to Galen and smiled.

Talon scrolled his eyes around to see if there was anything that he could use to get across the lake to the entrance of the Dark Tower, but Galen had spotted a small boat before he could. Galen was untying the boat that had been set aside near the entrance from the stone archway, and Talon was now getting into the boat. He had forgotten about the Cyclicorn that he had left in the halls of the chamber of the stone archway, and he realized this fact when he stepped into the boat. He thought to go back for her, but the boat was too small, making him decide that he would go back the same way that he came.

The boat rocked back and forth as he reached for the oars, and Galen also began to step into the boat. Water dripped from the ceiling of the cave and down the sides of the Dark Tower that stood just in their path. The boat was gentle and the water smooth as the boat cut its way through the ripples caused by the large drops of water from the cave ceiling. Talon stroked the wooden oars through the water, and in his mind, he had begun to remember a song that he had heard in the pub in Pastel. It made him think of all the ones that had been lost to the Requiem. His thoughts caused him to try to remember his father and his mother together. *It was too long ago*, he thought to himself as he stroked the water below. He had hoped that one day he would be able to remember his face, possibly an emotion that would help, but there was nothing. Talon had been subjected to many things that he had not been subjected to before, and he thought that perhaps he would someday remember his father's face. *Someday*, he thought to himself again. Galen was wondering where the tower would take them when they entered it, what would they find, and how would Talon react to it; and when it would all be over, he would ask Talon how it was that he was able to form the ball of fire from what appeared to be nothing.

11 YORK

TALON PLACED HIS HAND on the stone door to the entrance of the Dark Tower. Moisture streamed down as his hand caused the droplets of water to draw together and fall down the side of the door. Galen watched as Talon tried to open the door. Talon closed his eyes and placed his ear to the door as if he were trying to hear something on the other end. Moments later and his other hand was on the door. Galen did nothing but watch, and when the door did nothing, Talon stepped back from it and tried to form another ball of fire. However, before he could form it, the energy was dispersed at the entrance.

"Something is collecting the energy of the fusion," Talon said to Galen as he turned to look at Galen for guidance.

Talon looked around to figure out the riddle.

"Perhaps the door needs another element," Galen said as he stretched out his hand over the water.

Water streamed up out of the lake that separated the tower from the stone archway. Galen formed with his hand a globe of water. The water flowed around a point, and Galen moved the watery globe over to the entrance of the stone door. And before he could let the globe go, the door began drawing the water into the four corners of it. The door made the sound of stone sliding across stone, and the moment that it had been opened, torches that had been placed into the hall of the entrance had burst into flames, giving a beautiful light that flickered on the black stone walls that led into the castle.

Galen entered immediately. And as Talon followed him through the wide corridor, flames burst into life in front of them, and others snuffed themselves out as they left their vicinity. Moments later they emerged into a large courtyard that was enclosed by the cave ceiling. Stalactites had been cut and formed into a solid and smooth ceiling. Talon followed Galen into the entrance of the inner castle. The entrance to the inner castle was two very thick wooden doors that had chain links in the center of them, which were connected by steel rings that dangled from their hinges. Galen pulled on the chain links that were nailed to the tall doors. The doors opened into a bare hall, and it was clear that this castle was one of the oldest that they had found. It was of an earlier design and was not as sophisticated as the castle of Pastel and certainly not as well designed as Asscatan. It was that which made the castle so interesting to Galen. Talon though, thought that it was a good find. He, however, was not comfortable in this castle. It was too dark and dreary; it had a sinister feeling to it. Talon wasn't too keen on the idea of staying too long to investigate the castle despite his newfound power and confidence. He was not going to be subjected to an untimely death caused by his stupidity or ignorance. Galen was not afraid too much though. He had been exposed to many disheartening situations.

Galen walked through the hall and up into the chambers where one would have slept; he thought that he would try to find out what kind of people once lived there, if any at all. There was nothing that would denote that it was not inhabited because there were no indications of disarray, no spider webs, no dust; the utensils were still lying in their positions on the table in the middle of the food hall. There was no food on them, but it had seemed to Talon that they had been polished and set there for the next time that they had a celebration, whoever they were. It would very much surprise Talon if no one came out of a hidden room with a sword to defend themselves from the invading forces that had just penetrated their walls.

Talon imagined the first one to be someone from the dungeons coming out from behind a secret door and following would be hundreds more soldiers from a kingdom that the Order had no knowledge of, but nothing came out from beneath the floors and behind the walls. There were no soldiers to defend their posts, and there were no valiant men to protect the king and the queen. There was just the sound of wind whistling through the windows and cracks of the castle that created an absolutely queer feeling. It was about that time that Talon had decided it was time to leave. If no one was home now, they would be home later, and he was not about to be there when they returned.

Talon was still in the food hall when he had made his decision. Galen had walked off into the chambers and could have been anywhere in the castle by that time, however he was still near to Talon. He quickly followed Galen through the stone spiral staircases and up to the chambers. There were skulls and bloody swords on the way through the corridors and armors that had been pierced through and were being displayed down the halls to the library. Galen was quickly looking through the thousands of books that sat on the shelves of the massive library. The names of the books were in a different language that Galen had never seen before. He knew that he would not find anything in the library without more information, and for the time being, there was nowhere that he thought he could get that information but in the castle of Asscatan. Talon stepped into the library when Galen was making that conclusion.

"I'm going to look in the dungeons for clues," Galen said as he placed one of the books back onto the shelf.

The shelves of books were pillars of spiraled shelving. There were many different levels, and there was a balcony that led to another reading room that was another level up. There were approximately five spiral pillars of books with spiral staircases surrounding each one. The walls that surrounded the room and the walls that surrounded the reading chamber were the traditional shelving, and there was not one spot to put another book, all of them had been taken. It appeared that the previous owners of the castle had found other places to put their books because some were neatly stacked right side up on the floor, and there were chairs that had been dedicated to the cause of making a place for a book to sit.

Talon liked the library. It was not like the other parts of the castle. It could be said that the library had some personality—the kind that Talon liked, the kind that made him comfortable, not the kind that portrayed conquest and danger. But then Talon remembered that this was the only place in the castle that he felt this way, and he was not happy with the idea that they would now be traveling down to the dungeons. This was the most peculiar castle that Talon had ever seen.

Galen had looked for the symbol, but he could not make out a message being that all the books had been written in the same language that the symbols had been. That fact made Galen realize that they were not just symbols but letters of some sort, possibly a message of some kind. Galen had always wondered why it was that the gold sign at the entrance of the castle of Pastel had nothing written on it. It was a fact that reminded him of the things that they were now finding, and it was obvious that Pastel had many secrets that he had not known, and still does not know. For someone or some kingdom to have built what they had, they must have been a world power. Perhaps it was just that they liked to live underground that they built all these things. The whole truth of the matter had eluded him, but he would not allow it to hinder his first mission, and he would never stop till he had the whole truth.

Galen stepped cautiously down the steps to what he had thought might be the location of the dungeon. They traveled down through one of the chambers of the castle, but there were no chambers for criminals, and there were no chains to bind them. As they walked down the staircase, they came to the place where the water flowed underneath the castle, and there was a boat. Chains dangled from a hole in the ceiling, and a draw gate separated them from the exit to wherever it was that the river led. Torches burned on the walls, creating a soft reflection on the water that gently flowed in and out of the base of the castle. Light shone through the hole that extended through the center of the tower, and the chains that hung down through the well glistened in the light like jewels.

"No dungeons?" asked Galen, confused.

Talon simply looked emotionless into his eyes. Galen got in the boat and grabbed the oars.

"Get in, where there's a boat, there's a path that must be traveled, and in a quest such as ours, it is a path to knowledge."

Talon had at one time told himself that he would never forsake the opportunity for knowledge, but he had not known that at one time in Galen's life, he had also made the same promise to himself. Talon wanted to go back to wherever it was that Galen had hidden the Order so that he could lay his eyes upon Cypress and hold her in his arms. However, he knew that if ever he would want to truly be able to protect her, he would be required to take on the responsibility of taking in knowledge that would be lifesaving in the future. So, he reluctantly stepped into the boat and took the oars when Galen presented them to him for him to take hold of.

Talon was staring into the softly flowing water when Galen had reached out his hands to lift the large steel gate that opened up to the path that they would take through the castle tunnel. Chains clinked, and the water took different paths; water dripped, and pieces of plant from the floor of the river hung as the steel gate lifted into the wall of the tower. Talon softly rowed the boat through the tunnel that led through the castle. There were bridges that spanned across the tunnel, and the boat passed under them as the water flowed. The current was against them, so Talon was working at getting the boat through the water harder than usual. It was a good thing that they were heading upstream, Talon thought to himself as he pushed the water under the boat with every stroke. Talon thought that there was something to say about going upstream than going downstream. It seemed to him that they would make significant progress traveling up rather than down, and then he thought that perhaps it was that they were not traveling backward that made him comfortable, not the flow or the direction of the water. Whatever the case, he was confident that something good would come of it.

The path went on and on and in many different directions. Galen had pulled out a piece of parchment and a quill and began mapping out the tunnels from the entrance to the gate of the black castle. The quill scribbled and scratched across the parchment with the speed and skill of an excellent writer, every now and then being dipped into the rocking glass of ink that Galen always brought with him next to the tobacco and the pipe. He did think to acknowledge the fact that as long as Talon was in his vicinity, he would never have to use another match to light his pipe.

The ride in the boat was a calm and peaceful one, other than the unskilled rowing of Talon, but Galen didn't mind it too much that Talon was never properly trained in the skillful art of rowing a boat. He was more concerned about mapping the passageway so that they would be able to find their way back to the Black castle if they did indeed find something that was of any interest.

Galen was always the type to think far ahead of his situation so that he would not be placed inadvertently into a horrible one. This had helped him before in the past. And he had, after some time, made the action a habit much like that of the puffing on his pipe, but not as many people would be perturbed at his thinking ahead than they would of his known nasty habit of blowing smoke into the air.

Light had begun to show at the end of the tunnel from afar, and it was not long when the boat came to a stop on a bank of sand and dirt. Galen quickly got out of the boat and stepped onto the dry land. Light shone through the trees that surrounded the entrance to the damp forest. The forest was much like a rain forest, however, there was no rain because they were clearly underground. The river ran through the forest farther on, but it was Galen that thought it was a good idea to stop and look around.

Talon tied a rope to an old piece of wood that was lying on the sandy bank of the forest and stepped out of the boat. They could hear animals in the distance that were similar to the sounds of animals that were indigenous to a normal rain forest. Galen slowly made his way through the very large brush that surrounded the trees, through the ferns that were six feet tall, and in between the massive trees that stood scattered about in all directions as far as the eye could see, which wasn't very far at all. The brush perspired dew from every part, and the trees were damp with water. The temperature was much higher than that in the castle chambers. It was in the middle of the winter, and they had just walked into a tropical environment that Talon was absolutely not enjoying.

Talon had stopped to take off his jacket when Galen, who was ahead of him, let out a shriek. Talon rushed to where he had heard Galen's cry and found a large gorilla-like creature carrying Galen off into the forest. There was plenty of water around, so Talon didn't think that he would have a problem forming an orb that would scare the creature away. But something was hindering his ability to create the light: the environment was absorbing it. This was a place that Talon knew he would never want to be in again. Talon ran after the creature as it slowly dragged Galen across the ground, and when he reached them, he began to yell. He had picked up a large branch and was hitting the large animal with it. The animal stood on its feet and released Galen so that it could show itself strong in the face of an enemy. It was waving its hands violently and shouting into the depths of the forest behind it. It was at this time that Talon took the opportunity to get Galen to his feet. Galen had begun to run, but Talon was much faster, and they both could hear the creature running after them. Galen was almost out of breath when Talon spotted the end of the forest. Talon grabbed hold of Galen's hand and was now almost dragging him to the clearing just outside of the forest.

He had reached the end of the forest when Galen fell to the ground, and moments later, the creature had reached them and was trying to pull Galen back into the forest. Talon took one look backward into the eyes of the creature, and it immediately stopped. It was breathing hard and slowly releasing Galen from its claws as Talon watched from the clearing. It dropped to all fours and slowly backed away into the forest, still staring into the eyes of Talon. There was nothing that would have explained the reason that the creature finally stopped its pursuit. They were completely defenseless against it, but Talon was not about to find out why the creature had cowered. Galen was looking out into the clearing when Talon was raising him to his feet, and Talon didn't think that there was anything else that needed questioning until he heard the sound of a man calling out to them.

"Are you all right?" asked the man as he ran out to greet them. "You have got to have something wrong in your head to be roaming about in the Qwirl," he said as his armor clinked and clanked as he ran. "How did you get out of the city? You know that this is a forbidden place. The both of you could have been killed, and you"—he paused for a moment and looked Galen straight in the eyes— "you should be ashamed of yourself, why, at your age, you ought to know that this is a place where no one should ever be. I should put you into the dungeons for your stupidity," the man said as he unsheathed his sword and pointed it at them both. "I suppose that you're fortunate that I do not have that power," the man continued as he returned his sword to its place.

"Dungeons do not frighten me. I have been in them before. They do not stand a chance," Talon said as he shot a warm smile at the man in armor.

"What is this place?" asked Galen.

"Just what exactly do you mean 'what is this place?'" the man asked, offended.

"We are not from here. We have traveled far, and we wish to know where it is that this place is on a map," Talon said as he moved his hands around forming them into a square.

"What is a map?" the man asked, confused.

Talon's hands dropped in defeat at the mentality of the guard and said, "Just if you will, take us back into the city please."

"That I can do," the guard said as he gestured for the guard opposite of him to open the gate from far off. "Come with me, and we will get you back home," the guard said as he stepped through the grass of the clearing.

Galen looked around and saw the roof of the cave that hung down in certain places and connected to the roof of towers that surrounded the city of York. Once they had passed the threshold of the forest, the temperature had returned to a cooler atmosphere. The tower touched the ceiling of the cave that had been carved out of the stone of what Galen had thought must be a mountain, like the one of Pastel. It was manufactured much like Asscatan, a city that Talon knew nothing about, but it was not overrun with creatures. It didn't have the feel that everyone in the city had perished a horrible death.

The city had white stone walls, and the river from the forest expanded into a moat that circled the castle walls. Galen was beside himself at the knowledge that there was a working civilization living in the city and was thrilled to find out that they were not some extinct civilization that had been overrun millennia ago. He was going to find out all that he could about these people—their culture, their art, their entertainment. Had there been a time when they had lived somewhere else and had simply taken control of an ancient city? Did they know any of the city's secrets? There was a lot that he would be asking anyone who he thought could give him an answer.

The guard waved his hand in the air again to let the other guard know to open the gate and draw up the wooden doors. Slowly the gate and doors began to open, revealing a remarkably busy municipality. There were people selling food and fruit and fabric in the streets. People were dancing and playing music on the corners. The white stone was like that of Fable, but the city was designed in a more artistic fashion. It was the most fantastic thing that Galen had ever seen. The guard left them at the gate, and Galen and Talon walked slowly through the city and enjoyed every moment that they were there. Mirrors were embedded into the ceiling of the cave and were being fed light through tunnels cut through the side of the cave walls.

"I wonder if they have beer," Talon asked as he walked through the city streets with Galen.

"We should find the library if we can," said Galen as he pointed to the center of the city's castle.

People held out their product of whatever it was to sell at each stand; all the stands with goods were at the gate entrances, but most of them covered the entrances to the gates. That gave Galen the impression that the gates were no longer used. Talon passed through the merchants and into the housing section for people that lived there. They walked up the steps of the inner castle, but there were no royal guards stationed for the protection of the royalty. The doors were open, and there were commoners inside. Galen was wondering if they would have difficulty getting into the castle yard, but there had been no need for his stealth and cunning. Talon looked around with a large smile as he took each step.

"These people really do know how to live, don't they?" he said, staring at a woman dancing with a sort of tambourine in her hand as another played a stringed instrument and sang.

Galen was in the center hall of the inner castle when a woman came up to him and asked if there was anything that he was looking for. She thought that he looked like he was lost. She said that being lost was not something that was a very usual occurrence in York, and Galen agreed and said that he didn't need any help, and then he thanked her. Talon thought that his response was rather rude though. They could have gotten more information out of her, he thought to himself knowing that he would give Galen a hard time about it when there was nothing to do but pick at each other.

Galen had stopped asking people for directions by this time though because most of them just looked at him weirdly and kept walking. Like the woman said, there was never a time that she had met someone that didn't know their way around the city. After all, everyone that occupied the city had been born there, and they had never known another place. They had never gone anywhere outside of the confines of the wall, and never had anyone entered the forbidden Qwirl. It was just not something that any sane person would do.

Galen didn't pay attention to the judging eyes of the inhabitants of York, and besides, they were perfectly pleasant if he didn't mention that he was completely unaware of his location in the city. The light from the mirrors had begun to dim, and the night sky had begun to reflect into the city. No one questioned where it was that the light came from. They went about their lives in their own little world, and they talked gossip about the friends and neighbors that they had. Homes were cut out of the side of the cave as well, and staircases led to each place of lodging. The people who had accommodations in the caves were envied for the view that they had of the world, as they put it, a world of only a few miles in one direction and another few in the other.

Talon was absolutely fascinated that there could be a society that never wanted to escape the confines of the cave, never dreamed about a world that lay beyond the cave walls or even the castle walls. It was all too peculiar to him. Talon though was not, in the least, bothered by the way that the people lived. The old ones sat outside of their homes and smoked whatever it was that they desired. They would talk about the crops of next year and how they would feed them better to get a more luxurious crop so that they could eat even better, and they would have better-quality smoking and better-quality lives. They would watch their children play in the streets and in the fields that sat between the castle and the houses cut into the side of the walls of the cave; some of them were as high up as just below the ceiling of their world. Others would visit them and tell them that their family had been living in the Calyeran number 55 for over ten centuries and would offer to take them up to the house closest to the ceiling for dinner and watch the Aresats (stars) glisten in the mirrors of the cave.

Stories that the people had heard more than once echoed from house to house as the older ones told them to their grandchildren while they rocked in their rocking chairs. It was a place that even Talon thought he could call his home. It was evident, however, that if Talon and Galen were going to need a place to stay for that night, there would be none. All houses had been occupied for generations. They would have to tell someone that they were travelers from a different world and that they had found themselves here by surprise and that they would need a place to stay for the night. That would likely cause some trouble. Galen was very unhappy at the thought and reasoned that it would be better if they simply found a way out. Talon wasn't about to just pass through such a wonderful place, and he had already formulated a plan to get the whole city together.

Galen was in the center hall of the castle when Talon started calling out for all to hear news that would please the ears. Talon had been studying the way that stories were being told and heard their fondness of rhymes and new stories that needed to be told. Talon walked through the city with his hands in the air, calling out to the people, telling them that there was a new story that must be told and that all would be invited to hear it and its magnificence, behold. At the mention of a new story, not one of the people turned a deaf ear. They all listened intently to a man that they knew not, and the mystery was too much. Talon named a place and a time, and he threw in a few phrases that rhymed, knowing that every person would attend, and as Talon put it into words, their ears he would bend. When the light would dim and the night would set in, all must meet him in the middle of the court of the inner castle. That time being not too long warrants a great song. The people were grateful for the new story that the man would tell, and so they repeated his announcement in every street and on every corner in anticipation of what they called the new meet. Others would ask each other whose family he was from and what he could possibly have that was new to be told. Nonetheless, the spectators and the doubters were too overcome by their curiosity. Galen was not too happy about the attraction that Talon was creating, but he knew from what he had learned of the people that it would be a highly effective way of getting what they would need for the night.

It wasn't long when the light in the city dwindled down to a moonlight, and people began to collect themselves together at the entrance of the center hall of the inner castle. There were torches that had been lit and music played to the rhyming announcement that Talon had given all through the city not but an hour before, and there were people dancing in the streets just where they could see the inner castle. Galen and Talon were in the court, sitting down in the chairs that surrounded the fireplace, when they heard the mob outside. Voices fell silent and songs grew quiet as Galen and Talon walked out at the top of the stairs of the entrance to the inner castle.

"Most of you are wondering who it is that I am, and others are wondering who it is that stands beside me," Talon said with a smile, and Galen just stared into the crowd. "From what I know about these people, I would say that there has never been anyone who has traveled outside of these walls, or perhaps never done so and lived to tell the tale. And if I told you that we did not come from this place, this city, you would not readily accept such an explanation. However unusual the circumstances, it is the truth." Talon stopped talking to let the horrible truth sink into the superficially close-minded people. The mass of people gasped and began talking of stories that had been forbidden to be told. "You need not worry, this is not a story that is forbidden because it has never been told," Talon quickly responded to the offended crowd.

The reasoning was sound enough for them because they had stopped murmuring among themselves. Every eye was upon the two men that stood tall at the top of the stairs, and there were no sounds at all now that were coming from the crowd.

"I was born in a place called Fable," Talon began his story. "A place much like this one but with a difference in what occupied the space above my head. There were no stones or rock that lay above me, only phantoms of water that floated in an empty place, and the light that would give its light was that of one entity. It also moved about in the sky but always at the same time much like the light that comes and goes in this world. Then I came to a place where there were untold truths, and I was taught much. I was told of the Legacy."

Talon paused as some in the crowd nodded their head at the knowledge of the Legacy when one of the older men who had set his rocking chair in the middle of the street called out to Talon, saying:

"It was all a great truth to us all, my boy."

Everyone nodded his or her heads in agreement. Galen looked at Talon in confusion and spoke to the crowd.

"You know of the Legacy?" Galen asked while trying not to sound like an idiot.

"Absolutely. It is the foundation of the society," another older man shouted out from the crowd.

Galen stood there in amazement. A whole culture that had been preserved through the ages; it was by far the greatest find he had ever made—an ancient culture still here. Galen stood there without another word on his tongue and allowed Talon to tell his story further.

"I came to this place by the atrocities of wicked men and by the saving force of the Legacy, me and my friend Galen here. My name is Talon Barrett, and because we are not of this place, we will need a place to rest our head for the night until we find a way to get back to our world." The mob burst out in joyous song and laughter, talking, and telling, playing, and dancing to a song that was a wonderful precursor to the hospitality of the Yorkens. Talon saw the older man that was sitting in the rocking chair telling his young ones to walk up to Talon and Galen. The little boys walked up the steps through the rejoicing crowd and grabbed hold of Talon's arms, gesturing for him to follow them.

Talon and Galen followed the young children down the steps and to the old man that was now dragging his chair across the white stone of the city streets. Signs that hung from shops reflected light from the crystal mirrors, and moisture had collected in the streets from the water that surrounded the city. The old man gestured in all the loudness of the crowd for them to leave the mob and follow him. Galen and Talon followed the old man through the streets of York around the center castle and near the portion of the castle wall that ended at the cave wall where the homes were that were fabricated by carving out portions of the cave. The old man left the chair at the bottom of a staircase that led to many of the homes of the cave and began the long hike to the home closest to the cave ceiling. The old man instructed the young boy to carry the chair up to the house and to place it near the fireplace. Talon examined the homes with every step that he took; they were the most fascinating things that he had ever seen, and to think that he would probably be staying the night in such a wonderful place was very pleasing to him. Talon was glad that his plan had worked to his advantage and that they would not be staying the night in dungeons with a design that he had never seen before, a design that would be likely to his disadvantage. He could, in these circumstances, be willing to be patient to see Cypress because he knew that he would be sleeping in a soft, warm bed—a luxury that he had not experienced for some time now. The old man opened the small door to their home. Talon walked up the steps and across the balcony porch that led into the house. The house was quaint and comfortable, and the floors of the house were overlaid slats of wood that had been constructed to make the dwelling more contented. There was a fireplace that sat dead center to the home, and the living space surrounded it. Pictures of family members were plastered on the walls, and the stone had been painted with red paint. *Perhaps a stain from a fruit or something like that*, Talon thought to himself as he entered the living room. There were woven carpets that blanketed parts of the wooden floor and many little trinkets that had been set in inconspicuous places all around the house. The fireplace had fancy carvings of people fighting vicious creatures, one that looked like the one that carried off Galen in the Qwirl, and pictures of knights and horses. But when Galen asked about the carvings, the old man said that they were just legend, legends that no one ever questioned the validity of.

The fire crackled, and the smoke billowed just before it was sucked through the chimney that, according to the children in the house, led off into a nothingness that no one knew about. An older woman was preparing something in the kitchen, and there was another young person in the kitchen with her. Apparently, they had not gone to the gathering in the center of the city. Clocks ticked and chimed as the light from the mirrors shone through one of the holes that had been formed into a window. Talon could see the whole city from that window and yet again was surprised by the beauty of York. Talon turned to ask a question for the old man and almost knocked over a small stringed instrument, which made a deep humming sound from the nudge of his boot; he quickly reached over and saved the instrument from falling.

The old man was now sitting in the chair in front of the fire as it blazed and had reached for his pipe to light it. Talon thought it would be a good joke to light it with his mind, so he tried it. And much to his surprise, whatever it was that was hindering his manipulation of light had not affected him this time. The pipe burst into flames from the bowl, and the old man just about fell to his death to the floor.

"What in blazes?" the man shouted out in surprise, but his said nothing because of the man's unpleasant reaction.

Whatever there was left in the pipe had been torched by Talon's experiment, and the man was not happy about it. Thankfully, Galen was there to take the man's thought off the loss by offering him what he commonly smoked. The man quickly shoved the dry leaves into the bowl, lit a match, and puffed away. Moments later and he was not unhappy at all, and it was shown by a slight smile and one raised eyebrow.

"So, young man, you say that you are not from this place, correct?" the man said, still smiling and gesturing that whatever it was that Galen had given him, it was good.

Talon disdained the thought of smoking; it was an unscrupulous practice. The old man coughed and asked the question again, now paying attention to Talon.

"Yes, not from this place," Talon said as he stared out the window at the city below.

"Well, no worries, we shall have another place for you to rest your head in no time, and I hope that when you get to wherever it is that you are going, you will remember us and possibly come back to visit," the old man continued.

"If it is not too much trouble, we will," said Galen as he lit the pipe in his mouth with a match.

Dishes were clinking and clanking as the old woman washed them in the stone sink. The water was fed to all the complexes of the cave by a large wheel that had been constructed out of wood to pump the water up into a stone basin that was at the tallest point of the cave and off near the entrance of the river to the moat. Talon could see the wheel turning round and round as the water flowed.

"My name is Gooshwen Kavut, and I have lived here in the city of York for ninety-two years, and I've never seen anything outside of the walls of my home, and until now, I hadn't thought that there was anything but this place. The things you speak of are wondrous things, things that I will never see in my lifetime. But you must promise me that you will not deprive my young ones of that gift. We have never needed the use of the Legacy. It was something that everyone has learned in their youth, but we have never used it to our advantage. We have all that we need in this place, and for millennia, there has been peace because there has been no danger."

Gooshwen paused for a moment and leaned in closer to Galen with an expression that could only be caused by secrecy. His tone changed and his lips began to quiver as he whispered the words.

"Danger is something that every youth needs."

Galen looked at the old man and was wondering what it was that he was trying to get through to him and Talon. Whatever point it was that Gooshwen was trying to make, it had completely eluded Galen.

"We are already planning to take children that would be good for the cause, but we were completely unaware that this city existed," Galen said, knowing that the old man knew much more than what he was telling them.

"If you wish it, they are yours for the taking. I am an old man. Otherwise, I would be there to fight with you," Gooshwen said as Galen nodded in agreement.

Talon was completely at a loss. He hadn't the slightest clue as to what it was that they both were talking about, and it worried him. Talon had seen expressions on Galen's face that he had never seen before, expressions of concern and worry.

"When the time comes, so it will be," Galen said in response to Gooshwen. The old man nodded and left the conversation at that.

Talon was staring into the fireplace and sitting in a chair that Gooshwen had placed near the kitchen and near the fireplace. The night air was cold, and the crickets sounded out from the grassy pastures near the fields of trees and vines and fruit. The temperature in the cave had now dropped drastically, which made Talon more aware of the warmth of the fire. The woman walked out of the kitchen, and Gooshwen introduced her as his wife of many years; the little ones were his grandchildren. They would come to visit them every three days. She then introduced herself as Shannon Kavut; she explained to Galen that they were considered a sort of royalty to some and something else to everyone that didn't. She made sure that he knew that she didn't care what people thought of her. She was her own person, and her family would be themselves no matter what anyone said about them. It was hard for Galen to concentrate on what she was telling him because he either already had come to that conclusion himself or he was simply uninterested. He could not understand how Gooshwen knew what it was that the Order was planning to do; Galen hadn't completely worked it out himself yet. The addition of young ones that had already been trained the basics of the Legacy would be an unbelievably valuable addition to the team which would someday save the race of humanity. Perhaps Gooshwen didn't know anything but was wise enough to see that they would see great value in ones who knew the Legacy. There was, however, something that Gooshwen wasn't telling him; and he had hoped that before he left, he would have the answers to many of his questions.

Talon sat in the chair and tuned out the incessant droning on of Shannon with all her gossip and such. He stared into the fire and dreamed of what it would be like to hold Cypress in his arms and feel her presence. He thought of what it would be like to look into her deep blue-green eyes and lose himself in the touch of his face against hers. Dreams would only frustrate Talon though, and yet he could not find himself resisting them. Would he be able to make his dreams of Cypress into a reality? He didn't know if he truly had the courage and strength, and not knowing what the Order had in store for him was the most taxing uncertainty of them all. Galen was making plans that Talon didn't know about, and things that he didn't understand had already taken place—coming across the young man with the strange clock orb and coming across the strange tower castle that led him to this castle. It was all very fascinating to Talon, however, at the same time frightening. The Order had taken his life to places that he never thought existed and, in doing so, subjected him to the most frightening things that he had ever seen. The thought of it all caused Talon to curl up in the chair that he had been sitting on in front of the fireplace and clench the soft knitted blanket that Shannon had given him—while still talking about the time when she accidentally humiliated Ms. Dumsy at her dinner party—and fell asleep and, in so doing, hopefully wake up from the best nightmare that he had ever experienced.

12 KEYS TO A WARDROBE

TALON OPENED HIS EYES to find himself lying on a wooden cot that had been set in front of the fire. The light shone through the little house's window that gave a beautiful view of the city of York. Talon's hand had flopped over him while he was sleeping and was now hanging over the side of the cot. It was all wonderful—the stay in the little house, the view down into the city, the hospitality of the people, and the warm atmosphere. Shannon had been baking something in the kitchen when Talon awoke, and the scent was gently being carried through the air. Talon took a deep breath, savoring the smell of the berry bread, or at least that is what it smelt like to him. There was animal's meat that was frying also; it was a good addition to Talon's view of the house. He looked over to his left and then over to his right, but he could not see where it was that they had put Galen. Knowing Galen though, Talon thought to himself, he's already up and out on the porch, puffing away on his wretched pipe.

A cool breeze passed through the windows of the small house that carried a scent all its own: a mixture of pollen, grass, dirt and wet stone, rainwater, fruit, and a hint of parchment. Talon raised himself out of the cot into the sitting position. The room was bright from the morning light, and the fire was no longer blazing; it had been reduced to a glowing pile of coals. Talon looked around the room again and saw Galen knocked out on another cot on the opposite side of the fireplace. The round living room was a design that Talon had not seen before the night that he had stayed at the house. He attributed it to the trial and error of trying to find the most comfortable setting during construction of the house, and according to Talon, they had found it.

He saw Shannon rushing back and forth in the kitchen, collecting plates, and cutting up vegetables and onions to go with what it was that she had clearly been preparing for breakfast. Talon huddled over his cot in the sitting position with his arms grazing the wood frame of the cot and his head down low. His hair was getting long now, so he would have to soon cut it, he thought as he lifted himself out of the cot. He walked across the wooden floor, which creaked and grinded into the stone floor beneath it, and around the fireplace in the middle of the round room to the chair that was placed near the kitchen.

Mornings were always hard for Talon if there was nothing absolutely important to accomplish for the day, and then it would be the necessity of the tasks of that day that would push him out of the bed. But if there was nothing in particular that was going on, it would be especially hard for him to pull himself out of his sleepy attitude in the morning.

"Had a good sleep?" asked Shannon as she chopped something with a knife with a wooden floor plank beneath it.

"Yes, the best I've had in some time, thank you," Talon said with his hand to his forehead and his eyes still partly closed.

Talon thought that Galen would be up and about by now; it was a surprise that he wasn't. He had figured that it would be Galen waking him up in the morning, not the sweet smell of breakfast. Talon didn't know what time it really was though. Perhaps he had had too good of a sleep and woke himself up. Whatever it was that was the cause, he was up and out of bed before Galen, and it seemed to Talon that that might cause some problems.

"It appears that Gooshwen was up all night with Galen, telling him stories of the past and history and such things like that," said Shannon as she poured Talon some tea to help him wake up. He said nothing. "Would you like some tea?" she asked him politely.

Talon's head was now beginning to ache at the loud voice of Shannon, so he quickly answered the question with a "yes" as she brought the small clay cup and plate around and out of the kitchen to Talon.

"The young ones are not out of bed yet, I assume," said Talon as he took the first sip of his tea.

Talon tried not to make a scene when he gulped the extremely bitter substance down his throat and found himself gasping for air and spitting at the same time. He quickly raised his hand to his mouth to wipe the spit and tea from his face as Shannon made a small chuckle and walked back into the kitchen to flip the meat that had been frying. Talon was still exhausted even though he had had a good night's rest, and he knew that wherever it was that they would be traveling next would be just as demanding of Talon's strength. He wanted to figure out the mystery of the doors also but was not very enthused about taking the journey to wherever it would be. He had already seen the destruction of one home; he didn't want to see the destruction of another.

Galen opened his eyes to the light that was shining past the fireplace and onto his chest. His gray tunic was stained with dirt from being dragged through the moist floor of the Qwirl; he smiled at the memory even though it had been a dangerous one. He turned and looked at Talon sitting in the chair near the entrance to the kitchen with one hand rubbing his forehead and the other holding a cup while setting it on a small plate and hoped that he would be offered one also. Galen was not ready to be the one to slow the expedition down; there were questions that needed to be answered and secrets to be discovered. It had been one of the more productive years that

Galen had had in quite some time. *If only I can get myself out of this extremely uncomfortable cot that I have been sleeping in for half the night,* he thought to himself as he rested his hand on the wooden floor.

"No, I shall not be the one to slow us down," Galen mumbled as he pulled himself out of the cot and to his feet.

He made haste reaching into the left pocket of his gray tunic and pulling out his pipe to take a good puff after he had lit it. He turned and looked at Talon and gave him a serious look.

"We need to find the library and get to the one book that has this symbol," Galen said as he quickly pulled out a piece of parchment about the size of the palm of his hand.

Talon's attitude made an instantaneous turnabout when Galen retrieved the paper from his pocket, and he leaned in closer to have a better look at it.

"What does the symbol mean?" asked Talon as he examined it closely.

"It means that we will find something that needs to be found. And I, for one, am not going to sit around and wait for something that will never come without careful planning."

"Ah, that's it, careful planning." Talon said sarcastically.

Careful planning really meant a lot of pain and suffering for Talon. But since he had already been put through the fire, the things that he would have to experience would become less and less harmful to him, Talon thought to himself. He had been tempered like a piece of steel subjected to the harsh element of fire, and so naturally, he was content to accept the challenge even though Galen didn't know that Talon felt he had a choice.

Galen told Shannon that they could not stay for breakfast and that they would be on their way in just a few moments. She was quite disappointed because of the clear lack of gratitude as any self-respecting homemaker would be, but Galen didn't have time to notice. He folded up the cots that both of them had slept on and made his way to the door of the home. Talon followed Galen down the steps of the flats and through the grassy fields that lay inside the castle wall just before the center of the small extension of the castle. This lay in the center of the city in the center castle. They walked through the center castle and into the library after some searching for it and asking for directions.

There were not many Yorkens that were up at that time; it was their usual custom to enjoy the morning in their loving abodes, from their loving beds or cots, or whatever it was that they would choose to sleep in. But Talon and Galen had work to do, and they had begun searching the library through its many thousands of books for that one book which, for some reason, Galen thought had to be in the castle.

It was about midday when Talon found the book with *not* the same symbol. However, it had the same lettering, the same language, one that even the Yorkens didn't use. And it was the only one in the whole library with the symbol. It was also the only one with a solid wood cover. Galen did see differences in the book though. It didn't have any parchment papers in it, and the book opened. He opened it and found a key in the center of it with the symbol that was like the one that was displayed on one of the doors of Pastel. The iron key was rusted, and the rust had not been touched for some time. Galen asked why it was that no one ever took the key, and most of the people answered with the thought that it was absolutely uninteresting and that anyone in the city who could comprehend anything *simple* knew about the book. It was exactly what Galen had hoped they would find, so naturally, Galen walked about with a large grin on his face.

He strolled over to Talon with the book in his hand after examining it further.

"We will need to get through the same way that we came. I'm going to see if we can get an escort through the Qwirl," Galen said as he turned to head in the direction of the outer wall.

Talon nodded and followed Galen down the steps of the tower that the library was in, down the halls, through the court, and down the steps of the inner castle in the direction of the wall. By this time, Talon and Galen were more than famous to everyone. They were the topic of every conversation, and Galen knew that they would be able to get anything that they wanted out of anyone that they needed to get something out of. Galen marched into the main tower to the defenses of the castle, up the steps, and into the wall. Men in armor blanketed the halls, some with swords and some with bows, just standing at entrances and hallways and having not a worry or care in the world. Most of them had never been subjected to anything that could remotely be considered a battle, and Galen knew it. However, the extra bodies would be a good distraction while they made their way through the Qwirl.

"What say you?" Galen asked the commanding officer sitting at a desk in the middle of the army stationing room.

Galen had just asked if they would be able to get an escort through the Qwirl, and the commander was looking at him as a child would look at his father in complete misunderstanding. The commander's eyes blinked, and his face had become pale from the thought that he would be obligated to command an escort through the most dangerous part of their land.

"But some of us may be slain," the commander pleaded to Galen.

"Is there another way out of the city? By all means, tell us where it is, and I will take that way instead," Galen said as if he were looking over imaginary glasses.

"There is none other than that from which you have come, and that is the reason no one leaves this place, it means death to all that pass through the Qwirl. Well, all except for you two," the army officer said, still cowering in his chair.

"Come and show yourself a brave man and bring your bravest of the lot. Our lives are more than just important, and perhaps with some bravery, yours will be too," Galen said as he grabbed a sword off the desk and jabbed it into the air as though there was an enemy to be killed.

The commander's face revealed his defeat in his attempts to evade the responsibility of a law that even Galen didn't know about. All visitors were to be treated as royalty, and if they needed assistance on their journey home, the soldiers were to give that assistance. It was in their law. Galen just didn't know it yet. The soldier commander relinquished his stubbornness and agreed to provide an escort. Naturally, Galen was very pleased with the response to his inquiry.

Twenty men with armor and swords stood on each side of Talon and Galen. They marched across the grassy fields to the entrance of the Qwirl. The soldiers fidgeted as they marched and were obviously terrified. Not one of them had ever seen a fight, and they were about to enter a place of legendary danger and terror.

"If we run through the forest, there will be a better chance that your soldiers will go home alive, and make sure to tell them that the Legacy has no effect in the Qwirl," Talon whispered to the army commander as they marched on.

The commander kept his head in formation and only moved an eye toward Talon to acknowledge that he would obey the suggestion. He raised one arm into the air to gesture for the army to stop and rigidly about-faced. The small army escort stopped marching, and all attention was on the commander. Galen was in the center of the group in between the two lines created by frightened and young soldiers. There was only one soldier that didn't look like he was born the runt of the litter, and he stood towering at least four feet above the commander at his side and one foot above Talon and Galen. He carried an ax at his side and three spears. He faced the escort with the commander.

"WE WILL CHARGE THROUGH THE QWIRL IF WE DO SO WISH TO SURVIVE. IT IS YOUR DUTY AS A SOLDIER OF YORK TO PROTECT THE NON-HOSTILE STRANGERS WITH YOUR LIVES. HAVE I MADE MYSELF CLEAR, SOLDIERS?" the old commander said as he raised his hand for another order.

"CHARGE!"

The man dropped his hand and began running toward the Qwirl. And again screaming:

"CHARGE!"

Galen ran with Talon in the middle of the escort and through the forbidden forest. It was only moments after they entered the Qwirl when Talon heard screaming coming from the rear of the escort. Dark figures were hopping from tree to tree and swooping down to take hold of anything that they could get a hold of. Arrows were being shot in almost every direction; Talon heard a few arrows whiz past his head and then saw a large ball of fur tumble out of the trees in front of him to the ground. He quickly hopped over the thrashing creature as it grasped for the arrows in its chest. Talon could barely see what it was that was going on, so he didn't concentrate on dodging the large creatures. He concentrated on running in a straight line right behind the exceptionally large, very tall, and fiercely strong man with the ax. It didn't help that their armor portrayed the design of leaves and brush. They sort of looked like the depictions of the old Lore of the people of the Fondland. Dainty people of the forest and legend. *Earthy people*, he thought to himself as he followed the large man that continually swung the ax at his side toward any intruder into the line. Shadows of the animals leaped from tree to tree, and sudden thumps sounded as they landed to attack their prey. *It will not be long now*, Talon thought to himself as he ran with half of what was left of the escort. He could hear the river at the entrance of the castle tower when one of the large creatures blanketed with black hair and having a face almost that of a man stood strong in his path. Talon heard the release of five arrows as the creature moved toward him, but one only brushed the ear. Another arrow was stopped by the matted hair of the creature. The convoy stopped because Talon had stopped. Two arrows were embedded into the creature's chest, and it looked as if it hadn't even felt it.

This one was not like the others; it was much larger and obviously saw a great challenge that it thought it could overcome. Or perhaps it was an animalistic impulse that drove the huge creature unceasingly. Talon was staring into its face as it stepped closer to him. All action had stopped, and even the shadows in the trees had ceased. Its breathing was heavy in the hot, humid air, and it stepped even heavier toward Talon, looking nowhere but into Talon's eyes. The creature was on two feet now; and only the commander, two soldiers, the tall man, and Galen stood with Talon directly in the path of the visible boat and the entrance to the tunnels. The hot moisture of the forest dripped from the nostrils of the gorilla-like creature as it stared into the eyes of Talon. The creature was not as a gorilla was in stature; however, it stood tall like a man, but much taller than a normal man. Its face was long, and its head was large. The eyes were the most captivating features about the creature because they were soft and gentle, with all the colors of the forest that surrounded them. Its fur was long and, in some places, twisted. Its feet were lengthy, limber, and it appeared as if it were standing on its toes, which resembled the fingers of a man. It was not yelling or showing anger of any sort. Talon was compelled to believe that the creature meant no harm to him. But his comrades were not so fortunate, Talon thought to himself as he retreated toward the forest and the creature advanced toward him. Silence filled the trees, and all that could be heard was the breathing of the creature, the dewdrops that continually fell to the floor of the forest, and the sound of the river flowing against the stone of the tunnels nearby; all that could be seen were the terrified looks on the commander's, Galen's, and the tall man's faces. Talon knew that there was something peculiar about the creature. The others were smaller, and they were brown. It stared intently into Talon's eyes and then dropped to all fours again, snorted, and shook its head as if it were pulling on something in a certain direction. The creature stood in front of Talon, gesturing to the left repeatedly. Talon stared into the eyes of the creature.

"Do not harm them," he said as he pointed past the beast to Galen and the group of soldiers that surrounded him.

Talon was weary but he followed; he had no choice. There would be no way that he would be able to get past the creature; it was clearly too fast. Talon's hands shook at the thought that he had no protective powers, and he would soon be walking in submission to the beast; however, it was the beast that showed the most submission.

The beast stepped to the side and began to travel to its left and the right of Talon. There was nothing that Talon could see ahead of him once he had begun to follow the creature, just high brush, and tall tree roots. As he walked, more of the smaller creatures followed them. Talon felt queer when they had gone some time into the forest, the portions of the forest where there was very little light.

As it seemed to Talon, the forest had disappeared and opened up into another clearing, but this one was much different. It was caused by a large tower centered in the clearing. Trees had fallen toward the object and were laid down in a circular pattern. Talon was now feeling almost sickly. He felt as if there was a wind that was passing through his body and it was blowing on his organs inside of it, as if he had been opened and was completely exposed. The creature stopped in its tracks and cried into the darkness of the forest. Then he turned toward Talon and looked into his eyes again. The beast was trying to communicate, somehow, with him, Talon thought as he slowly walked toward the tower. From what Talon could see, it looked like an enlarged rook on a chessboard of black stone. Perhaps Talon had been playing too much chess. It was simply a small tower, and it was drawing energy from the entire surroundings. The trees that were still standing were dead, and the grass that surrounded the tower spiraled in a pattern, and each blade of grass had died. Talon had thought that odd. It was the sight of the grass that caused Talon to come to the conclusion that there was a space-time disruption in the area, and it was centered on that tower.

The creature stepped toward Talon and used its left arm to reveal a key that hung around its neck. It pulled the key out from amongst its fur and slowly walked toward Talon with the key in its hand. The key was not like the others that Galen had found, and it was not like the key around the Musician's neck. It shimmered in the creature's hand, and the gold chain hung down the side of the large black hide hands of the beast. The key was gold and in a spherical shape. Talon had seen only one thing like it before; the key resembled the shape and size of the orb that caused his grandfather to go back and forth through time. Talon reached out and took the key from the creature as it kneeled on one knee and presented it to Talon. Talon didn't know how it all fit together, and he wasn't sure that he would tell Galen what had transpired or how he had reached the black tower which created the distortion in time alive—that is, if Galen and the others were still alive themselves. The creature snorted and pulled its hand away from Talon as he took the key from the beast's hand.

"Thank you." Talon couldn't help but feel that he needed to be respectful to the beast, seeing that it had been so with him.

The creature turned and went back into the forest, going the other direction. Talon took the same way back from what he could make out that had been his previous path through the forest from the river. He shoved the orb into his pocket and made his way through the forest to the river.

Galen and the four other soldiers were waiting for them in total shock of the situation. No one knew what had happened or why it was that the beast had chosen Talon to follow it into the forest, and no one asked either. Talon knew that Galen would expect a full report, but the others were content to be completely oblivious of the situation. Talon shuffled his way to the entrance of the tunnel and to the boat. Everyone was looking at Talon as if he had performed a miracle, and they all shoved themselves into the boat. The stream would take them back through the tunnels, so it was all right that Talon had no room in the boat to scull. The soldiers and their commander were too afraid to go back through the Qwirl in fear for their lives, so Galen had agreed that they could come with Talon and him to wherever it was that they were going.

The tunnels were their usual disgust as the boat was being carried through them. Rats scurried across stone piping and along stone edges where there was very little water. Talon had taken one of the oars and was directing the boat to which direction that he wanted it to go by holding the oar in between his legs and under his seat into the water. He would twist the oar in his hand if he wanted to go right or left, but for the most part, the boat was being gently carried by the water downstream to the gate of the Dark Tower. Talon couldn't help but wonder why it was that the creature had taken him to that strange place and where it was that it had gotten the spherical gold key. The key was remarkably similar to the orb that his grandfather was carrying around with him, but there were distinct differences in its design. Talon thought that it might be a key to the tower, or perhaps it was not a key at all. Talon was confused. It had seemed that the creature knew Talon somehow, which made him even more confused. But whatever the case, he had a spherical object in the pocket of his tunic that was given to him by an extremely intelligent creature and was shown a strange tower that had the ability to disrupt the flow of the space-time continuum. If he had told any of his friends back in the city of Myth, they would have never believed him.

Talon had remembered his life that he once had in Myth and the small business that he had been trying to keep alive, the friends that worked for him, and the unexciting notion of it all. He would miss the company of their idiotic life that they led with Talon's continuous dependency on his mother and his endless studies and research. His great-grandfather was a clockmaker, his grandfather was a clockmaker, and so he figured that he would try to follow in their footsteps a little. He was not a clockmaker though; he was an engineer and architect. Talon remembered the first time that he laid eyes on Pastel—the pictures on the walls, on the ceiling, on the carpets, and everywhere there was a blank spot. And these were not ordinary paintings, not at all. They were beautiful works of art; something that a true engineer or architect could deeply appreciate.

The boat hit hard against the side of the tunnel wall, which caused everyone to stop thinking about what it was that they were pondering on, including Talon. The boat skidded and shook until Talon used the other paddle to push the boat away from the wall. Talon had stopped dreaming about the old Pastel castle that lay in ruins along with the Pastel Mountain that once shone so brightly in the light of the night sky. He stopped dreaming of what his old friends in Myth would say when he would lift something in the air to impress them, those foolish young men. He could never return; no matter what feeling he had for his brothers in business, he could never return.

Galen lifted his hands into the air toward the large steel gate that closed off the path of the tunnels to the castle tower, and it lifted slowly in unison with the movement of his hands. Talon docked the boat where they had originally taken it and headed up through the passageways behind Galen into the library of the Dark Tower. He searched and searched each and every book for a symbol that would at best resemble the symbol etched into the key. He searched in the shelving, under the chairs, through each book that lay on the ground until he realized that he had not searched the personal reading desk that sat on the top floor, which could be seen from the bottom floor. The desk lay there, untouched for what seemed only a few hours, and it had dawned on Galen that whoever owned the castle wall would have found the key and would have stored it in a safe place, such as a reading desk that only he or she could have access to. He quickly climbed the spiral staircase that led into the partial upper floor that looked down on the whole library, walked across the upper floor to the desk that lay in the far-left corner of the room, and began opening drawers to see if his hunch was correct. Suddenly, after the unveiling of the fifth drawer, there it lay like a beautiful woman in a meadow of red flowers. Galen picked up the gold key that had been lying in a bed of red satin and quickly draped the gold chain around his neck. He looked further for other items that may be of value to the cause but could find nothing. The soldiers looked around at the books that lay on the floor and in the shelves and were in awe of the many different languages and markings that they had never seen before. Galen closed the drawers and shelves that he had been looking through; he put the books back on the shelves and repositioned the books that he had knocked down, with a smile. He had found what it was that he was looking for, and if there was something that needed looking for again, he would have many good places to look.

Talon's sphere of light shone brightly in the darkness of the spiral path up to the doorway of the castle of Pastel. Galen watched as the soldiers were still out of breath from passing through the evaporation archway. It was all a new and strange world to them, and they were unsure of what was to become of them in this world. Galen turned to the commander,

"Corel, is there no mention of a world outside of the city of York?"

"Only the forbidden stories that we were not allowed to tell anyone in the city. If there was one caught telling such a story, they were to be fed to the Cane," Corel said with fear in his voice.

"What are Cane?" Galen asked as the commander held his head high and frantically searched his surroundings for something that would jump out and snatch him away.

"They are probably waiting for us on the other side of this wretched place." Corel paused for a moment and said, "That was the name of the creatures that own the Qwirl."

"Ah yes, that would make all the sense in the world," Galen said as Talon interrupted with a question in a sarcastic tone.

"In which world would you be referring to?"

Galen said nothing in return to the disrespectful remark because of the sight of the entrance to what was left of Pastel.

Talon's orb emitted streams of fire toward the door, and the door opened with a loud hissing sound as the air from the chamber was depressurized into the opposite chamber. Galen sped out in front of Talon and pulled the rusted key from around his neck. He quickly looked for the symbol of the key on each door. Galen searched and searched each door until he realized that the key that he had was the key to the first door that had already been demolished. The symbol was carved into each corner of the door, and what was left of the first door shown slightly in the bottom right corner of the door. The rusted key didn't match any of the twelve doors.

Galen was extremely disappointed. He had not found a way into any other door and was feeling quite sorry for himself and turned toward Talon as if he knew something that Galen didn't. But Talon looked away and said nothing; he was leading Fire along out into the chamber. Galen knew that the key was to unlock something that was especially important, so he thought to keep it around his neck until he found out where it was that the key belonged. Galen though had had enough excitement in such a short time and wanted to go home to Asscatan, and so that was what he would do.

"All in its good time," Galen mumbled to himself as he passed through the entrance of the demolished passageway to the train that led to Asscatan.

He would take the mystery home with him and ponder on it; then he would return with an educated hypothesis.

"Yes, that is what I shall do," Galen mumbled to himself again.

The guards followed Galen and Talon through the passageway into dangers that they knew nothing about, and they were not prepared for what was to come. However, that would not mean that they didn't have the capability to be brave or valiant in any manner. They certainly would need such resiliency for the adventure that lay ahead of them. Talon was only concerned about how it was that they were going to transport the Cyclicorn on a train. *Galen would figure something out*, Talon thought as he followed Galen through the dark corridor with only the light of Talon's sphere to shine the way.

Cypress looked out into the dark light that shone through the tunnels onto the cave floor of Asscatan. She, though at times made things hard for Galen, was happy that he had made the effort to go back into the dangerous outside to save Talon from his predicament. Cypress knew that it would not be an easy task if it were the Ministry that had captured Talon; it would not be like their capture of Sol. There would be guards at every corner; they would most likely have guards posted in the forest. It would be one of his hardest missions. She was looking at the trees in the near moonlight that shone down when suddenly, her countenance changed. They must have been followed when they made the attempt to save Sol's life. It would be all that the enemy would have needed to follow them back to the city of Pastel, stealthily watching them enter the castle through the stables, and the mission would be accomplished.

"That is exactly what happened," she said as she grabbed hold of the stone wall that she stood on.

She led the Ministry to them. It was a very careless thing to do. It was she who had wondered why it was that the Ministry hadn't taken them right then and there. They didn't care about Sol; they wanted the Order's secrets, and they got them. She was worried now. Would they try to do the same thing with Galen? Would they follow him through the tunnels without his knowledge? Would Galen lead them straight to the underground city of Asscatan before they even had a chance to repair their previous mistake, or had they thought that they had won? The thought had begun to make her sick to her stomach. This she could not let happen. She could not allow Galen to lead the Ministry to the new city. She would have to somehow stop them from entering the city at all costs—even though she would perhaps never see Talon or Galen again. There had already been too much loss. She could not allow that to happen again. Cypress had made up her mind; she was going to go back through the tunnels and close the entrance the only way that she knew how. There were going to be no more lives lost because of her stupidity, she thought to herself.

Galen had only been gone for a day, and Cypress knew that it would take at least three days for him to return with Talon: one day to get to the Ministry; one day to plan, attack, and escape; and another to return. So, she knew that Galen was still two days from reaching the entrance to the city of Asscatan, and that would give her ample time to close the passageway from the train tunnels. *I must do it; I just have to do it whether I love Talon and Galen or not. The entire future of the Order is not worth their lives*, she thought to herself as she began walking through the shimmering light that was cast down onto the city's floor below. *This is something that absolutely must be done*, she thought convincing herself again as a tear began to fall down her cheek.

Galen was driving the train when he saw Cypress in the tunnel passageway. With outstretched hands, she barely dodged the incoming train. She lay on the tunnel floor as it went whizzing by and then came to a shrieking stop after some time. The lanterns from the engine shone dimly in the darkness of the tunnel, and if it hadn't been for the train's one lantern in the front of it, Cypress might have been dead. Breathing hard and in total shock of the premature arrival of Galen, Cypress sprang to her feet and began to run to where the train had settled. The questions began to race through her head as fast as the engine had raced past her. Had something gone wrong, and Galen got away free? Had he been successfully faster than

Cypress had expected? Was Talon with him or was Galen in the train at all, or was it a Ministry army that had come to finally destroy what was left of the Order? She crept along the floor of the tunnel of the train passage in disbelief that whomever it was that was on that train could possibly be a friend and not a foe. It was not an enemy that stepped out to greet her though she had thought that at first, judging from the way that the man stepped out of the train and began walking in her direction. Talon stopped in the light of the lanterns on the side of the train and smiled at Cypress as she stood there with her hands out in front of her tunic.

"What's the matter, never seen an apparition before?" Talon asked as he reached out his hands, gesturing for her to jump into them.

Cypress didn't have to think twice about showing how much she was glad to have him back and near her; she didn't, at that point in time, care whether it was a trap from the Ministry or a vision from desperation. Talon was near her, and she was going to enjoy all of what she felt from his presence. She would never let him out of her sight again. It would be an endless job of making sure that Talon would always be all right and safe in her arms even though he was not in her arms—she was in his. Galen was not far behind when he saw Talon and Cypress holding each other.

"Why was it that you were in the tunnels in front of the train?" Galen asked Cypress as he walked up to them from behind.

"Did anyone follow you?" she ignored his question.

"No, we were not followed," Talon said as he held her in his arms.

"Never mind the question," Cypress said as she hugged Talon closer.

"We need to get the train out of the tunnels, and I need to get to the library and see if I can find anything that resembles this symbol," Galen said as he pulled the rusted key out of his tunic and showed it to Cypress.

She looked at the key in fascination and then turned to hold Talon closer to her as she thought of how wonderful it was to have him back in her arms. Galen walked to the front of the train, took the break off, and started the engine on into the train station. Talon and Cypress walked the rest of the way through the tunnel.

Talon marveled at the amazing sight of the city of Asscatan with its many trees and lush gardens that was, in many ways, similar to the city of York, just on a larger scale. They held each other shoulder to shoulder as they walked along the railroad tracks and over the railroad ties that led to the entrance of the train station. It was all that Talon could do to look away from Cypress just to see where it was that he was going. All that he could do to realize that if he had truly lost her, he would have very possibly become a vicious and detached person without a care in the world. *What would hold me back from becoming the greatest and most dangerous creature that ever roamed the earth?* he thought to himself as he held that thing that would do just that in his arms. It took everything that he had inside him not to stop, turn her around, and tell her that he could never live another moment without her lips pressed tightly against his. It would take everything that Talon had to not tell her that he truly did love her, not some kind of fashionable love but the kind that would make him want to die if another had taken her, which would cause the deadliest jealousy that any man could muster up in his heart. It would take all the man that he thought he was—all of it, and only he knew it. Every moment on would be a sort of torture to him. He would not be able to truly tell her how he felt about her until he could be confident that she felt the same way toward him. He would have a battle in his heart that would rage on until he knew that that who he so desperately desired desperately desired him in return.

Talon held her as close as he could and was at the same time mortally afraid of her finding out that he loved her. *It will pass*, he told himself as he walked along the floor of the train station and into the courtyard of the inner castle.

The architecture had begun to take his mind off his love and pain and into the spirit of the moment of realizing that he was in his new home, and that it was the most beautiful thing that he had ever seen. Galen had stopped the train by now and was headed to the library through the courtyard. He sped past Talon and Cypress talking about how beautiful the castle was made and how it didn't seem possible that one could create such an amazing accomplishment. They would be left to create their own civilization that could live on and on past the ages and through the depths of time until it was that time when the millennial war would come upon them. Talon thought that it was all so important now that one become skilled in the art of the Legacy; it would be a necessity.

Talon and Cypress walked through the castle to the library and sat in one of the sofas that lay toward the back of the library. The large fireplace burst into flames when they walked over and sat down. Deep in the large corner of the wall that lay in front of them there was a wooden wardrobe that was about as tall as the ceiling itself, about twenty-three feet. Talon didn't pay it any mind as he watched the fire rage on, and Galen was too busy fussing through the books that lay on the shelves. Cypress lay next to Talon on the sofa with a book that she could read and a piece of fossil that she had torn down from one of the exhibits. It showed all the different creatures that were now extinct, and it was all so interesting to Cypress. It was in this state in the darkness of the love of Talon that he saw the symbol directly surrounding the center of a keyhole that lay to the right side of the wardrobe's solid wooden door. Talon jumped out of his chair, and Cypress slid and crashed at the seat of the sofa.

"Galen," Talon cried with a loud voice. "It's the symbol on the key, you must come quick," Talon said as he stood there in shock.

Cypress hadn't noticed it before, the fact that there was a door in the library. That fact to her would have made the experience of cleaning the room more interesting. Possibly, if she had seen the symbol on the key, she would have known. Whatever the case, it was Galen that was the one who was the most interested in the door that looked like an entrance into a wardrobe; and as he pulled the gold key from off his neck, he knew that there was something unexpected, something that would change the beliefs of the Order forever. And that would not be the end of it.

13 A MINISTRY EYE

JACK'S HANDS SHOOK as he entered the Ministry guard. Men and women in tunics of all different colors filled the courtyards and streets of the Ministry castle. Someone would ask him where it was that he had been, and he would have to tell them that he was on guard and was attacked by men that he knew nothing about. The Ministry magistrate would look at him again, this time with a different look, and tell him that he wanted the truth. Jack would tell him that he lay in the forest near Myth for over a month and a mysterious woman had helped him to his health. That was the plan. Jack would lie, lie, lie, and hope that he would get away with it. *That was the plan?* he asked himself as he entered into the main chambers of the council room. *It's not a very good one*, he thought again. Jack had seen what the Ministry had done to the castle of Pastel and knew that if they could link him to the Order in any way, he would not stand trial. He would not be brought to the high inquisitor; it would be a quick and untimely death that he would receive and nothing less.

The castle of the Ministry was very large; it extended in all directions, all except for the section where Auzgool sat blocked by the lake and river. There was no moat, just an extreme amount of guards that stood at their posts when the gate to the castle was open during the day. The castle had very tall towers that had walls, which linked them together, and only one large gate, which led from the outer wall, protecting the many tax stations and inner businesses that lay in the inner section of the outer wall. The center castle grounds were full of religious elders, politicians, and Ministry members, and another wall separated them from the stationary merchants that sat inside the confines of the outer wall. Most of the produce was shipped from areas like Myth and the Fondland where there were peasants and farmers that were almost taxed out of their livelihoods. The castle stood tall and strong high on the top of Ministry Mountain, and the light from the sun beamed down upon it and its gray stone and mortar. Snow blanketed the tops of the towers and the tops of the eight-foot-thick walls; it covered the ground in the courtyards and melted its way through the sewers of the castle. Everyone had their best warm clothes underneath their most expensive tunics.

Jack crunched the snow under his feet as he walked and thought about what he had seen and heard in the city of Pastel. It was too much that he had tolerated from the Ministry, and he wished that he did not have to take another step into the Ministry castle. He wished that he never would have to look at another Ministry official in the face and talk to the viperous beings that inhabited the castle. He had hoped that he would find one like him, one that would feel disgusted when they heard what it was that the Ministry was up to, what it was that they had done. *This is a wicked place*, he thought to himself as he walked into the main Ministry hall to report in and tell his lie.

Jack's face was distorted at the thought of all that the Order had been trying to accomplish all these years, and he felt sorry that the Order had lost their home; he hoped that they were alive. It was not even Jack that had known about the raid that had taken place against the Order. He hadn't known whether they knew the location of Pastel or not, and it was a complete surprise to him when the Order had told him to return to the Ministry.

It was not but a few hours that had passed when Jack began to hear screams and see fire coming from Pastel as he watched from the forest. He could not return to aid them though; he could not risk his being discovered. That was what hurt his heart the most, and if he were all that was left of the Order, it would be him that would have the advantage over the Ministry, not the Ministry over him. He was too important to the Order's cause, and he didn't like having to remind himself of that fact. Jack had known that it was not the Ministry that made the initial attack on him or on Talon and Cypress; the Ministry didn't have that kind of foreknowledge or power. He was curious to find out who had made that attack and whom the woman with the lamp was, where she came from, and what it was that she wanted.

Talon and Cypress didn't tell Jack as much as he would have wanted, and it made him unsure. There were many questions that Jack felt that he absolutely needed the answer to. He knew, however, that the Ministry was the attacker of Pastel. It was all too obvious that the Ministry had used their control of the land to influence the Requiem, and only the Requiem could have created such a scene that could be seen from the forest of Myth. It was natural for Jack to worry about these things though, because he was walking into the heart of the operation.

Jack walked past the guards to the entrance of the high inquisitor's office to report in and was met by a man in black clothing, that of a gentleman. The man's tunic was unveiled and draped over the back on his dress uniform, and there was a label that had been sewed to the man's sleeve, which read, High Inquisitor's First Aide. The man carried a long black cane that he tapped against the ground as he walked, and when he reached Jack, it was the custom to cower at such a high-ranking official, which Jack did quite skillfully.

"I was just brought word that you had entered the Ministry. Welcome back, friend," the middle-aged man said as he held out his hand, placed it on Jack's shoulder, and smiled gracefully in a calculated fashion. "The high inquisitor wishes for me to teach you a lesson, won't you come with me," the man said in an even more sarcastic manner than before, before Jack had a chance to give a reason why it was that he did not report on time and why he had been missing for over a month.

It took Jack by surprise, the fact that the official didn't ask him where he had been, and what did he mean by him teaching him a lesson? It was all very strange, and before Jack could come to the conclusion that there was something wrong with the way that his known acquaintance was treating him, he was unsatisfactorily assured.

"There's nothing to worry about. Just a few things that need to be cleared up while you're still with us in the Ministry."

Jack didn't know whether he would have been better off never coming back to the Ministry or making a run for it at that very crucial moment. If he had ran, he would not have survived. He would be shot down within a few yards of his acquaintance calling out to the guard's archers to attack. If he had stayed out of the Ministry, he would not be carrying out his duty. It would be better for him to die in the Ministry without it knowing that he was truly a part of the Order. But Jack didn't know whether he was being taken to his death or not, and so he quickly made the decision to be oblivious to the dangers around him and to do what he had set out to do: successfully re-infiltrate the Ministry.

The man took Jack by the shoulder and gently led him through the hall that ran through the center on the main inner wall of the Ministry castle. Light shone through the slits that had been designed as protection windows for archers. And the castle floor was immaculate, nothing but the best for the Ministry grounds; there were servants whose only job was to continually sweep the floors of the castle all day long, and it was highly effective in making an impression on neighboring kingdom leaders that would come to visit for some business. Jack walked tall through the corridors of the inner siege wall as the light flickered on and off of him as they passed the windows. Merchant-servants, and maidservants passed as they walked, and Jack kept a smile on his face the whole time. It was his new plan to boast about how he escaped the capture of the Order and the attack that left him for almost dead; it would show himself more of a member of the Ministry.

"Yes, that would be sufficient," Jack caught himself saying under his breath as the official turned his head quickly to catch him at something.

Jack just acted as if he had said nothing at all, and it had seemed to work quite nicely.

It was a long walk past sections of the castle that he had never seen before, and he would never have guessed that he would be near them without a stealthy plan. Jack could hear people in the many layers of the castle wall, talking and singing, fighting and yelling. Soldiers sat along the walls in a non-casual manner though it had been ages from a time when they had had any trouble directly in the Ministry castle. It was counted as a sort of job security to become a Ministry army soldier. There was never a time when the Ministry had been questioned in their actions, and there were severe consequences for anyone that disobeyed anything that was ordered by the Ministry officials. It had appeared that the Ministry was in a very comfortable position in time; however, there were only a select few that knew of the Order's threat to the Ministry and all that it could do to their kingdom. What Jack didn't know was the reason that he was now being brought into places that at one time to him had been out of his jurisdiction.

He had not a clue of what was happening, and yet he could not truly feel that he was exempt from an explanation of his not-so-distant past. The tall man's tunic flowed gently behind him, and as he walked across the floor it brushed the stone slightly with every step that led to a place that became darker and more of a mystery to Jack. It would all become much clearer to him in the end, Jack thought to himself as they both stepped slowly down the steps into, what seemed to Jack, the endless darkness of the Ministry castle.

Deeper and deeper into the castle they walked as the tall man held Jack's shoulder tightly. It was in the darkness that the man stopped walking. The man turned in the darkness and pushed Jack to follow him. Light shone through the crack of a door and then passed over Jack as the tall man pushed the door open.

"Have you been stripped of your rank before?" the man asked Jack as he opened the door, not looking at him. "I shall have to show you what it is like," the man said as he smiled and turned to look at Jack in the light of the window that shone through the door of the chamber. "I was instructed to escort you to the mistress's chamber for a special assignment. It appears that you have attracted some wanted attention, good path to you, my friend."

One moment later and the man was no longer by the side of Jack. Jack entered the room and saw a woman dressed in a very eloquent manner of clothing; she sat tall and strong in her seat.

"Come in, I have been expecting you," the woman said with a smile in her voice.

Jack didn't hesitate to obey the order, and he quickly walked over to greet her in a respectful manner.

"What is it that you wish of me, my lord?" Jack asked with fear in his voice.

This was a woman that he had only heard about; he had never laid his eyes on her for she had never once shown herself to him. The most powerful woman in the kingdom of the Ministry was sitting in front of him, and Jack was beginning to think that she was either going to try to snake information out of him or tell him that there was a special mission that she would have him accomplish. He could not think of any reason that she would trust him enough to go on a special mission, so he had prepared himself to be careful of every word that came out of his mouth.

"I have a very important mission for you, Jack. It would involve you changing your name and pledging your life to my cause no matter what it is that your job requires of you. Can you do that for me?" the woman asked very politely as if Jack had any choice in the matter at all. He didn't hesitate and immediately said,

"Yes, my mistress, I most certainly can." And he finished with a "Thank you for the opportunity to serve you in every which way I can, Head Mistress."

He thought that perhaps he was laying the charm on too thick with his corny response to her question. But if the consequence was that she really was going to send him on a special mission, it would give him all that he needed to lift himself into a higher entry level of secrecy which, as one of the members of the Order, was the reason that he had already spent ten years infiltrating the Ministry: to find its secrets that it didn't tell even its own people that were not on some level of trust in the organization. It was all that he needed, and he was going to get it, he thought to himself as he stood kneeling on one knee, staring at the stone floor that lay beneath the lady's office desk that she sat behind.

"It is my understanding that you were attacked on the road in the forest of Myth. Have you any idea of who your attackers were?" Jack hesitated in the sudden fear that somehow, the Ministry had already known about his unfortunate experience.

"No, I do not know who they were or what was going on at the time. It happened all too fast," he said, still with his head facing the floor.

"We are glad, nonetheless, that you escaped and that you are here with us again," she said as she shuffled some papers that lay on her desk. "What if I told you who your attackers were and it was so unbelievable that the truth would go against all of your beliefs and values, those parallel to the beliefs of the Ministry?"

The woman had stopped shuffling her papers and was now looking deeply at Jack, but his eyes were still facing the ground.

"I'm not sure what you mean, mistress," Jack said in a confused tone of voice.

He had not known that there were Ministry guards that had been trained to use the Legacy; he had not known that there was a secret organization that even the Order had no knowledge of that sat in the heart of the Ministry. He had not known that Talon had been abducted by this elite Ministry organization, and he had absolutely no idea that Morastah Barrett, the head mistress of the Ministry, knew about the time barrier. He did not know that she would put so much trust in him, and he was amazed at the notion. After she had explained the concept of the time barriers with very little detail, she revealed to him the existence of that secret Ministry order.

"Those men that had come after you were after Ministry secrets that not even you knew, whatever was the reason that you were so far from your patrol does not matter. What is of importance is that you have knowledge, by way of contact, of a group of people that still live in the first world, and you must know where we, as the Ministry, stand with such humans,"

Morastah raised herself from her chair with a grace and subtlety all her own. She gestured for Jack to follow her, and he was up off his knee before she asked it of him. She opened the door to her chambers and began walking through the darkness of the castle walls of the Ministry. The farther down they went, the denser the darkness became. Jack could hear the dripping condensation of water down the walls in the darkness through the words of Morastah as she explained that the Ministry castle was built on a foundation of a castle that once was owned by the founders' first ancestors, the first humans to enter through the barrier to this world, the second world in time.

Jack knew nothing about the twelve doors that Galen had found and the secrets that just the first two doors had revealed, and so it was naturally a very fascinating thing when Morastah brought him into a chamber that lit its own torches.

"This chamber was left open as the ancestors of the Ministry fled for their lives. No one knew where it was that they went, it is a mystery that has been such for many ages now. There are, however, many secrets that were discovered by the study of how the chamber was built and information that has been gathered from a now-deceased organization that called themselves the Order. There is, however, a continuous problem that we are facing, that of the kingdom of man that is somehow sending troops through the barrier."

The light from the torches flickered on Morastah's face as she gently waved her hands in the air as she spoke. She had stopped walking when they had reached the chamber with the open door, but after a few moments, she continued through the open door to the next chamber. Jack walked through the door to the second chamber and saw four men in blue tunics sitting in each corner of the chamber room. Morastah had begun to explain that the men were always there, concentrating on sealing the rift of the barrier, which is the reason that soldiers are passing through it. There was an arch that protruded from the wall in the back of the chamber, and when Jack asked about the stone archway, Morastah told him that it was only there to complement the design of the room. It had no real importance, and Jack quickly lost interest.

"Your new assignment is to learn what we know of the Legacy as it is stated by ones who use the power that is given by our occupying another realm. You will learn all that there is to know about it, all that we know about it, and you will eventually become a tracker guard which is in the Ministry the highest-ranking Legacy official that there is, and you will serve me. You are the only man that has seen the Legacy at its full capacity, and that makes you, to me, the most valuable commodity that one could have. You will be taught by our Legacy commander, and you will learn well. Do you understand all that I have said to you?" she asked Jack as if she would scold him if he answered with any questions on the matter.

"I have, thank you, Head Mistress."

"You no longer have a name. You will be called by nothing but a look of ordinance."

Jack answered back with another:

"Yes, Head Mistress."

She smiled at him with approval and headed back through the chamber to the inner parts of the walls of the Ministry castle and began directing him to his new quarters, which were stationed in the center tower of the Ministry castle that led directly to the chambers of the ancient ruins; the ruins that lay under the Ministry castle.

"This is your new place of dwelling. Here is where you will learn the Legacy, this is where you will become a true servant of mine. You will stay here and wait for your teacher until he comes," Morastah said as she looked at him in his eyes and then shut the door.

Jack took off his tunic and sat on the bed that lay dead center in the castle tower. He had not been treated in this fashion in the Ministry at any time, and he was very pleased that his little adventure with the men from the first world had not taken his life or, worse, given him away as an eye for the Order.

The room was very pleasant to look at; there were afghans that hung from the walls of stone and expensive carpets that lay on the floor. Cloth was draped over his bed, which hung down from the bedposts that extended almost to the ceiling of the room. The ceiling was tall and had a cone shape that extended from the base of the wood and stone of the castle tower. Beams of wood crossed over the section where the stone met with the roofing and under the cone roof itself. Windows with eloquent designs in the stained glass reflected many colors as the sun's light shone through. Jack looked around the room for some clue as to what the Ministry would use to train him in the ways of the Legacy. He would have to act as if he knew nothing at all if he were to survive, and he would need to be very convincing. It didn't seem that difficult of a task for Jack; he had been acting his way through the Ministry for quite some time now, and he was used to the strain of being another person inside and someone else on the outside. Only time would tell if he would be successful, and he thought that perhaps he might learn something new from the Ministry. He had studied his whole life in the Order but nothing that would entail a study of a more sinister Legacy, perhaps a deadly one. It would make him a well-rounded man, he thought to himself as he picked at the red quilt that lay under him on the bed. They would probably teach him how to kill with one thought anyone that he wanted to or torture someone with his mind—things that the Order wouldn't teach him; things that if he had a more imaginative imagination, he would be able to figure out himself. But just what would he test it on? he asked himself with his hand to his chin in deep thought. No matter what he would learn or not learn, he would have to find a way to send a message to Galen, if he was still alive.

The third window to the right was not closed completely, and there was a cool breeze that came in from off the icy mountains that lay just a few miles north of his position, the position of the Ministry castle. There was a birdcage that lay off to the right of the entrance of the sleeping chamber, but there was no bird in it. It gave Jack the idea that he could send his bird to find Galen, and once Galen was found, he would give him a message. Jack turned and opened the window closest to him and pulled out a small wooden whistle. Jack blew, and an almost unrecognizable shrieking sound echoed out along the land, through the trees of the forest of Myth, and down into the valleys of Orland. He would sit and wait on the windowsill for the bird, not the Ministry official. He would sit and wait for a glimmer of hope that would make it easier to carry on in his battle with the Ministry and now the battle with the men that were coming through the barrier from the first land. It would be more difficult than Jack had thought—the war that would come and the prevention of human extinction. He could not help but realize that he stood in an organization that knew of the Legacy and the cause of it and yet refused to accept that with that great power came the responsibility of protecting the human civilization from the imminent war that is to come, and still they hid the truth for power. He saw no logical conclusion for the deceptive delusion of the Ministry.

He sat on the stone that encased the frame of the stained glass with his hand clenched to his wooden whistle that had a tassel of red cloth laced through the small hole at the base of it and watched the trees from the forest of Myth shake and sway as the cool wind blew through them. He watched as the sun glistened on the freshly fallen snow that blanketed every portion of the Ministry ground that had not been cleaned of it, and waited for his eagle to find him.

Galen stared at the key as he slipped it into the keyhole of the wardrobe. The key slid in with very little force. He could hear the tumblers slide up and down the tall forks of the key as it slipped into place. And moments later he gave it a quick twist, and the door opened with a loud click that echoed through Asscatan's library room. Talon shivered as the sound waves from the echoes passed through his body only to continually bounce through the halls of the ancient castle grounds. The wardrobe door opened without Galen having to push or pull on it, and a light shone through a window about the size of his hand. The small window changed the light from the sun that entered the small book room through the stained glass into deep reds and bright greens. The picture was a short man in armor of gray that held a sword up twice the size of his body. A peculiar picture to place on a window, Galen thought as he entered the tight space. A six-foot stretch of carpet paved the passage to the reading and writing desk that sat against the right wall from the entrance to the wardrobe. Books lay in shelves that surrounded the entire space of the small library office that the wardrobe had been converted into.

"Or perhaps it was made deliberately so that no one would have too much interest in the office. A wardrobe isn't always a place that one might be interested in, unless they were female," Galen said out loud without realizing it and with a smile.

Cypress was now looking over Talon's shoulder to see what it was that Galen and Talon had found. She was curious as to how Galen had the key to the wardrobe but wasn't curious enough to ask.

Galen sat in the chair and looked around to all the books that surrounded him and saw many that were in their language, many that he could read. The books that were up above the desk and the books that lay on the desk were the ones that Galen could read; the books that were on the shelves behind him were in that same confusing language that he didn't even come close to understanding, and all the books were very, very old. It had appeared that no one had been in the room for quite some time, which was the same conclusion drawn from the state of the castle itself.

Galen took a look at the first book that he could see in his language. It was entitled *Songs and Hymns of the Aintianta Trans*. Galen opened the book and saw handwritten text of old songs and celebrations that went on for about three hundred pages. There were weird notations that had a resemblance to notes and scores for music; however, it was too foreign for Galen to understand. He set the book down and picked up the one that was just under it, which was entitled *Dragons: The Lie and the Truth of Their*

Legend. That was a subject that Galen would definitely be interested in after he had settled the business at hand—the business of finding another key, if there was one to find. It had been so far a journey that had taken him to places that he could have never imagined, an escape from his enemy and a discovery all so amazing. It would be foolish on his part to neglect the opportunity that had been continually presenting itself. He had not found the key to the other doors, and Galen knew that it very well would be absolutely necessary for the Order's survival. He searched the shelves book by book as the others now, including Bristle, watched since there was only room enough for one person in the wardrobe.

There was a special glimmer in Bristle's eyes once he had seen the book room in the wardrobe. It had reminded him of his small book room that he had in the tree house in Pastel. Bristle had managed to save some of his books and bring them along with him in his trusted leather bag that he always kept at his right side. There was not much that could separate Bristle from the secrets of the Order, the secrets that lay in the leather bag. He would find new additions for that bag, hopefully, and they would come from the wardrobe, Bristle knew it.

Galen's hand forced its way around a book that lay at the very bottom of the shelf on the left wall from the entrance. The wood was rough and coarse; he brushed his thumb over the symbol that was engraved on the cover of it and took a deep breath as he pulled it from the shelf. This book was not like the others; it was solid with metal hinges and had many signs on it. There was a puzzle on the back that required the matching of symbols obviously to open the lock to get whatever was in the book. However, it was more like a box than a book, and Galen saw the difference immediately. The symbols were foreign to Galen, and he was absolutely clueless as to which order they should be positioned in order to open the box. Bristle could barely see the symbols on the box as Galen retrieved it from the shelf. He tried to see some patterns in the symbols so that he could match them to each other, and everyone looked through the tall door of the wardrobe.

The puzzle was circular in shape, and it lay under a thin layer of wood that was fixed onto the box with two brass hinges. The thin layer of wood opened when Galen had taken the book out of the shelf, which inadvertently revealed the key puzzle embossed about an inch into the wood underneath the small wooden door. The puzzle had symbols facing each other in a circular pattern, and each circle layer of symbols had a smaller diameter as the rings of symbols reached the center of the puzzle. There were precisely four rings that could be spun to match up with the ring symbols just below it or above it.

Galen looked at the key puzzle and slowly moved the ring in one direction to see if he could hear anything going on inside the workings of the lock, but he heard nothing. Galen set the box on its face and put his ear to the lock as he twisted the rings in this direction and that direction, and yet there was nothing that Galen could do to open the box. He had hoped that he would be able to open the box in a non barbaric fashion, but the puzzle left him no choice. Galen lifted his head off from the box that lay on the desk and put his right hand over the puzzle; he was going to destroy the box. He would not let anything get in the way of him finding out the secrets that lay just outside of his grasp with the requirement of another key in order to get through the other doors of Pastel. Galen concentrated, and the box's puzzle began to spin out of control; the more that he tried to use the Legacy against the box, the faster the energy would be sucked into the box through the puzzle, making it spin. Galen had to stop; he was beginning to get exhausted.

"It is a lock that has been designed to divert the usage of time against it," Talon said as he moved in closer to Galen and into the doorway of the wardrobe.

Galen said nothing because he knew that Talon was right; he had come to the same conclusion. They would have to find out how to open the box the hard way, Galen thought to himself as he looked at the box in defeat. Galen turned to Bristle for advice, knowing that he would have some, but Bristle was no longer there in the library with them. Then Galen placed the box in the far right corner of the desk. The light from the sun shone through the little window onto the box, showing the little man with the sword twice his height, and the man took the shape of the extravagantly designed box.

Galen took a long breath and reached for the next book that was in his language that sat on the shelf just above the desk. He would ask Bristle what he thought he could do with the box when he returned from where it was that he had gone. He opened the exceptionally large book that had the title *History of the Ancient Human Ancestors and the Secrets of a Fallen Race*. This book was also written by hand, and Galen quickly shuffled his way through the other books written in his language and realized that they were all written by hand. It was when Galen began to read the first sentence of the history of the ancestors that Bristle came running up to the wardrobe with a hammer in his hand.

"What's that for?" Galen barked as he watched Bristle breathing hard with the hammer in his hand.

"To break the box, you old fool," Bristle said with a smirk on his face.

"And what made you come to the conclusion that a hammer would work if the Legacy would not?"

Galen asked with a perturbed tone of voice.

Bristle looked at Galen as if he was about to explain something very difficult to a child, and Galen could see it in his face.

"The fact that you were not able to enter the first door of the chamber to Pastel with the Legacy, but a large tree in the hand of a very powerful man was."

Galen looked at him in amazement of the truth that he had not thought of it first and then gestured for Bristle to give his hypothesis a try, with a surprised look. Bristle lifted the hammer to give it a good whack, and it was one moment before the hammer hit the box when Galen shouted for Bristle to stop.

"I think that it would be in our best interests if we tried all of our options before destroying the artifact," Galen said as he held out his hand, stopping the hammer from hitting the box by just a small measure.

Bristle didn't quite understand what it was that Galen was talking about; he thought that they had weighed all their options and made the decision to destroy the box. *What could there be more to think about?* Bristle thought to himself as he pulled the hammer from its frozen position over the wooden box. Galen leaned over and took a look at Talon who was standing behind Bristle, watching and waiting with no real interest. Talon was still happy that he was near Cypress in the flesh and near to her in heart.

The opening of the box could be done at a later time, according to Talon. He wasn't too concerned with it. Besides, Talon wanted to get some rest from the stressful ordeal of his journey, and he wanted to take that rest with Cypress, not with an ancient box with another something to tax his mind power. Now, though, in Talon's gaze into the nothingness of his daydream of him and Cypress together, Galen was staring at Talon, expecting him to do something for him. It hadn't dawned on Talon that he had a special skill that no one had ever seen in over millions of years with a possibility of no one having seen it at all. It wasn't till Galen called out Talon's name that he responded with a "Huh?" as Galen waved one hand in his direction for him to come into the wardrobe and for Bristle to get out of it.

Bristle was still at a loss at Galen's reaction. He had really thought that they had considered all their options, and there was only one option, that of destroying the box with a hammer. Talon walked into the wardrobe after Bristle had walked out, wondering why it was that Galen had made such a fuss.

"Would you please show us some light, Talon?" asked Galen once Talon had settled next to him.

Talon, still wondering what Galen was talking about, had forgotten for a short moment that he could in fact show a sphere of light and that in the past, it had been the key to opening the door to York, which in Galen's view, was not such a small skill. The peculiar way that the key had used the energy of the Legacy was the reason that Galen thought there might be some use in Talon trying his special skill on the key. It only took a few moments for Talon to realize that Galen wanted him to use his light to open the box, if it was indeed possible, so Talon obeyed Galen and worked to make the orb of light in the palm of his hand. Talon was completely unaware of the expressions that were being given by his awesome display of power as the light began to tumble and turn, hovering just over the palm of his hand. Expressions of fear, panic, satisfaction, and awe gripped the Order members as they stared without blinking. Talon was concentrating on the work of the moment; he was not concerned with what the others of the Order thought of him, all except for Cypress. But she had already known that he would do great things, and it would be no surprise to her that he had accomplished this great thing. He was, however, quite wrong about Cypress's feeling toward him at that moment; she had not known that he would take such great leaps in the knowledge of the Legacy, and she had not known that he would be able to accomplish the amazing accomplishment of bending light and fire. It was something that she had never thought was possible, and yet the ball of fire stood there suspended in the clutches of time and slowly drifting into the box's key. The key absorbed each particle of light and infused them into the correct symbols. Shifting the rings in either direction it began to line the symbols up. It was exactly what the box had needed to open, a light user—someone who was not of the world that the box was constructed in, someone who was immensely powerful in the simple teachings of the Legacy. When the symbols had aligned, the rings stopped turning, and the box made a loud click and then parted exactly down the center. Inside the box was blue and red velvet that encased another key. The key shimmered in the light that was fed to the wardrobe by the small window in the back of it.

Again, Galen was right in his presumptions, and he was proud of himself. Galen, however, knew nothing about the key that the creature had given Talon, and Talon liked the fact that he knew something that Galen didn't. Talon thought that he would keep it that way for some time. It would be what made his confidence more pronounced, and it would quite possibly lead Talon to a different conclusion of things as they progressed in the mystery of the twelve doors and the many keys. There was an unsettling thought that had begun to occur in Talon though—a thought that the key that the creature had given to him had nothing to do with the doors, a thought that would make the significance of his grandfather's appearance of the utmost importance, perhaps an importance that would outweigh the importance of what it was that the Order was trying to accomplish. This was something that had begun to cause fear in Talon—fear even after all that he had been through, after all that he had accomplished.

Galen had allowed the stress of the situation to pass, and the help from Talon was all that it took to allow Galen to do just that, relax. He would now be able to read the handwritten books that sat in front of him and perhaps learn a great deal. It was the book that talked about the history of the ancestors that had caught his eye; he would read all that he could out of it to see if he could get an answer as to where it was that the castle had really come from.

It was Galen's suspicion that he had not known nearly enough about his heritage, the Legacy, and the ancient people that built and lived in the castles of Pastel. When he opened the book, it was the first sentence that had absolutely amazed him. The Order had known that it was the Order's descendants that had created the castle of Pastel and likely the other castles that followed from the two doors in the secret chamber; that had been what he was told for some time by the man who found him in the orphanage, the man that knew his name before he did. However, it was to Galen's surprise that the first sentence of a book that lay in his hand, and that had sat on a shelf for thousands of years, said something much different about the past of the Order and the past of the castles of Pastel. And as he read further, it was in his disbelief of what he had heard from the words on the page that led him to realize that it did indeed make all the sense in his world. The fact that the ancestors of the Order came through the border to a place that had been abandoned, a place that had been peaceful, a world unoccupied and yet ready and prepared for them. Castles and kingdoms that were not theirs were left as a legacy; they were left as an inheritance to them—an inheritance that they could not ignore, a history, a power that was not theirs and a kingdom left untouched.

14 Eyes in the Dark

THICK GLOOM covered the land as the moon's light beamed through the halo of dark clouds. Thunder struck the ground far off in the distance as the whole world was blanketed in darkness. Strange noises came from the trees, and the earth was cold and desolate. Talon folded his hands and sat in a chair that would only be fit for a Dark Lord. He lifted his head from staring at his hands with his mind but could not be seen beneath his black cloak. He could feel the long coarse fingernails, which he had allowed to grow, and he pondered on the hundreds of years of his life. He could barely remember the thought of Cypress's face, and the Orders had long faded away through the pain of old age, through the pain of the seven-year war that had finally been lost, and through his continuous battle against the dark kingdoms. He had fought for so long, he had toiled his entire life, finally he had found a solution—a solution that would turn the tables of time toward his benefit, toward the memory of the Order. Talon's breath shone through the freezing night air, but the air did not bother him, no more than usual. He had stopped worrying about such things long ago and was more concerned with his plan, what he would do to restore the peace in the land. Talon's dark figure unfolded its hands and laid them to his sides onto the stone seat that lay in the center of the Dark Tower. He had remembered thinking that the castle would not be a suitable place for him to live; but now, after all that he had been through, it was a peaceful place, dark and secluded and much to his liking. It had a charm all its own, and Talon was content to rule his kingdom from this place.

Because of the archway, no one truly knew the location of the Dark Tower, not even Talon; and this was what had helped him to survive. After the archway had been destroyed near the passageway of Pastel, he had accidentally found the frequency of the evaporation portal, which led to the Dark Tower while running for his life from the Dark Lord's minions; he had barely escaped. It would all soon make no difference at all, the fight that the Dark Lord had against Talon and the fight against the growth of the Ministry in the second world. Time had already been changed by Talon, and the Dark Lord had no knowledge of it.

Talon raised his hand and gestured for the nearest guard who had been standing near him.

"What is the progress of the Black Sighthur?" Talon asked the man with a soldier's armor as he shivered under his tunic.

"The Sighthur has not returned from the second world, master," the soldier responded in a fearful voice.

Angry, Talon reached out his hand toward the man in armor and began to clench his fist.

"It is something that you could not understand, something that no mere man could. I must succeed at my goal, and no incompetence of any man soldier could understand how useless they really are. But have no fear, if I succeed, your death from the disposition of men will not have taken place. It is likely that you would live in pastures of green, with a son to your house, and that would be the best for a farmer made soldier. As you can see, that would be a better life for you. However, in the here and now, you have continually shown a lack of insight, and for that, you will be repaid with your death," Talon said as the soldier grasped at his neck and hung from the ground as life fled from his body.

Talon released the dead soldier to fall to the ground in an awkward position and returned to his deep thought. Other soldiers and servants quickly came from dark places in the hall to dispose of the body. One at a time, the soldier's armor was stripped from his body and then the carcass was taken away. Any man that had an unsatisfactory report died in such a way, and each time, Talon would say the same thing before he brought upon their deaths. Talon remembered the first night that he had met Cypress and the man that had led him to her. He never saw his face though; and Talon, still to this day, had been wondering who the man in the pub in the city of Myth had been. He traced his thoughts to the time of the old man that sat mumbling in the corner of the tavern with a beer that had been untouched. Talon remembered the words as if they were in his own time: He would find her by the side of the road. He would find her by the side of the road. Her name was Cypress. Her name was Cypress. The words mauled in Talon's mind over and over, much was what the man at the bar had spoken, the thoughts that he had written on a parchment in front of him. Talon would probably not have ever seen the woman walking on the side of the path, let alone stopped for her if those words had not been ringing in his ears just hours before he passed by the Ministry castle to get to Fable. Talon had not known the man before that day and would never see him again, but he had always been open-minded to anomalies in his life, even before the Order had turned him into a powerful man through the Legacy. Talon owed his life to the Order many times over, and he would soon give it to them on a platter and to himself also. Talon relished the thought of a peaceful world as some place that he could truly call home, not as the person he is now, but as the person he was. He enjoyed having the power that he had, and he liked the wars that he had to fight against the Dark Lord. However, he knew that a life such as that which he was now living would not do; it would not do at all. Too many lives had been sacrificed for Talon to have such a life, the life of a Dark Lord. It had been but a night that had passed when Talon had last seen and felt Cypress; he was taking a large risk at her seeing him in the tunnels at the train. Talon had not been through that door before and was beginning to wonder what it was that the Order had found on the other end of the train tunnel. He had to return to his own time though; he could not be there long. There was too much that still had to be done.

In the night, his mind had begun to change, he could still remember the death of the Order by the Requiem the night that they had attacked Pastel; however, there was now a new memory that had begun to emerge. It hit him like a flash of light just after he had impaled the giant with his sword. And when he returned to his natural timeline, many things had changed, but it was not enough. He had hoped that he would not have to destroy the Ministry with his soldiers; however, it was all too obvious that the Ministry was too powerful for the Order even after Talon had saved their lives. Talon had not anticipated this, and he would have to now formulate a plan to destroy the Ministry himself. This would not be an easy task with the borders of the first world being patrolled by the Dark Lord, and that was what troubled Talon the most.

He raised himself from his stone seat as light from the flickering lamp candles shone on his dark tunic, his face concealed by it. All in the hall of the Dark Tower stood strong as Talon raised himself to his feet. Talon looked into the darkness through the tall pillars of the hall to a person that he could not see with his own eyes; he had lost them along with the war that had ruined his four-hundred-year life. He now saw through the eyes of the Legacy. It had taken all this time to find a way to pass through the barrier without the unnatural distortion of the universe, which unifies the two worlds, and Talon was not even the one that had figured it out. The key was in the tower and it was that which had made the distortion in time the first time that it had been opened. However somehow the Dark Lord had acquired his first key and was now using it to pass through the barrier in the future where Cypress still lives. The clockmaker had created a key portal. The design was complicated though and it was difficult to pinpoint the times that Talon needed to bring the Order back. The portal still stands open, however, and Talon knows that though he is personally more powerful than the Dark Lord, his troops are in a lesser number. It was that truth that was bothering Talon the most. He would have to accomplish his plan as his resources would slowly be dismantled, and yet his armies were still unable to keep all the Dark Lord's troops from entering the portal. Here and there, they would slip through the hands of a man from Talon's troops, and it would make Talon less tolerant of their incompetence as a whole.

Talon had control of the eastern mountainous planes of Zebulan and the surrounding areas, which was where the portal was created by the Dark Lord, and somehow his spies would penetrate the borders of the eastern line and the castle walls of Bareness. Talon could not understand how this could happen; but every so often, it did, and he disliked it very much.

Talon walked up the stairs to his library where everything was kept in pristine shape. He had run out of space on the shelves and was now finding himself placing the books neatly on the floor and in chairs that he never sat on. No one would come and visit the second Dark Lord because they were afraid that he would kill them because they were trying to get too close to him. Talon had lost friends and lovers, not to the enemy that stood with him in time, but the enemy of death itself and old age. He didn't understand in all his searching through his many books of old language why it was that he had lived such a long life, but to him it no longer mattered. He had learned to live with truths that had not been revealed to him, and he had learned to not get comfortable with any woman because he would likely outlive her only to feel the effects of the evilest of evil's death. He would not fear the death of his body or the death of the life that he had lived because it would be the life that was to come, the life that he would relive in peace that would matter.

"Yes, it is that life," Talon mumbled to himself from underneath his cloak hood with a smile as he shuffled his way through parchment papers that had been put aside in his desk, which looked down on the whole library.

Talon pulled the paper out from beneath the shelving of his desk and lifted the quill with his mind to write. Though he had no eyes to look upon the paper, it was the eyes of the Legacy that painted a clear picture of the surroundings wherever Talon was. Because of this skill, he could see behind himself, through walls, so far as there were no places that distorted the energy of time. Some would say that he had better sight than anyone, and they would not be far from the truth. There was another that could do such a thing, and both Bristle and Talon read how to do it out of the same book. It was almost discombobulating to have two lives of memories rushing through his head all at once, but Talon could handle it well. The quill drew lines of battle formations and land formations—plans that would need to succeed if the Order was to have any hope at life. Talon paused in his writing for a moment to look down at the key that lay around his neck. The Dark Lord knew that Talon would not risk opening another portal in desperation, but Talon knew that if he were successful, he would destroy the Ministry with one swift stroke of the blade, and all would be as it should be. The Dark Lord would not know that the Ministry would be his target, and it would throw the Dark Lord off his track if Talon created a new portal in the land of the Dark Lord. Talon would have to find a way to get his troops into the Dark Lord's lands though.

"No, there must be a better way," Talon said to himself as the quill continued its drawing of the land.

Talon sat there in the chair, near the desk with his arms laid palms down on the wood. *The land where the original portal is, is neutral land*, he thought to himself, still leaning against the desk and sitting in the chair, waiting for an answer to come to him. He knew that it would be absolutely necessary to open a new portal. He would let the Dark Lord in and move his troops away from the first portal. He would move them to the area of the new portal, which would not be far off from the first. Talon, however, would direct the entrance of the portal to the second world to inside the center of the Ministry castle. *That would be the simplest way of doing it*, Talon thought to himself, now sitting fully in his chair and drawing out the place in which his army would enter the castle grounds. The Dark Lord would send his legions through the first portal, which exits days away from the Ministry castle, and before the Dark Lord could realize that his plan would be flawed, the end of his world it would be, and the beginning of the Order's. Talon's wrinkled and gaunt face smiled in the light of the candles, which surrounded the library common room.

"Yes, that is how it will take place," Talon said as the quill scribbled some more lines to show where he would send his troops once they were inside the Ministry castle.

He opened the drawer to his left at the bottom of the desk to find a gold key lying in red satin. Talon looked down at the key as if he could show some kind of love for the object. It was its mystery that captivated him. Talon had looked in all places that he thought he could look inside the Dark Tower but found no place that the key would fit into. The key sat there under his desk for over four hundred years without being used for any good. Talon would sometimes become angry at the thought that someone had made a key that could be used for no purpose. He would often fall in love with the colors that the key would emit in his mind through the Legacy. The key had sat for many years under his desk without his knowledge. He had long last given up on finding the place where it belonged and now only kept it to look at for his own pleasure. In his time, Talon had never come across his grandfather excluding the accidental happening in the pub in the city of Myth where his grandfather had been on one of his last-time expeditions as an old man. He had been going over his notes, memorizing them so that he would save on ink and parchment; Talon's grandfather was that kind of fanatic scientist that was what had made him so brilliant. Talon was reaching for the key in his lust when a loud thump came echoing from the door. He looked toward the door and whispered into the air,

"Who comes to me?"

The wooden door cracked open, and only one eye and a sliver of face shone through the crack of the door. The steel ring handle that had been nailed to the door shook as though it was afraid to open, but it was only the small man who held the door firm in his sweaty hand that caused the ring to vibrate in fear.

"Speak!" Talon shouted at the waste of his precious time because of the fear of a man.

"The Black Sighthur, master, and she wishes to give you her report," said the small man still partially hidden by the door.

"Good, you may leave," Talon said as he raised one hand to gesture for the man to do what he had said, leave. The hand met the drawer to close it before she walked into the reading chamber. A woman with a lamp emerged from behind the door as the small man ran off through the halls into the great hall. She reached for her tunic hood and unveiled herself. A young woman stood at the entrance of the door and quickly kneeled in service to the Dark Lord. Her hair was black and her skin pale white with a hint of pink. Her eyes were deep green that shone like the daughter of an Ancient, and she was tall and skinny. She laid the lamp to the stone floor and raised her head toward Talon that now towered over her from atop the balcony of the reading common room.

"What news do you bring from Myth, daughter of the fallen?" Talon asked as he gripped the four–foot stone wall that met him at the end of the balcony.

"Villinovious is forming an army and is heading toward the east, toward the portal. He will try to break the barrier of troops to send them through the portal, my lord. We will no longer be able to stand against such an army, my lord," she said as she raised herself to stand tall.

"Good, it will give us a reason to fall back without Villinovious becoming suspicious. He knows that we would rather let the second world fall if it meant our extinction."

The woman looked confused but would absolutely not question her master; she would not make a mistake that would most absolutely cost her life.

"You will pull back our forces and send them to the Requiem fog. Have them wait for me in the center of the Ministry castle ruins. Do not have them march fiercely, have them walk as cowards being driven from their land," Talon said as he stared into the woman's eyes through the Legacy.

"As you wish, my lord," responded the woman as she withdrew the lamp from off the floor and returned the hood of her tunic to its proper place, concealing her face in darkness.

Talon could not recognize the time of the day by looking out at the sun; it hadn't shown its face for all the time that Talon had lived in the first world, and his blindness was a look at the world as none had seen before. His life of hiding in the Dark Tower was not that of a king or lord, and he was tired of living in the shadows, living as a memory of an old world that had long passed away. Talon grasped the orb that hung around his neck in a sentimental way; he had hoped that his grandfather would come out of nowhere and tell him what would transpire from his next action, but there would be no one to help him. It had been that way for so long; it would not change.

Talon looked through the chamber window of his room only to see the darkness, rain, lightning, and thunder that would never stop their continuous thrashing of the surface of the earth. Talon's chamber opened without any notice. Slowly and smoothly as its hinges screeched, a large creature emerged from behind the door. Talon turned to look at the creature from the Qwirl as it held its hands low and its arms to the side.

"Why is it that you have come here, Salon?" Talon asked with confusion in his tone of voice.

Salon said nothing because it could not, but it could make its intentions known. Salon held out his hand as he had once done before when he had expected Talon's help against the Dark Lord. Talon had seen the death of the Order behind the library wall the night that the Requiem had invaded the castle of Pastel, and had grown powerful from his rage. When he created the orb of fire to consume the bodies of his fallen friends in respect of their lives, the door to the Dark Tower had opened. It was not something that Talon had expected, and with all his knowledge of time and space, he would find a way to go back through time and save their lives. It would be his lifelong mission. Talon, however, had not thought that it would take such a long time for him to realize the solution but was glad that he was gifted with such a long life to see his goal accomplished.

Salon held out his hand, gesturing for Talon to give him the clock orb. Talon did not quite understand what it was that Salon was trying to tell him, so Talon entered his mind to speak to him.

"Give me the key that your troops may enter into the portal and accomplish this deed."

Talon heard these words and slowly walked down the steps of the chamber to confront the creature. He reached out his hand and closed the open palm of Salon's hand gently to gesture that he would not comply.

"No, my old and wise friend, I cannot. There is another way, and I am going to take it. I have already put it into place, it is only a matter of time."

Salon retrieved his hand from Talon's and shook its head in agreement. Talon took another look at the world that the first world had become and knew that once he left the confines of the Dark Tower, he would be in immediate danger. Villinovious had many soldiers patrolling the outer regions of the area of the second world where the Pastel ruins were located. The moment that he left the chamber and the mountain cave, he would have to fight his way through the labyrinth of hidden deadly creatures that the Dark Lord had at his command.

Talon held the reins of the horse tight as the darkness from the clouds lurked overhead. Deep grays and reds overshadowed the land. He looked over the land, as he stood tall on the back of his horse. The strong wind whipped Talon's black tunic here and there as he stood on the top of what was left of the Pastel Mountain. Demolished stone and dirt lay where the Pastel castle had once been. According to Talon, the destruction of the Ministry castle had not come soon enough. It was the Ministry that had brought the Order to an untimely end, and he was going to do the same to the Ministry.

He remembered the time when his mother had tracked him down, betrayed the Order, and locked him away in prison. His mother would pay for the things that she had done to him. She would pay all over again for her deceit and betrayal. Talon would make certain of it.

He looked down into the valley and could see the teeming soldiers of the Dark Lord like ants that filled the valley and contaminated the land. Talon remembered the woman with the lamp that he had never found the identity of and felt a compassion for the phantom that had once been there in his life to save him over and over, but she had not shown herself for some time, and Talon had expected to never see her again. *The one person that had shown the kind of power that I now displayed in my kingdom, perhaps I would not feel so alone*, Talon thought to himself as he rode down the mountain to the place where the center of the Pastel city ruins were. Before he would create the portal, he would need to direct his army of first-world cats and men toward the area of the Ministry ruins. Talon rode down what was left of the mountain and began heading in the direction of the Requiem fog near the Ministry ruins. There, his forces would find no battle but that which Talon would instigate, no battle but the absolute destruction of the kingdom of the Ministry.

Talon rode through the forest into direct battle. The wind blew harder and harder against him as he rode along the path through the forest. He drew his sword and killed all the strange beasts of the first world with one swift stroke of the blade that came near to him. Talon did not like to slay with the Legacy; he felt that it was an improper way of using the power that was given him by the universe, and he would not show it disrespect unless it was absolutely necessary or if someone or something angered him enough. At each turn, a beast of the Dark Lord jumped out to make the kill but was only met by the end of a blunt sword. Blood burst at contact, and the sword was off to its next assignment from Talon. Left and then right, Talon swung the blade for destruction.

The cold winds blew through the forest and snow blanketed the ground as Talon rode across the forest floor. Trees and brush could not blind the Cyclicorn that he rode because, with the help of Talon, it too could see beyond the barriers of light. The horse jumped over the large tree roots and through the tall ferns that would usually prevent the horse from seeing its way through the forest. It was unafraid of the creatures of the first world; it trusted that Talon could protect it. The black-and-brown hair on the horse glistened in the queer light of the moon that barely shone through the trees of the forest and the clouds of darkness. Talon would often fight his way through the Dark Lord's beasts, and the small ones he did not fear. It was the beasts that were the size of a small mountain that Talon would sometimes find trouble with; and as he had hoped that he would not encounter one of the large beasts, he continued fighting his way through the forest. Deep in the forest, the large creature had heard the call of the small beasts; and though Talon had countless times slain ones such as this one, they would not think to not confront him again. Talon would have to use the Legacy now; that is if he did not find a path in the forest that would go around the great beast.

He brought his horse to a sliding stop in the snow and dirt. He could hear the cries and roars of the creature off in the distance, but it would not be long when it would close in on his scent. Talon could sense the end of the forest and could still hear the creature when he started after the path around the creature and to the Ministry Mountain. Though he had evaded it for now, he was still some distance from the Ministry and the fog of the Requiem. He was nearing the hills of the Ministry kingdom ruins when he emerged from the forest.

Breathing hard in the cool night air, Talon reached to place his sword back into its sheath. Soon he would be with his army; they were near the fog now and close to the place where he would open the portal. Only the key could close a portal through time; Talon had only left the portal open so that he would have some leverage on the Dark Lord. He knew that as long as the portal was open, Villinovious would continue to send the bulk of his forces to conquer the area near the time portal, and Talon would be able to keep an eye on what the Dark Lord was doing with his troops. Though some had slipped through the grasp of Talon's forces, it was still the most advantageous maneuver that Talon could make. The creatures didn't like the hills and the mountains, and the Dark Lord could do nothing to make them patrol those areas. Those were the few places that Talon had learned to hide whenever he was not in the spirit of fighting his way through some area of the land. Talon had rested his horse at the top of the hills of the Ministry ruins and could see the demolished foundations of the stone fortresses and the partially destroyed stone walls that surrounded them. Talon could now see the army that he would lead into the heart of the Ministry castle grounds and take the future by force. He would leave none alive, and he would hope to seal the time barrier before he faded out of existence. That would be an unsure thing, and even Talon could not know what the future would be from that time forward. He had faith that it would be a better world without the Ministry, and he was willing to risk the long life that he had already lived for a better one.

Talon looked across the plains and through the hills at his army still two days away and marching slowly in the darkness of the land with only the cold as their friend, with only the thought that the Dark Lord would take the bait and begin entering through the portal, which led to the center of the forest and be days away from Talon and his army. Talon would open a new portal dead center to the Ministry and take the city down stone by stone, and slowly the future would change, and he would no longer have the life that he had led for so many years. Talon would wait for the end of his system of things; he would wait for his army to conquer on the top of his hill—the top of his waste of a world that he had known for so long. He and his horse would stand tall and embrace the feeling of change and for the first time feel light at heart at the reality that was to come.

Fog cradled the soldiers as they marched through the part of the forest that mixed with the fog of the Requiem. Many of the men were afraid and confused at the thought of the Dark Lord pulling back his forces and having them act in such a way. They all would stay true to the cause of the Lord, but many of them could not see how evil could beget goodness. How doing bad things could turn into a good deed on the part of the Lord. They, however, would never voice their concerns to the Sighthur, let alone Talon; it would only bring about the evil, which is said to beget good, upon them.

The soldiers marched through the fog with their heads held low as the Sighthur had commanded, and the action of the soldiers caused the creatures of the forest to not attack, besides the fact that the soldiers were entering a place that the creatures would not dare go. It was not something that an animal enjoyed too much—an animal from the first world. Fog was something that could not only cloud the light but also the thoughts of a creature without the skill of a focused mind, and so they never entered the fog. The soldiers could see the many creatures that lurked in the forest just within their sight in the fog. There were some that would act the brave and ravenous animal and would be quickly slain at the edge of the fog by the sword of a watchful warrior.

The fog was consuming for the soldiers; it shone the dim blue light through the black and, for a guardsman, made visibility not but an arm's length in front of him. The soldiers stayed close though, they did not stray at all. Cold seeped through their armor and beneath their skin. Many had left the reason that they had once had and lived a life, as the Dark Lord would have if he had been there right by their side. There was no mercy that would be bestowed to the enemy. There was no compassion, and if another man was found that was not on their side, it was them who had chosen their fate—the fate of a death by the sword.

Though Talon was not much different from Villinovious, Talon had a purpose, and he was not the one who had caused all the pain. Villinovious had brought the war early and had no regard for the ancient ways of war. He was a king that had been left behind and had his own agenda as to how he thought the world should be. His reach did not stay in the confines of the first world; he brought his evil through the barrier and was relentless to his cause, the elimination of man from the known universe. Talon had become malevolent as he combated that evil, and the ones that once knew him were still loyal to him—the ones from the city of York—and even though he had become evil, he was working to return the world to its proper place in time. Often the soldiers would reason in such a manner, and it would help them bear the pain of seeing Talon kill one of their friends and family; it would help the passing of the memory of having to discard the lifeless body of a brother or a father that had incidentally angered Talon, and they would know that Talon was indeed correct in thinking that if he was successful in his mission, it would be as if they had never died. But it only helped with the pain. There were many times that there had been an attempt at Talon's life to no avail, and yet it would be the anger of a loved one that would cause only another death with the same thing said as a dirge just before the life fled from their body.

It was an often occurrence that would take place: Talon leaving troops to die in the land as if they were something expendable. It was only a small occurrence, the use of Talon's troops for some strategic advantage, but this time Talon would use the troops for the most important job of all—the annihilation of the Ministry. His army would not have a chance to be proud of their victory. They would not even remember the life that they had once lived. They would vanish into the inner workings of the strands of time, having been discarded by the cosmos as something to be snuffed out. They would be hidden in time as they were now being hidden in the fog of the Requiem. They could hear the condensation of the water falling off the trees to the mud that their feet sloshed through; with every step, it became harder and harder for them to carry their own weight. For a day they had been walking in their armor, and the Sighthur was not going to allow them to slow down; they needed to reach the place that Talon had ordered within the time allotted, or as always, something awful would happen.

"They would camp in the fog, and Talon would meet them there to tell them where they would be going next." The Sighthur kept telling herself over and over so that she would not make any mistake at Talon's orders to do so. She had led many battles for Talon against the Dark Lord Villinovious, and for the first time, Talon had not told her everything that she would need to know to win the battle. She was being treated, in her opinion, as a message runner, and she was very unhappy about it. She would, however, not let her malcontent show to Talon. She would not tell him that she could run the armies without his help because no matter how much she thought that to be the truth, there was something in the back of her mind telling her that that was not the case and that she could not do the things that Talon could do. Perhaps it was her common sense that no other man-child had. She didn't know or understand all the things that Talon was after, and she knew that he did not tell her everything that he discovered or planned, and it was best for her. She knew that to be the truth, and whatever it was that was bothering her, she would always somehow be reminded that she was the one in the cold, in the fog physically, and Talon was the one that lived in the cold of his heart and body. No matter what surroundings he was placed in, it was his sorrow that would continually consume him. *Thankfully so*, she thought to herself because if it were not for Talon's sorrow and determination to set the universe right, they would have no chance of survival at all.

The Sighthur sat on a large stone when the horse of Talon could be heard from a distance through the fog. The sound was eloquent in form and strong in stature. Fog parted as Talon passed through it to get to his army. By way of his use of the Legacy, the fog cleared, and walls of fog were created all around the camp. When the army noticed that he had entered the camp, the sound of a horn trumpeted an alarm for the masses to spring up from their sleep and go out to greet him. The Sighthur raised herself from the stone quickly and took hold of Talon's horse. Talon dismounted and began walking across the mud to his tent that the Sighthur had erected for him to sleep in. He stopped and faced the twelve thousand strong soldiers that stood by their tents in the fog and raised one hand in greeting and for absolute silence. The army, upon seeing his raised hand, left the station of their encampments and quickly got into formation.

"In three days, we will pass out of the fog and travel in the direction of the ruins of the Ministry castle grounds. There you will station yourself at my side where I will lead you into the greatest battle that you have ever known, the greatest victory. As I speak, Villinoviou's troops are falling into the place that I have taken you from, the place of the guard of the second portal. He will not be able to resist this temptation to create his greatest devastation. However, I will lead you in through a new portal that will be opened in the heart of the enemy where you will pillage and destroy the true enemy, and while the armies of Villinovious would be days from the battle, we will have won the war, we will have won the peace. That is the battle that we are to fight, that is the battle that we are to win. And so be it, that we have lived a life that would have truly mattered, a life that would be worthy of repair, the life of men. This is the destiny that cannot be changed by any other means. It cannot be changed by the wickedness of man. It cannot be changed by the wickedness of an Ancient. It cannot be changed, so when the time comes, fight as if that day would be your last and first day of life because that is what it shall be and that is the truth, not the lie."

15 PARALLEL DESTRUCTION

A MESSAGE HUNG by a thin piece of leather, which was tied to the leg of an eagle. Jack quickly grabbed the small sliver of leather and untied the message from the bird, opened it, and began to read,

"My dear and oldest friend, it was of no surprise that you had sent this bird, and I am happy to report that the Order has survived the attack of our enemy and have a new home."

Jack's face changed immediately from his usual sadness of being marooned in the Ministry castle to a relieved expression. The fact that the Order had lived through what seemed to be an impossible attack was something that Jack had not anticipated. He had begun to believe that he was the only one left, not hearing a word for over a month now; and now that they were deep into winter, his spirits had begun to diminish. Now that Jack knew that the Order was indeed still alive, he would know where to send the bird with a message of the new information about the Ministry, and the place that they had put him. He would be able to tell Galen that the Ministry had a secret organization, which had been under their noses the entire time. That was Jack's job, to infiltrate the deepest places of the Ministry and to find all their secrets that could possibly be found. He had reached a crucial moment of his assignment—a place where it would be the information that was real and not propagandized. It would be that information that he would send to Galen, the truth of the secrets of the Ministry. It was at this point that Jack had felt the most useful, the most powerful.

He took the parchment from off his desk and turned it on its back. He pulled the drawer open and took the ink out of it, and then he took the quill and dipped it into the ink bottle and began to write the secrets of the Ministry down. If Jack had used another piece of parchment, Galen would have rejected the message because it would mean that the bird could have been intercepted and the message changed, or Jack could have been discovered. Using the back of the parchment would not be known as the common way of communication. Jack squeezed what he could onto the back of the parchment and paraphrased his note so that he would have more space. There was so much to tell Galen on one piece of a four-inch-by-four-inch parchment, but after some time, Jack had succeeded in telling Galen that there was a secret order in the Ministry and that he had been inducted into that organization, that there was a secret passageway through the underbelly of the Ministry castle and he would gain greater knowledge of the Ministry's view of the Legacy; that they even had an understanding of the Legacy, and there were soldiers being pushed through a hole in the time barrier. He continued his note telling Galen that Cypress and Talon were the victims of three soldiers from the first world, and there were four men in a room that were continuously trying to seal that breech in time. Yes, it really was, for Jack, the most productive day that he had had; and finally, the Order was going to hear the truth about the Ministry.

The fire in the library blazed as the ice that had begun to cover Asscatan created a cold chill through the chasms and tunnels of the Pastel entrances. Asscatan was deep in the season of winter, and it was beginning to show the effects of it. Black ice covered the stone floor of the castle, and the grassy green pastures inside the cave of Asscatan were beginning to turn yellow. Galen sat in front of the fire in the library, reading the book that had told about the history of the known first settlers of the first world. He had begun to reason that the ancestors of the Order were not the first to occupy the second dimension, and his curiosity would almost cause anxiety for him. Though he and the Order were now safe from the Ministry and now that Galen had contacted Jack, they would soon be able to come out of hiding again. Though the information from the history book was disturbing to Galen, he could not close it, he could not resist turning to the next page. There was much missing in the book; however, according to the ancestors of the Order, they knew nothing of the creatures that had once settled there or what it was that had caused them to leave. Galen knew that he would not need to look elsewhere for that crucial information. He had hoped that there was in some place a record of those events, and though Galen was taking a small break from his search for the clues and keys to the other doors, he was confident that the answers would spring up.

Talon and Cypress sat talking to each other as Galen told them something that the Order had not known about the ancestors of the Order every few minutes. It was still disheartening for Galen to go on and on about something that he had no knowledge of until that very moment of enlightenment. The Order had prided themselves on the thought that they had the whole truth, that nothing was left out about their ancestors and what had happened after settlement. It was a grave mistake to assume that their ancestors created the castle of Pastel. Galen knew that someone else had constructed the castles and it would only be a matter of time till he did find out the whole truth, no matter what the cost. He was turning through more of his pages when he remembered something that no one else had paid attention to—the fact that the train tracks passed through the cave and into another tunnel. Galen thought it was possible that the tunnel led off into a dead end, and then he thought to question the reason that the people who had created Asscatan had spent the time to make a very elaborate bridge that passed over the castle and into the other tunnel. Then it dawned on him that the train must lead to another place, possibly a place that would be the secret behind one of the doors that he did not have a key for. But Galen was resting from the long journey through the Qwirl from York. Talon was the one who had spent all his time telling the others of the Order about the city of York—the city much like Asscatan, but with people in it, people that knew the Legacy and people that could not use it because of the tower that drained the Legacy straight from the air. They were an interesting people to Talon, and he made sure that all the Order knew of it; he spent some time telling James of his fun that he had had in the city and hoped that he would go back.

"This could be a useful thing," Talon blurted out the words as he thought them. Everyone looked in his direction when he said it, and the room went silent; and before anyone could ask Talon what he meant by the saying, he was already telling them.

"The people in York could help us. You said that we were about to go to war; we have a ready-made army at our disposal that already knows the Legacy," Talon said as he turned his head toward Cypress, emphasizing that it was her that had said that they were going to war soon.

Galen's eyebrows lifted as the thought entered his mind as well.

"Yes, they would be of help, but they would not be enough, and most of them have not seen a day of battle; some would not live to see the battle to come, and they too would have to be convinced that there is a war to be fought and that it would mean their lives," Galen said as he pulled the pipe from his lips. "But first, I must find out where it is that the train tracks lead," he continued while looking at Talon.

"Then we should not be sitting here, wasting our time reading old books when we could find the truth out in the real world and not behind the written word," Talon said, frustrated with the Order's stagnation.

Talon hated reading books; he had done it for so long in his private schooling all day long, and he thought that once he had matured, he would no longer need to see another book. His life had taken a serious turn though, and to Talon's knowledge he would need to begin reading again to learn the Legacy. That made him extremely uncomfortable. He remembered his covenant to himself though, that he would never break. The one that he made in prison, and if that meant reading all the books in the world, then that is what he would do. The answers that they needed were not in the book that Galen was reading though, according to Talon, and he was absolutely tired of sitting and waiting for another battle to come their way. Talon knew that there were secrets that needed to be found but couldn't be found in Galen's book, and he was becoming anxious.

Though Talon was near Cypress, it was of no consolation, knowing the work that he needed to do. He wanted to find the secrets of the orb that the Qwirl monster had given him, and he wanted to find out what was behind the doors of Pastel. There were too many mysteries that needed to be solved behind those doors, and it was possible that Galen had at least one of the keys to one of the doors; it would only be a matter of going to the chamber and matching the symbols, and perhaps Galen would take out his notes and jot down the symbols and to which doors they belonged so that they would know whether they had the right key or not immediately.

Jack held the bird firm in his hand as he opened the window to let it free. He thought that this would be a turning point in the Order's timeline destination. The Order would know where the Ministry stood with the Legacy and that they would now need to concentrate on a new foe and find a way to destroy the Dark Lord that threatened their land or find and seal the time portal that had been opened. He thought that it might be a hard concept to handle though because of Galen and the Order's beliefs that there would be no way for anyone to enter through the barrier except during the time of the seven-year war, which was some time away from them. Whatever the case, there was some truth, that Cypress, Talon, and Jack had been attacked by ones who knew the Legacy and knew the Legacy well. That was something that Galen could not deny—that and the fact that the mysterious woman with the lamp had shown that it was not only the Order that was capable of learning the Legacy on their own. Which is what Jack thought—that she must have learned the Legacy on her own and that she was very skilled because of her long years of life. The truth on the matter of the woman with the lamp was a truth not yet seen though; Jack could only hypothesize. He was now writing a more detailed letter to the Order— one that would have his special stamp on it, one that Galen would accept as a true message to the Order from Jack, one that he could send by bird later on, after the hawk returned.

The quill had begun to write in Jack's hand when he heard a knock on the door. He was never paid visits by anyone other than his Legacy teacher that he had been continually deceiving by appearing to make very rapid progress in the art of the Legacy. The man was an old man, and he had been through many battles that once raged at the Ministry borders only but ninety years ago, a time that Jack had never seen. His name was Corgono. It was only moments after the knock had occurred, and Corgono was emerging through Jack's chamber door as he quickly shoved the note back into a drawer in the desk. Corgono wore a dark blue tunic that had many different designs in it with reds and lighter blues. It was obviously one of high stature. It was an awkward time for Corgono to be coming to him; they usually did not have their sessions in the dawn of the night. Jack had been kept up in the tower with his food fed to him by a maidservant. He saw nothing of the outside, and he heard nothing of the happenings of the outer world other than that of the Order of the Ministry. Corgono was not there to visit Jack, however; he was there to give him a message. It seemed the prudent thing to do since no one but Corgono was to see where it was that Jack had been taken or in what tower. The maid was always blindfolded when she entered through his door, and sometimes Jack could hear her fall down the steps of the tower with the food and end up crying at the bottom of the stairs, and then it was not long when there would be another who would come to feed him. So, the best way to give a quick message to Jack would be to have Corgono stoop to a low that he had not been subjected to for quite some time.

The old man sat at the foot of Jack's bed as he always did after he entered the room. There was nothing different about the man other than his task at hand. He spoke in a deep and dark voice almost as if the voice was something that he had fabricated over his long life, a voice that he had deliberately made to sound evil. This man was not an evil man though as some would suggest. He lived a life of solitude for the Ministry, and there was nothing that he would not do for their cause. He too was one that had been deceived by the cunning of the Ministry guard, and he had lived his life accordingly. Corgono laid his hand on Jack's bed and caressed the clean quilt underneath his hands.

"There will be a celebration tonight, a celebration of the death of the Order. Because you are now one of the Ministry guards, you will be expected to attend. Your nights of involuntary solitude are over, my friend. It has been told that you were executed for treachery and you no longer have a place in the courts of the Ministry just as it has been said of us all. It is here that you will spend your long days, here with the Ministry guard of the Legacy. Here you will be given secrets that not even the Order had known, secrets that will be told to you farther down into your future. For now, though, you will celebrate the end of the Order with your brethren and your freedom from this tower," Corgono said, still staring deep into the softness of the fabric.

Corgono didn't strike Jack as a person the way that he thought he would; it was as if a child with an advanced mind occupied the heart and body of an ancient man. It was things like the caressing of certain objects that made Corgono seem very lost to Jack; and at times, Jack felt pity on the man that had lived his long life with the Ministry, had lived his long life with the bosom friend of a lie. Jack had wondered what this disturbed man would have become if the life of the Ministry had not consumed him. Jack would attend the celebration, knowing full well that the Order had not been destroyed; they had had casualties, but they were stronger than they had been in all their years. Jack would go, knowing that he would have a better understanding of the deadly enemy of the Order, and he would enjoy doing it. Corgono turned and looked at the stars that shone through the window of the tower as if he were longing for something. Jack had never asked about the long life that Corgono had lived. Sometimes, Corgono would accidentally divulge information that he was not intending to originally— things that were important to him, things that would influence him emotionally, things that might cause him to be a sympathizer to the Order. It was too soon to tell at this point though; but Jack, with enough time, would be able to, and he knew it. At this point in time, Jack would go to the festival wherever it would be held, and he would mingle with the enemy to find weaknesses like that which he suspected in Corgono, and he would probably find them.

Bristle was sitting in one of the train cars when Galen had called out that the train was about to move. Talon, Cypress, James, Mary, Bristle, and Galen were all that was left of the Order now, and they were not looking back to their old ways of foolishness, thinking that they were invincible enough to try to sway the Ministry into noninterference. He tried to contact the others of the Order however it had appeared that they had met their demise in another fashion that Galen knew not of. He knew that it would be a risky thing sending Cypress to enter the Ministry castle and bargain with the enemy, to try to make peace with the unreasonable; but he had to try, he had to give them one last chance, and it was that which caused them many special lives that didn't need to be lost. Galen thought that it was all so pointless, the loss of life and the dispute with the Ministry. He had hoped that they would turn from their stupidity; obviously, he gave them too much credit.

Cypress looked out the window as the train began to move, turning around the turntable. The track met up to the set that ran across the city and over the bridge. All of the Order was now ready to find what it was that would be on the other end of the tunnels, and as always, Cypress was concerned about the danger more than anyone else. The Order had changed their views on the danger that could be in a world that they knew not. They would never make the mistake of thinking that they were in a fortress and would not be harmed by the Ministry or, as Galen had put it when he received Jack's message, a new threat that grew in the second world. Not knowing who the enemy was, which was harassing not only the Order but also the Ministry, was a humbling experience for the Order. If the Ministry was having problems as Jack had put it in his letter, then they were in a danger that they knew not the magnitude of.

As the train began to move, Cypress began to get more and more uneasy at the thought of the Order entering a place that they had not yet been. There were mysteries about Asscatan that they had not yet uncovered—she was sure of it—and yet they were moving on. She looked down at the city of Asscatan as they traveled slowly across the train bridge which crossed the city. The lights on the sides of the car had been lit by Talon so that when they entered the tunnels, they would have light. Cypress looked out at the small tunnels that emitted light and began to calm at the thought that there might be another castle city like that of Asscatan, perhaps another York. But whether they would find a hospitable environment or not, she thought that they would find something of importance, not a dead end; after all, the people who built the castle must have had a reason for going through all the trouble of creating the tunnels that exited the city as well as entered the city. She was confident that they would find something.

Bristle worked the controls of the train engine as the Order sat in the fourth car near the back. Galen had settled himself at the back of the car and had closed off all lights that might enter through the windows with the curtains that hung at each window. The train bounced on the tracks as it chugged on to its destination through the tunnels. Talon looked up and out through his window and saw holes that had been made for the smoke to pass through in the ceiling of the tunnel. He had wondered why the tunnels were not filling up with smoke once they had entered them. It had been about a month since Talon had been in the train, and he was enjoying the sound and feel of the ride. He knew that there would probably be danger that they would meet somewhere along the path; though York was a peaceful place, each city had their deadly secrets—secrets like the Dark Tower, which led the way to the Qwirl.

Where there is good there is always something evil to combat with it. Talon remembered that he had seen the consistency of evil in all cities that he had been to, even that of the white city of Fable. Fable was the truest of all examples of evil with the face of an angel. A city blanketed in superficial beauty and yet beneath it, a darkness that could contend with that of the Ministry. Talon would never again be fooled by the beauty of something. He would never be fooled by love, and those who had deceived him would pay for their treachery; he would make sure of it.

Galen was not concerned about the danger that they would be facing in the tunnels, if there would be any at all. He knew that all things were not absolute, and it could very possibly be nothing that met them at the end of the tunnel. Galen was always filled with hope when it came to things of his heart. He loved a good mystery, and whatever the cost, he would search it out and find the answer. He was determined to find out what it was that Talon was keeping from him and what it was that the creature of the Qwirl had said to Talon if anything at all; why the creature had stopped the attack on them, and why Talon had acted as if nothing out of the ordinary had happened. It was a mystery that Galen was not going to push the finding out of. He would take it slow and allow the inexperience of Talon to reveal what it was that had happened in the Qwirl; he was in no rush. He didn't think of Talon as an enemy because of Talon's nondisclosure of the happening, but Galen was unsure of his new intentions now that he was beginning to acquire power through the Legacy. Galen always thought that power in the hands of an inexperienced one was dangerous not only to everyone around them but also to themselves. It was the future of Talon that Galen feared. Talon allowed his love for Cypress, which was very clear to Galen now at this point, to cloud much of his judgment. He would not lose hope in Talon, however. He was a faithful man—faithful to his cause, faithful to his family. And nothing in the world—no war, no jealousy, and no mistrust—could change that fact. For now, Galen would sit and wait for Talon to come and tell him what had happened in the Qwirl. He would lie back in his chair with the light closed off from his immediate surroundings and enjoy the peacefulness of the moment where nothing was jumping out at him to take his life and there were no secrets to be solved and no one to be angry at. "*Yes, that is what I shall do,*" Galen thought to himself out loud as the train car shook through the tunnels of Asscatan.

Bristle's eyes were not shut; however, they were wide open to the danger that might be in front of them at each passing moment. Only he could see the consuming darkness that the train continually plunged into at a high speed. He had never seen the Qwirl and the city of York or the Dark Tower and the dangers that could have been lurking in them, but all that was happening was making Bristle nervous as to what they would find down the corridors of the tunnel. His hand shook at the thought of something being in the way of the train, and he began to think that he was much too old for this kind of thing. It was his curiosity that had made him go on, much like Galen's curiosity. He was, at that moment, finding a place of bravery that he had never known. He was not the type to enter freely into danger, and yet at that moment, he was the one driving the lot of them into an extremely dangerous place; that is what he kept telling himself—that they were headed into a very dangerous place and they would probably not be coming back to their comfortable home, that they would never step back onto the floor stone of the place that he had come to love so much.

Bristle was staring into the endless black when a shimmer of nightlight had begun to show through the straight tunnel up ahead. Bristle immediately brought the train to a slow crawl on the tracks, and the train slowly emerged into a cave much like that of Asscatan. The starry night sky glistened through crystals that had been embedded into the ceiling. Bristle pulled the whistle on the engine, and the train cried through wood and stone. Talon looked out the window and saw the city of York beneath them. He remembered looking out through the window from the stone houses at the other end of the city. He looked down below them, and his thoughts were confirmed when he saw the water tower pass underneath the stone ledge of tracks. Obviously, the track was never seen by anyone because of their location in the city; it was a complete surprise to Talon, and he quickly jumped up out of his dining chair and rushed over to Galen's, which had been closed off by curtains.

"Galen, you're not going to believe it," Talon said as he forced his way through the thin hallway, which ran through the center of the train car.

Galen, however, had not been sleeping, and once the train had sounded, he was looking out the window for himself. Talon was right; Galen couldn't believe his eyes, and he had wished that they had seen the train track somehow from below. It would have made their getting home much easier than passing through the Qwirl. Then Galen thought that they would not have found the key if it had not happened that way, and he was glad once again that they had had the experience with the Qwirl monsters though many lives had been lost. This was indeed a pleasant surprise for him; it appeared that they would be able to have easier access to the castle of York, which would grant many opportunities.

The track was made to circle the city and pass back through the tunnel that they entered through. Galen could see the path for the track that had the switch underneath it. As the train would pass back in the other direction, it would automatically flip the switch underneath the track and would allow the train to go back through the tunnel to the city of Asscatan.

The train slowly passed, and to Bristle's surprise, it had begun to slow without his making it. There were obviously switches that controlled the speed of the train as well. As it came to a slow stop, Bristle noticed a section of the ledge track that widened out deeper into the cave wall, and there were markings that had been etched into the cave wall that could not be seen from afar.

The train slowly came to a gentle stop, and then Bristle heard a snapping sound beneath the engine. The stone that was in the widened-out section of the track ledge began to invert at the seams, creating a passageway with stairs down into the city of York. Galen and Talon were the first to get out of the train when it had stopped and were immediately heading down the passageway of steps as Cypress quickly followed. This had, by far, been the best day of the week for Bristle; he was going to get to see the fabled city of York without having to pass through the Qwirl, and that was good enough for him.

People down below began to awake and come out of their houses and chambers of the castle of York to see the train that had appeared out of nowhere and was now sitting on a ledge that could barely be seen from below. They would not have been able to see the ledge unless the train was there, and now that the train was in fact there, they did indeed see it. They had gone about their days without ever having the knowledge that there was a track on a ledge that led out of their world. No one had had to make maintenance on the water wheel that passed under the ledge that the tracks were nailed to, and even if they had, they probably would not have noticed the ledge. Others would not have cared that a ledge existed, but now there was a beautiful train that sat on it and there were people that were coming down the steps of a secret doorway that no Yorken had seen.

The smoke seemed to disappear as it was sucked through a small slit in the ceiling of the cave, which could not be seen from any place in the cave, not even that of the station of the train. It was a fine sight from the floor of the city; it didn't matter where you stood; it was still a very fine sight to see the train sitting on the ledge that overlooked the entire city, much like a toy train that circled the room.

Yorkens hadn't seen a train before or the technology that could spawn such a device, and there was no one in the city that had ever thought of anything close to it. These people invented things that amplified their stationary living and improved their stagnant life. Galen was the first to emerge from the stone chamber door that lay just at the base of the river, which flowed underneath the spinning wheel keeping the water tower filled with water. It was not something that Galen was surprised about, but the people that were watching the opening of a door of stone which emerged right out of the wall was something that was very amazing.

There were many things that the Yorkens had not been subjected to before the visit of Talon and Galen. When some of the men and women recognized Galen and Talon, they would remember the things that were told about their coming to their city and the stories that they told about the sky, but it was the strange steel creature that they had brought along with them that the people were curious about. Many of them wanted to know the story about how they had captured the creature, and some of them were smart enough to realize that it was not a creature but of a man's design, and they wanted to hear the story about who had built it and how they had acquired it if they themselves were not the creators of this great machine. Galen would not waste time telling them foolish stories of their time with the Ministry; he was once again close to the Dark Tower, which was the fastest route to the twelve doors; and as Galen remembered it, they would be granted safe passage through the forest of the Qwirl. And there was a door to be opened. He would have to first take the Order home before he used the passageway; however, there was now a faster route from Asscatan to the twelve doors of Pastel, and Galen was glad to know it. It would be of very good use, and once he returned the Order, he—or he and Talon—could go through the Qwirl and through the Dark Tower to the doors of Pastel. *Perhaps I would pay a visit to the Musician and retrieve the key from his neck*, Galen thought to himself as he walked to greet the people that had come out of their homes to find out what it was that was happening that they had not seen before.

.

278

Jack followed Corgono down the steps of the castle of the Ministry and watched the man eloquently pass from step to step down the spiral hall with grace and power that made it appear as if he were hovering in the air. His cloak gently brushed against the floor of each step as he hauntingly made his way down to the inner places of the Ministry castle. All had gone to sleep outside of the castle walls, and all the merchants had ceased selling their merchandise inside the outer walls of the inner Ministry castle. Jack remembered the message that he had just finished writing when Corgono had entered through the door of his tower chamber. Jack was glad that he was able to get out of the tower; he had been in there too long for his taste and was beginning to not feel himself. Perhaps it was the dark things that Corgono was having him use the Legacy for. Jack had never killed anything before, and he certainly had not used the Legacy to do it. There were things that Corgono had made him do that were not to his liking, and being completely surrounded by the darkness of the things that he was being forced to do had begun to weigh at his heart. Oftentimes, Corgono would bring a man who was to face the executioner; instead, they made him face the deadly power of the Legacy. Jack knew that he would have to do all that he could to not allow the discovery of his involvement with the Order if he was going to survive; if Corgono noticed anything strange in the way that he would act toward something that he would have him do, Corgono would have killed him right then and there. The Ministry could not allow anyone to go free with the knowledge of the Legacy; it would undermine all that they were trying to accomplish as Corgono would often put into words, but Jack knew that they were not trying to accomplish anything at all. They were trying to inhibit accomplishment and knowledge; any one person could know that if they were not influenced by the Ministry. It would be one of the most dangerous things for Jack to do, to try to turn Corgono to the side of the Order, but he knew that he would have to try.

Large stone slabs passed in the darkness of shadows cast down through each crack as the light from torches filled the halls of the Ministry guard. Jack had been through these halls once before when his acquaintance had taken him to the head mistress's chamber, but Corgono didn't stop anywhere near her chambers; he walked deeper into the fortress of the Ministry Guard where the most misled of them all were stationed and celebrating their conquest of the city of Pastel. Jack knew how hard it would have been if death had indeed been the eventuality of the Order; he was, however, glad that he would not need to experience such emotions as those which would be evoked by the celebration of his dearest friends' death. It was only when Corgono had stopped and turned toward Jack to show himself in the light of a torch that he had begun to get nervous, and as always, his hand had begun to shake.

The light of the torch in the steel holster connected to the stone wall shone brightly on Corgono and the door that he had stopped in front of as the light cast his daunting shadow on the wood that was the door. Corgono held out his hand from beneath his cloak and forced the door open with his mind. Loud music and men's voices rang in the distance of the large rectangular chamber that apparently, to Jack, sat underneath the inner Ministry castle wall. Men held their ales high in the air and splashed the substance all over the wood of the tables, and the women that danced on them. Jack had noticed an empty throne that sat at the far end of the mead hall, and torches filled the air with a yellow light that made the atmosphere gentle and pleasing to the eye. There, however, was none gentle and pleasing to the eye in that room to Jack. The women wouldn't even be able to excite him because of who it was that owned them; no matter what their beauty was, there was nothing they had that he wanted.

The chamber was tall and long with marble floors and monumental statues that came down from tall pillars. Soldiers had mouthfuls of crab and fish and delicacies of meat of all kinds. Beer and wine kegs were set up at each corner of the hall. There was no wood other than that of the wood table that sat in the center of the hall. Marble had been laid along the walls, and polished stone stood underneath their feet. They all shouted and bellowed with laughter and danced with one another at the thought that the Order was gone and would never plague the righteousness of the Ministry with their foolishness.

Jack stood behind Corgono who showed no enthusiasm toward the death of the Order. It was with Corgono that Jack felt comfortable the most though he was likely the evilest of them all. It was likely that Corgono was the one who had tailed Cypress and Talon the night that they had come for Sol, and it was likely that Corgono was the one that orchestrated the attack on the Order himself, possibly himself alone. Corgono, however, was not like the others of his kind; and though he would like to have thought that about himself, Corgono was much more intelligent and had seen organizations much like the Ministry fall in one night.

It was the light that had begun to grow in the center of the room that Corgono had made a mention of by his movement in that direction. Corgono flung his cloak behind him as if he were there to protect Jack. Corgono kneeled on the floor when the light had begun to grow wider. The celebrating guards were, however, completely unaware of the hovering point of light until it had grown to the size of one soldier in length. Plasma shock had begun to strike the room, peeling marble tiles from off the walls and pillars. Still the time disturbances had begun to grow; everyone was ignorant of what was happening. Some thought it was a bomb and dropped their drinks to reach out with the Legacy and contain the blast, but nothing happened besides that of the disturbance growing larger and the strikes of plasma lightning that occasionally knocked a guard off his feet. Stone flew through the air as the disturbance began to widen as though it were being controlled. Jack didn't know what to think of the disturbance and was afraid that he would have to use more than what he had shown Corgono that he knew of the Legacy to survive; that was if it was indeed an attack on the Ministry. The portal widened and began to encompass the long wall of the hall. Lightning began to strike more violently when the length of the portal stopped at the length of the room. Corgono held his hands forward at the mass of blue light that stretched from one side of the room to the other. With his hand stretched out toward the portal, his cloak whipped in the strong wind that had begun to circulate through the hall. The striking of the lightning did not stop, and every now and then it would strike a guard dead to the ground. Once the portal reached the length of the room, soldiers began to pour out of it one line the length of the hall at a time. The first wave of men that carried swords used them against what was left of the guard, and seeing that he would not have a chance against an army that had infiltrated the deepest part of the city Corgono had begun to head back the way that they had entered, and Jack quickly followed.

Wave after wave of soldiers marched through the hall with only one intention, that of annihilating the Ministry before its time. There was nothing that could come against soldiers that used the sword and the Legacy to fight, not taking into account that it was a ten-thousand-man army that Talon had unleashed against the Ministry.

Jack was moving fast through the chasms of the castle, but Corgono was much faster than he, and he knew more about where he was in the castle than anyone could. Jack slowly began to fall behind. He could hear the soldiers killing ones in their sleep and pulling them out of their beds. Jack could only think of one thing that he could do, that being, getting to the gate and heading toward the mountain of Pastel. He had, after a few moments, lost sight of Corgono through narrow passageways in the castle, and he began to feel the fear come over him, the fear that he had been led not toward the outside of the castle but deeper into the heart of the Ministry. At the moment that Jack thought that he could not survive in a place where he did not know where he was, he felt what seemed to him to be the force against his right leg. And because he felt no pain at just that moment, he went to take his next step down into the darkness into the place where Corgono must have been; and when there was nothing to step with, he fell to the ground. It was at his fall to the steps that he realized that his right leg had been severed off and that he was being pursued by a man in dark armor. Jack lay on the steps of the Ministry in the light of one of its torches that hung on the stone wall and began to feel the scorching pain from the absence of his right leg and the exposed knee. The soldier did not slow as he ran to pick up his sword that was about the length of Jack altogether in height. Time began to slow for Jack as the man that had thrown the sword to cut him in half advanced toward him. The sound began to flee from his mind as time began to slow. Jack saw the soldier slowly and swiftly pick the sword up from off the ground. The armor hung from the man like a leaf on a tree that was blowing in a strong wind. The soldier's hand was now clenching the handle of the sword with more force as the blade was slowly lifted from the steps. Jack felt his heart pumping pain to his appendage with every moment that slowly passed. The soldier lifted the sword over his head, and the blade came down upon Jack. The last thing that Jack saw was the bright blinding glare that passed from the peaceful torchlight down the blade of the sword and the emotionless face of a man-soldier in his peripheral.

16 THE DEADLY FOREST

SHE COULD SEE the smoke rising from the city as she laid the lamp on the desk in the chamber that was, at one time, Jack's. The chamber was destroyed, things were thrown around and left on the floor, and part of the desk had been demolished by a sword. She remembered what it was that she had seen when the last man had been killed outside the city. Once his head had fallen to the ground, the soldiers that entered from beneath the city and who had destroyed the Ministry faded away as if they were a dream. She looked back on the scene of the last fallen man of the Ministry and the man that led the army on his horse in his black and tattered cloak, and remembered the things that she had heard coming from the man's mouth— the things that she could not believe. But after the soldiers had faded, she found it harder and harder to remember what it was that she was doing near the city. After seeing the devastation, she was curious enough to have a look at what had happened to the Ministry, and she felt that she had changed, but she could not explain it. Soon she was completely unaware of who it was that had attacked and destroyed the Ministry. Because of her knowledge of the Legacy, though, she knew that something had been changed.

Now after walking through the mess of the Ministry walls, she found herself drawn to the place where Jack had left the message for Galen, and she opened the drawer to see that what was left inside was still there; she didn't know how she knew it would be there, but it was there when she looked. In reading the letter, she wondered where it was that she had been when the attack on the Ministry had taken place. There was a gap in her memory that would not be filled. She looked down at the message in her hand and wondered why it was that she had picked it up to read it. All that had transpired in the Ministry had left her completely now, and she stood with the note in her hand and the lamp on the demolished desk and knew that she would need to take the letter to Galen. She had stood outside the city and watched its destruction, and she had entered to find out why it had been done, and she could not think of anything to do but to give the note to Galen. She knew where they were; she was also there when the Ministry had taken the city of Pastel and the castle of Pastel. She had entered then and had seen the Requiem; her once-allied people that she depended on endangering the lives of the ones that she held in the highest regard in the world of man. She had seen them flee, and she had seen the man in black kill the Requiem with his sword once they had left. She had followed them through the dark tunnels with the lamp covered, and she had seen their new home. She was glad that the Ministry had not destroyed the Order, and after seeing what had happened to Jack, she would soon join them in their endeavor.

The woman with the lamp slowly walked down the steps of the tower and across parts of stone walls that had collapsed; she walked through the halls that ran through the walls of the inner castle and out into the streets. She looked at the bodies that lay dismembered in the streets, against the walls of huts and merchant stations that had been left to burn. She knew that there were people that would have come to the aid of the Order, people that had lost their lives that night, and it angered her that the death of the Ministry was not carried out in a better fashion. She knew that it was not the Order that had made the attack though, and she had begun to wonder who it was that had attacked the Ministry. She knew the Dark Lord had been sending soldiers to take the land of the second world, but taking the

Ministry was not something that she thought the Dark Lord would do. She had captured some of his spies and retrieved information from them, but there wasn't that much that she could get. She was only able to gather the Dark Lord's name, where he was from, and why he was against the humans in the second world.

The woman clenched her hand around the paper more tightly. It folded and crumpled under the handle of the lamp as she held it tighter. She knew that she would definitely take the message and tell the Order what it was that they needed to know about the Ministry before they were sent on their way to do what it was that they must.

Galen had decided that he would not open the door to which he had the key before he had more information. It had proven to be an almost-deadly adventure for Galen, passing through the Qwirl even though Talon had somehow saved his life. He would take into suggestion the thoughts of the Order and would not take too many more risks with his and Talon's life unless it would be absolutely necessary. Though Talon had gained the creatures of the Qwirl, Galen would not risk the death of anyone of the Order. He had remembered how the creatures had treated Galen's escort and did not want that to happen to his dearest friends.

Galen was, after one day, ready to return home to the castle of Asscatan; however, he would have to go on and find the truth about his heritage. The Order's understanding of their history had proven to be flawed, and if they would expect to win the war against the first world, they would have to know the truth, the whole truth.

Talon sat in the train with Cypress and was slowly beginning to show his affection toward her. She too had begun to tell Talon how much she enjoyed his presence. The future was something that Talon was most concerned about; he was unsure what the war that was soon to come would cause in their lives, what future it would have in store for them. Talon held Cypress close to him in the train and remembered the time when he had thought that she had been killed. He remembered the pain that that thought had caused in his heart. He would never let anything happen to Cypress now, no matter what it would take to save her life. Bristle had had a good time in the city of York and had enjoyed the company of the ones that knew the Legacy; it had been a very long time since he had been around so many that had learned it freely. He remembered all that had once been a part of the Order, and now there were so few that were left. He too was afraid of what the future had in store for the Order and, at times, felt as if they would lose this battle and eventually lose the war because of the domination of the Ministry.

"Talon," Galen said in a strong voice.

Talon immediately responded by whipping his head around and facing Galen.

"Take the others of the Order back through the tunnels and keep sure that they are not to be harmed," Galen continued.

Talon made a confused look at Galen and agreed with a nod of his head.

"I'm going back to pay a visit to the Musician. He had something that the Order needs," Galen said as he closed the door of the train car.

Talon knew that Galen was going alone for a reason that was important, and at first, He was not sure that he wanted to comply with

Galen's wishes, but the thought of staying with Cypress was one that he would not pass up. Talon knew that there would be little time left to spend with Cypress once the true fighting would begin, and he was not going to pass up the opportunity to protect Cypress. She, on the other hand, was not the slightest happy with Galen going off alone to see the Musician. The lady with the lamp had said that he could not be trusted, and she had just suggested that Galen not put his life in unnecessary danger. She had reached for the door as Galen had closed it, but there was nothing that she could do. Galen had made up his mind, and that was that. She turned to look at Talon as if to ask him without words why he had let him go off alone, but she knew that she would get this answer: Galen was his own person and Talon felt that he had no right telling him what it was that he should do.

Galen was already down the steps of the train station staircase that led down to the city. He would wait to see what he could find out from the Musician before he entered the door that the key from the wardrobe fit in. He was going to get some answers before he leaped into the fire. Bristle had started the train when Galen had begun to enter the Qwirl from the entrance of the castle gate. He did not ask for an escort this time. He had hoped that the creatures would have remembered him and his companion Talon. He knew that this would be the riskiest thing of all, trusting that the Qwirl would honor its agreement with Talon to not harm his companions, but Galen would take the chance because they had honored the agreement when they had left before into the Dark Tower.

The trees were tall and damp just as they had been before the winter had fallen upon the land, and though it was deathly cold outside the walls of the cave and tunnels of York, it had seemed that there was only one season for the Qwirl, hot and humid. He began to enter through the tall trees that were rutted, that had twisted in all directions along the floor of the forest. Galen could hear the trees moving as the creatures of the Qwirl moved along them, but he was not afraid of death. He had, long ago when he was just a young man, promised himself that he would never let fear take complete hold of him. He slowly walked through the forest and ducked under the low branches that spiraled down to the floor of the forest and back up along the other trees. Some of the trees flowed from one to the other creating a thick nest of vine-like branches that spanned from tree to tree. It was a very beautiful thing once you did not have to worry about being torn apart by the keepers of the Qwirl.

Galen stepped over tall roots that would spring out of the ground and wrap around the base of other trees like it. Ferns and other thick brush covered most of the floor of the forest, and there was not much that could be seen from any one point of the forest. At last, Galen had reached the end of the Qwirl and was stunned by the sight of the boat. He was going to walk along the inner edges of the tunnels. He did not expect to see the boat sitting, waiting for him on the sandy outlet of the water tunnel; it was indeed, for him, a very pleasant surprise.

Galen pulled out the map that he had made of the tunnels the first time he had come through them with Talon and placed it on the deck of the small boat. He bent down and reached for four small stones that had found themselves laying on the sandy outlet of the water tunnel, dried them off with his cloak, and placed them at each corner of the map to hold it in place as he navigated through the tunnels to get to the Dark Tower. Occasionally, Galen would glance at the map and then back to the tunnels of the Dark Tower. He kept thinking to himself that it was a particularly good stroke of fortune that they had found the passage to York; it took a whole day off the trip from Asscatan to the twelve doors, and that would be very advantageous. He, however, was not going to open the door before he had paid a visit to the Musician. When he had reached the gate to the under part of the Dark Tower, he used the Legacy to raise it as he had done before. The water dripped and fell to the rushing water as he raised the seal gate and rowed the boat to the stone pole that he had tied the boat to the last time that he had come to this place. Galen was not worried about what might happen to him, it was obvious that there was no one that inhabited the castle though it somehow was able to keep itself in such a clean condition. This was a mystery that he could handle not ever finding out about. He knew the important mysteries from the unimportant ones.

The darkness that had begun to fall came with the snow that whizzed around Galen's body. His face felt as if it were going to freeze and fall off; but underneath all that he was wearing, underneath his cloak and the regular clothes, he was warmer than usual in a blizzard. The ruins of Pastel were not exempt to the power of the elements, and it was the clearest of all portrayed by the expression on Galen's face. Snow whipped and spun through the air in the chamber that once was a part of a very prestigious library and castle. He stood there in the cold and took time to acknowledge what it was that the Order had truly lost. It was more than just a home; it was a fragment of their history, the history of the Order. There was nothing that Galen had once held so dear to his heart than that of the Pastel castle and the people that lived in it, and he was relieved that the Order had made away with their lives. Looking up and out through the place that was once the ceiling of Pastel castle he imagined what it had been before the very mountain of Pastel had been brought down. Now as a passerby, one would look at the mountain and would not believe that there was once a great place that had stood there; they would not believe that what was once a towering mountain could look like a cratered hill. It was a desolate volcano to Galen now, but without the death-dealing magma. It was, to him, the secrets that were once held in the Pastel Mountain that would never be found, and that was the death that was continually coming forth from its hole. Now filled with the darkness of the night and the cold from the death of his home, Galen would press on and do what he knew that he must.

Though the journey to the twelve doors was shorter than it had been before, Galen was still exhausted by the trip. Now he would have to travel deep into the forest of Myth and find the Musician and answers that the Musician must have.

Deep whistling hummed through the trees of the forest of Myth as the wind and snow passed through it at high speeds. Galen clenched his cloak around himself tighter to keep the cold wind from entering through the warmth of his clothes, but there was very little that he could do to prevent the cold from passing through his body and into his soul. He was now, not sure whether he would be able to find the Musician in all the mess of the deadly forest. Galen would not give up; though his travel had exhausted him, he would press on to the end no matter what it would take. He looked into the darkness and realized that he was lost; it had been so long since he had navigated the forest, and he was completely unaware of where he was. He had begun to worry at the thought that the Ministry still would have spies in the area, and the cold had begun to weigh upon him. The white, heavy, falling snow, clouded his senses, and he was losing concentration. He had begun to slow as the snow accumulated at his feet with every step. They crunched and scraped as the flakes of snow met the bottom of his feet. The snow was now as high as the length from the ground to his knees, and he had to step over two feet of it just to move another step.

A light began to blur into sight in front of him as he took one of his leaping steps over the impossible powder. Slowly the light began to get brighter; Galen paused in his tracks and realized that this light was not one that anyone should be happy about. As the funnel of light came near to him, his immediate reaction was to move out from the path of it. He plunged himself into the cold snow that showed a bright blue until the funnel of light that was passing horizontally along the ground whizzed by him. The beam barely missed contact with Galen and did not touch the ground but a few feet from the place that he had previously been. With an impact like that of a large stone, the beam of light came in to contact with the snow and dirt underneath it, throwing dirt-melted snow and tree wood into the air. Galen, still inside of the indentation of his body in the snow breathed hard and quickly made for a run through the trees and snow which, for a time, had been ridiculously hard. Galen thought to use the Legacy to move the snow and wind out of his way. Falling snow and fallen snow parted as he used the Legacy to move the wind from behind him as a combatant against the wind that was beating at him from the front. Galen stretched out his hand as he concentrated on parting the elements at war with him and could hear the beam of fire and light consuming its way toward him.

Trees fell against each other as the fire consumed them making its way toward the running Galen. He turned to look behind him and knew that he would have to destroy the wielder of the Legacy to survive, and he went toward the source of the stream of fire. Galen turned the rest of his body toward the source of the stream of light and allowed the forces of the wind and snow to pass over him. He looked into the center of the funnel and reached out with his mind a force that would snuff out the fire. Galen held out his hand before him and concentrated on lifting the surrounding wind and snow. With a clenched hand, he pulled all the snow up off the ground within a radius of fifty feet. As he concentrated on the incoming devastation, he used the wind that was already heading toward the streaming fire to push the wall of ice toward the devastating light. The disk of snow lifted from the ground and high into the trees; it shifted and spun as Galen used the Legacy to keep it steady in the air. There was a great darkness that had overshadowed Galen when the disk of hovering snow congealed above his head. With a forceful push of his hands, the large spinning disk of ice and strong wind hurled itself through the air and through the trees toward the light that now was not far off from Galen.

The impact of the ice to the fire was a brilliant one. Ice melted as the pillar of fire began to pass through it, but the wind kept the fire from progressing past the ice. Slowly the water that had once been ice began to encircle the pillar of fire; steam had begun to spew out of the pillar of water, but he used the Legacy to contain the vapor and push it back into his pillar. Soon the column of water had completely overtaken the fire and had passed the person that had been manipulating it; once this had happened, the huge mass of water plummeted to the ground, sending out an encompassing sound.

The water had instantaneously begun to flow down the mountain of the forest of Myth, creating a small flood and cutting dirt and rock out of the mountain. Galen stood there in absolute exhaustion. He fell to his knees as the snow fell gently around him. With both hands on the ground, he sat there for some time to catch his breath.

Galen had thought that he was too old for war and that he would soon come to his death. He knew that he would never find his enemy's body to know whether or not he had met his demise at the hand of the Legacy, and Galen was too exhausted to go and investigate. The fact that he was no longer being attacked was something that told him that his enemy had indeed been defeated. He also knew that there were too many things that he didn't know about the Legacy and who the ones were that wielded it; but obviously, there were ones in the world that were very powerful now.

Galen remembered the paraphrased message from Jack and thought that it could have been one of the Dark Lord's minions. Galen knew that he would soon find out when he would receive the detailed letter from Jack. That information was becoming more and more valuable by the hour to Galen.

His breath could barely be seen through the shifting wind and snow; he stood there clenching his cloak because of the cold. It was when Galen thought that he would not be able to get up off his knees that his body found the strength to do so. Slowly he reached for the ground so as to lift himself off of it. The cold had begun to consume him, but he would be able to move on; he was not yet near the center of the forest where the Musician lived.

After some time, he left the place where the battle had raged and assumed that he had destroyed the soldier of the Legacy. When he had used the Legacy, he had not worried about the cold, and it was that which had begun to relieve him from it. He thought that he would use the Legacy to stay warm, but he had lost too much of his concentration and energy to the battle. It would only make him vulnerable to the elements of cold. He kept telling himself that he would soon be near the Musician's house, and if he simply took one step over another, he would make it to his destination; after some time, though, he realized that he was lost and he was perhaps nowhere near the center of the forest. Galen did not like getting lost especially if every step that he took was one that became harder just after the next. He looked out into the darkness of the night through the trees and felt as if he had already failed in his mission. There was just too much that had happened to him; he was old, and he could not withstand these kinds of things as battling for his life. He would not be able to withstand the pain of seeing the death of the ones that he had been told would die. A tear had begun to fall down his cheek, but before it could fall to the snow below his feet, it had stopped and had frozen onto his face.

He remembered the things that he had heard from the old man's voice. He was not sure what it was that the old man had meant by his words when he was a child in the orphanage, but he had come to him. He was a young man, and he had a striking resemblance to Talon. The words were soft and gentle, and yet they foretold a doom for Galen and the Order. Galen had not, at the time, known what he was talking about because he had not yet met the Order and their cause. He stood weak in the fast-moving wind and snow; he stood still and looked back into his memories of the gentleman that had told him how he would meet his demise. However, for Galen, he felt as if things had changed, and what the man had said would not come true; he could not explain it to himself, the feeling. But for him, things had changed, and changed drastically.

Galen looked to the sky after he had found himself at the edge of the forest near the land of Moolon. The lights of the small villages and inhabitants of the land could be seen from where he had found himself. The blizzard had ended; and Galen was, once again, beginning to feel his fingers and his face. The light from the moon shone brightly in the crystal clear night sky and down through the forest trees to the forest floor that glowed from the light of the moon on the snow that covered it. Galen had found himself far from the place that he had originally intended, and he was feeling set back in his endeavor to meet with the Musician. He was tempted to go down and find someone who would help him, but he was not fond of people who didn't use the Legacy; it would be a mentally aggravating experience for Galen, though it would be a physical comfort to him. He had a mission, and he would need to carry it out. He would fight through his pain and discomfort.

Though he could not be trusted, as Talon and Cypress had stated, Galen had a feeling that the Musician would dress up his wounds whether it was to the Musician's advantage or not. The Musician struck him as the kind of person that did not truly care about others—a sort of person that had the ability to be devious and cunningly symptomatic to get his way—and Galen thought that perhaps he could use the disposition of the Musician to his advantage to get the key. He had hoped that the Musician would not place too much value in the key and perhaps bargain for it. That, however, was something yet to be seen.

Galen would press on through the newly fallen snow and find the mysterious man that had hid himself in what Galen thought to be the first creation of the first settler in the second world. He had stood there for some time, looking at the scene of the small cities of the Fondland that could be seen from far off. Galen was glad that the storm had ended, and he was beginning to get his strength back. He turned and looked at the small shelter that he had quickly made from the snow; looking at it as if it were a lost love, someone that had been there in his time of need. It had been faithful and true to him as no other had been before, and he was now going to leave the small snow shelter that he had made using his last bit of strength for the Legacy to get it done faster than usual. The small slick icy mound stared back at him through the eyes of the bright blue moon and the small shimmers of the light of the cities of Moolon. It was there in that small sanctuary that Galen had taken refuge from the storm, and he was now going to leave it behind.

He was beginning to get nervous at the thought of entering the chamber alone, but there had been no one there, and Galen was beginning to get worried about the little man that could have been in very grave danger. Before he had come to this place, he had not thought about the horror that could have befallen the Musician; and now that he had not found him at all in the forest, he was beginning to think that the man came to a deadly end. Galen had searched through the forest from the edge to the center where he had found the Musician before. He looked and looked but was also unsuccessful in finding his home. Every time he would come to a place that had an unusual hill in the mountain of the forest, he would investigate; and so far, he had searched six unusual places that he had found along the way to the center of the forest. Galen now knew exactly where he was going, and it had not been long since the last snowflake had fallen. The Musician had hidden his home well. Galen recalled the first time that he had encountered the man, they had walked right past his home, and he had not noticed the difference in the terrain other than the little hill that protruded out of the slant of the natural mountain dead in the middle of the forest. Galen thought that perhaps the man had created decoys all around the entrance to his home, that would point to a central place inside the perimeter of decoys; and he had searched that area already and found nothing but natural phenomenon.

Galen was clearing away the vines and brush that had, to him, appeared to be unnatural when he saw something in his peripheral vision. It was not something he had seen before, and it was not as dark a figure as he had thought it at first, when he slowly turned around to look fully. Galen stood there not knowing what he should do, and with open eyes, he knew fully that the person that stood near to him was not the Musician; it was much too large in height. Galen, still on his guard, thinking that he had not finished off his attacker, turned to face the person that had been lurking just out of his sight for so long. It was apparent that the person had been watching him for some time without his knowledge.

The figure did nothing as Galen positioned himself to strike. Galen, with his hands held out in front of him, was sure of the person that was standing before him, now in close proximity. It had seemed as if the figure had closed in; Galen kept his eyes wide-open. All that he had thought about the figure had vanished once she revealed the small hand lamp that she was previously holding behind her. He, at once, knew that she was the woman that he had been so secretly anxious to meet, and suddenly she was standing in front of him. He didn't know exactly why it was that she had shown herself, but he had a suspicion that it was the battle that had attracted her. Before Galen thought to ask what it was that she was doing near him, it had crossed his mind that she, being so powerful, as Talon and Cypress described, could be his attacker; but it was quickly ruled out by his logic that she would still be attacking him. All of Galen's enemies never stopped unless he had killed them; they would fight to the end.

The woman stood tall in the snow, and there was a small trail of her tracks and the tracks of her gray cloak that skimmed the ground as she walked. She was much lighter than Galen, and so she did not sink into the snow as he did. He turned his attention from the lamp that she had been hiding behind her back to the cloak that stood soaked from the snow under her feet. Her face could not be seen behind the darkness of the cloak hood that concealed her identity. Galen noticed that the woman had a strange consistency of hiding herself, and he wondered what she could possibly have to hide; he thought about it only for a moment though and continued studying the woman that had saved the lives of the two people that Galen loved the most. He could see though that the woman knew more about their situation than he could possibly know. Galen turned to ask her what it was that she wanted of him, but she interrupted his thought.

"Your very good friend of mine left this to you. He gave his life as an unwilling sacrifice to the death of the Ministry."

Galen looked down at the piece of parchment that lay crumpled in the hand that was free from the lamp. He was unsure of what the message had meant; he knew nothing of the death of the Ministry, and he was unaware of anyone's sacrifice.

When the woman saw through the shadow of her cloak that Galen had absolutely no idea of what it was that she was trying to tell him, she held out the parchment that had been taken from Jack's demolished desk, which sat in the ruins of the Ministry castle, and spoke:

"Jack, your very good friend, has been killed."

She paused and waited for a response from Galen, but there was none to be seen; he had felt the news of his friend's death too hard. He stood there in the snow and stared into the nothingness recalling memories of the times that he had had with Jack before he had been given the assignment to spy on the Ministry. The reason that Jack had been killed was not the concern of Galen; there were many things that could have happened to him through his assignment that Galen had given him. He couldn't help but feel that Jack's death was his fault. The woman saw the reaction of Galen and waited to continue until he could be calm enough in his mind to listen to the reason that Jack had been killed; she knew that at that moment, he would not hear the reason. Just that Jack had been killed, everything else had been clouded by the pain of his loss. Curiosity began to get the better of Galen though once some time had passed, and his mind began to experience the loss of his very good friend; Galen made no response to the woman though, but she was watching him and knew just the right time to speak again.

"The Ministry had been overtaken by a force that I have never seen before and will never seen again."

She remembered the feeling that she got when she held Jack's message in her hand, the feeling that something had been changed using the Legacy. And though she was unaware of exactly how it was that she had lost a portion of her memory, she knew that she had lost a very important part of her that could not be recovered using any means.

"I found the Ministry in ruins, and there was something that had changed, something that I can't fully explain. Perhaps if you had experienced it, you too would understand what it was that I felt."

Galen looked at her and knew exactly what it was that she was talking about; he had faced the same feeling when he recalled the time when the man had told him how it was that he would die, something that Galen would not tell anyone whether he actually knew the person's eventuality or not, let alone tell a person at the age that Galen was at the time. He had felt it too; time had changed, and for some reason, he had felt that it had changed for the better. When he looked back on the feeling that he had after it had been changed, he could not explain it either.

Galen slowly held out his hand and gently grabbed hold of the letter that Jack had written. He slowly unfolded it and began to read. All the information that Jack had gathered on the four men and the Dark Lord that had been sending men and animals through the barrier was there in that letter in great detail; there was nothing left unwritten. The light from the moon shone brightly on the parchment, but for Galen, the letter was hard to see because of the glow that the moon created.

He couldn't help but think that all that Jack had done was completely in vain now that the Ministry had somehow met their demise, and when Galen thought about it, he could not understand where an army could have come from and had been so efficient in the destruction of the Ministry. The woman described it as the most total destruction that she had seen since the wars of the early times. As Galen knew it, there was no army alive that could have done such a thing, and the mystery was beginning to plague him. Galen was not happy about how the woman was so apt to accept the destruction of the Ministry with no explanation, but when he thought about how he would act, he suspected that he would be forced to feel the same way about the situation. She, in reality, revealed nothing of how she felt to Galen; he had only made assumptions at her thoughts. Galen looked down at the parchment in his hand and stared at the message that had been written with Jack's hand, and so it was that he knew that the woman was not lying to him. It was when Galen looked at the writing and the letters themselves that the emotion had begun to take him once again.

"Your new friend, the one named Talon Barrett, it was I who released him from Auzgool. He may have seen me and he may have not, but I was the one who lifted him over the ice to the forest, if he would like to know the truth," the woman said, interrupting Galen's pain. "Do not be in pain. Your friend died for a worthy cause, and nothing other than time can change that truth."

Galen looked into the dark place where the woman's face was hidden behind the hood of her cloak.

"Thank you for your help. I doubt that anyone could have done it better than you, and I am very grateful that you have brought me this information, but forgive me for asking. What is it that you want from the Order?" Galen asked as he folded the wrinkled parchment and placed it in his pocket underneath his cloak.

"I want you to succeed in your mission to save this world. I too would like for the world to continue peacefully, but you must remember, evil will always be where there is good. It is the human condition, and the truth cannot be changed through superficial fighting. It must be fought with time. I think that that is what we have witnessed for the first time, someone who knew that the Ministry could not be destroyed without the manipulation of time. There are many things that you will need to know, but this is not the place and time for such truths to be revealed. I will leave you now, and you will do what you must. There is a great threat growing in the first world, and you will need to learn how to combat it. I cannot tell you these things because I do not know how to fight such a battle. You will need to teach yourself in which way you should walk."

The woman began to turn around and walk back the way that she came from in the forest. Galen didn't know how he would be able to fight a battle without an army, and he certainly did not know how he would fight a battle in the first world, which Galen thought would be the most appropriate thing to do. He certainly could not fight a battle without knowing his own origins, the origins of the Order. A lack of knowledge could be the most detrimental thing of all to their cause. Galen was glad that he had someone so powerful on his side, and he was glad that she had been keeping watch over them. He, however, didn't think that she would be so efficient at finding information and getting things accomplished before the Order could, things like that of breaking Talon out of prison before the Order. She had proven to be a good friend to them. He was also glad that she was not his original attacker.

Galen looked up through the trees at the bright moon and knew that he still had hours of night left to accomplish his finding the Musician, and so that was what he would do; he would find the secrets to the key that hung around the Musician's neck, and he would eventually find out what was behind the door that the Musician's key opened.

17 A Colossus Solution

H E HAD NOT SEEN IT before, but now that he had looked harder and was not shaken from the attack upon him, Galen was able to concentrate deeper on the place where the Musician had hidden his home, the home that so closely resembled the castle of Pastel. He gently pulled back the fallen brush and dead leaves that were covered in snow. The chamber door was not but two feet beneath the fallen snow and the dead brush that the Musician had placed so that his home would be concealed. Galen picked up a water-saturated stick and tapped on the stone chamber wall that entered through the Musician's home. As he knocked on the stone door, he could hear small creatures scurrying through the forest. The chamber door sat there for some time and did nothing. Galen was not going to enter the man's home unless he had a good reason to do so. He had looked around the chamber door to see if there had been a forced entry, but there were no signs of it. He knew though that there would be no signs of forced entry if the person breaking in knew how to use the Legacy, but still Galen had a feeling that the Musician was not harmed but was hiding in his home for just that reason—safety. He stared at the motionless stone door just in front of him. Moments later, the door began to open, and the little man stood there in front of him. When the man saw Galen, he smiled and reached out a hand to greet him, but Galen greeted him in words.

"I had hoped that you were in good health and that the goings-on around you had not affected you, friend,"

Galen said as the man smiled at him and waved his hand to gesture for him to come inside his home. He followed the small man in through the chamber and down inside to the entrance to his small castle. The Musician had left the door open when he had departed to go see who it was that was knocking at his door, and the light from the fire and candles that were burning shone a gentle flickering yellow on all the things in the house.

As usual, the Musician laid the cane that he always took with him to the side of the entrance as Galen stepped through beside him. Galen remembered the inside of the Musician's house the first time that he had been in it. So many things that had happened that were unexpected had already occurred, and Galen was ready for the worst from the Musician. He would not leave without the key; he would not leave without the answers that the Musician had accumulated over the years. He would fight to the death for these secrets; he was not going to entertain the idea of the Musician telling him that he could not have them.

Galen looked at the warm atmosphere of the house that did not truly belong to the Musician; he did not take it as a reflection of the Musician's quality of personality. Galen knew that the Musician was hiding something, and it was not just the secrets of the key. He could not really place his finger on the feeling that he had about the Musician, but he knew that there was something unnatural about the small man; and Galen, after the night that he had been having, was not about to play games with him. Galen kept a strong and stern face as he entered, and the Musician paid the usual attention to him with his superficial greetings and his wasted words. To Galen, they fell upon the ears of the stone walls; and though the small man would continue with his foolishness, he had noticed that the expression on Galen's face had not changed. Galen recalled the words that had been spoken to Talon and Cypress by the woman with the lamp, the words that described the Musician as a man that could not be trusted. The woman with the lamp had proven herself again and again to Galen, and he could see that she was a wise and trustworthy person, and he would heed the warnings that came from her about the Musician. He would be incredibly careful in which way that he would allow himself to be led by the man. Galen looked past the sayings of the Musician and paid close attention to the things that were in the room. Before, the Musician had been careless and revealed the fact that he had a key which could be traced to the castle of Pastel.

"And you, how have you been these past days since I last saw you?" the Musician spewed from his lips.

It was only then that Galen dignified the man with a response.

"You know quite well how I have been, don't you, Musician?" Galen said, looking at the man intensely. "It has not been a secret, what has happened to the Order and the Ministry, and I have a very good idea that you know a great deal about what has happened. You will not plague me with your idiotic greetings anymore, Musician. I am not a man to be toyed with. You knew what I had seen before I left this place because you made good time in hiding it so that I could only get a glance at it, and you know full well what the significance of that key is. You will reveal it to me, or I will take you where you stand."

Galen was sitting down when the Musician had been talking to him, but now, Galen was out of his chair tall enough to touch the low ceiling of the small house with an expression on his face that the Musician would never forget. The small man jumped out of his chair and ran to the corner of the room and hid underneath the small table that sat near the kitchen. He squealed and yelped at the thought that he had allowed something into his house that could do so much harm to him. Galen was breathing hard, and the light that had once filled the room flared brighter than before. This was the side of the Musician that Galen needed to know, whether he would be a real threat to his cause or a small obstacle. The Musician had become, to Galen, a small pet that he had scared into the corner of its own mind.

"Mine, it's mine, you can't have it, I won't let you have it," the Musician kept whimpering to himself in the darkness of the shadows of the table.

Galen allowed his anger to subside in him, and the light naturally began to come to its normal flame. He sat in the chair that was next to the fire and reached out his hand to the small man who was to the left of him under the table. Galen flicked his wrist, and his hand jerked toward him gesturing for the man to come out of hiding.

"Do not take me for a fool, my friend. I only wish for you to give me answers that would not only save my life and the Order's but also yours. I am not a cruel man, but I do not tolerate stupidity,"

Galen, still resting his hand on the arm of the little chair, gentled the tone of his voice. He got out of it. Then descending he sat on the floor with each leg underneath the other as the Musician clenched the key that lay against his chest.

"If I must prove it to you, then I will, but you must tell me exactly what the key means to you that I may find a way to appease you the pain it gives to you."

He could see that the possession of the key gave the Musician pain, and he couldn't understand why. One thing was sure though, the key meant more to the small man than he had anticipated; and though Galen knew that he could forcibly take the key from him, he really did not want to harm him.

Galen sat on the floor of the polished stone, each sandal under each knee, and put out a hand to let the Musician know that he was not going to harm him and that he only wanted real answers to his questions, not lies and deceit.

The Musician stood there, coiled up in a ball with the key close to his chest and did not look at Galen when he spoke to him.

"I cannot tell you anything about the key, you must find out by yourself, but I can tell you the way in which you can walk," the Musician mumbled through his teeth.

He slowly pulled the chain from around his neck; he had double-looped the chain so that the key would not hang down to his knees. He slowly pulled the key, the size of his hand, from beneath his garments and placed it into Galen's hand. The chain made a soft metal sound as it brushed along the polished stone floor and made its way into Galen's hand. He used his other hand to wrap the chain around the key and placed it with the other key in his pocket underneath his cloak and in his warm clothes.

"Where is it that you wish for me to go, my foolish friend?" Galen said as he reached out to help the Musician back onto his feet.

The Musician took his hand trembling and came out from beneath the table to sit on the chair next to the fire. Galen stood back up onto his feet, walked over to his chair near the fire, and planted himself also. Galen placed his hand on the Musician's to comfort him. He made a small and broken smile at the thought of someone actually trying to help not just the world but also him.

"I didn't mean to frighten you, but I absolutely need to know who my true friends are, and it seems that though you are untrustworthy, you do have the ability to be brave to the cause of the world, and that makes you a friend enough. I will go where you tell me to go, and I will find the answer if it takes my life," Galen said as he withdrew his hand from the Musician's and relaxed it on his armrest.

"You must go to the land of the second world, the land of the Colossus. First, I must give you something that belongs to the Order, and I will not answer any other questions on the matter once I give it to you. You must understand that I do not wish to become a slave of it any longer. I will not be a slave to my former way of life," the Musician said as he got out of his chair and began walking back to the place where he slept.

Galen stayed in his chair and rubbed the end of the key with his thumb and said, "I understand."

Moments later, the small man came whipping himself around the corner of the hallway with a sword, the complete height of the Musician. He struggled with it as he brought it out to give it to Galen and threw it to the ground because it had become too heavy for him. The sword had the symbol of the key etched into the blade. It seemed to be an ancient knight's sword because the strap was thick and sturdy, and it had that style of blade attached to a long black handle. Galen reached down from his chair to the large sword that lay on the ground; he unsheathed it and raised the point of the blade to the ceiling. Holding it firmly, he looked at the symbol embossed deep into the metal. Galen did not expect the Musician to be so willing to get rid of something so beautiful. He knew from what the Musician had said that the sword linked him to his previous way of life. Galen did not know how, and he was going to respect the privacy of the small man. He had what he came for and more, and that was all that he would try to press out him. If the man had somehow crossed him, he would know where it was that the Musician would be hiding and there would be no escape. The sword glistened and shone bright in the light of the fire from the fireplace and the lamps that were lit all around the room. It was stunning to him, but he knew that it was a weapon that would be used to kill, so its outward beauty did not portray its true self. Galen hated the glorification of war. He had hoped that he would not have to use it in such a way and then thought that it would be foolish to think that in war, one would not have to fight for all that they believed in. Galen could see the Musician's gaze pass along the length of the sword when he didn't think that he was being watched; it looked to Galen as though the sword had some power over the small man. Then there were many things that Galen knew nothing about. The sword would prove to be a secret that could test the winds of time. Galen turned it in his hands and let the magnificence of its design begin to consume the Musician. He had hoped that he would gain more knowledge of the scope of the hold that the sword had on the Musician by flaunting its beauty, and he was right. The small man stared at the sword as though it was the most beautiful woman that he had ever seen. Galen quickly returned the sword to its sheath and watched the Musician's gaze follow every movement of the sword.

"Does it have a name?" He asked, thinking that the question would not offend the man.

"It has none that can be uttered without the destruction of that person," the Musician said as he looked down at the polished stone floor that lay at their feet. Galen knew nothing of what the Musician was talking about and decided that he would not ask any more questions about the sword. He began to think of how uttering the name of a sword could evoke destruction and thought of all the designs that the ancestors had created, objects that could focus the energy of time, and quickly came to the decision that he would never utter the name that was inscribed on the blade and that perhaps the Musician was indeed trying to protect Galen from some unknown power that could come against him. The Musician took his eye off the sword and stared into Galen's eyes as he had never done before and leaned forward in his place where he had been standing.

"There is another key in the place of the second world originators, the Colossus," the Musician said as he pulled himself back from his urgency toward Galen.

"I will go where it is that you have told me to go in the suggestion that you are someone who can truly help the cause of the Order."

When Galen said this, it was as if a very great load had been lifted off the Musician. He got out of the chair and reached down his hand to the small man in thanks and as a comfort to him.

"Your belongings could not be in better hands. I will keep great care of them and will return them to you when I am finished with them."

The Musician looked up at Galen and smiled a soft smile that he had never before seen from the small man. Galen tied the leather sheath around his waist and made his way in the direction of the door to the forest. The Musician opened the door and took hold of the small walking stick that he had always placed at the entrance of his home and stood leaning on it, watching the key and his sword pass through the boundaries of his home for the first time since the time he had watched his father take them out to war over three hundred years in the past. A tear began to fall as the tall man, not looking back, carried the only memory his father he had left. To the Musician, that was all a long time ago, and they had found a new purpose, a new path into war as they had done once before. The Musician, however, couldn't resist the thought that the items had not protected his father three hundred years in the past, that they would not protect Galen and that they would soon find another path possibly into the wrong hands. The door closed behind Galen as the Musician watched him walk out through the stone corridor of the forest that had been made by the Ancients, but the Musician would never tell Galen that; he would soon find out.

Galen pushed the brush off him as he exited the house of the Musician and stumbled into the tall snow. He would not get any sleep, and he knew that he would have a long journey to the Colossus; their mountains were treacherous and tall. He would do what the Musician told him to do because, though he did not fully trust the Musician, he had felt the urgency of his situation. The new addition to Galen's body hung at his side with a weight that had reminded him of his times of war that he had spent defending the world from evil. Once again, in a time that he thought not possible, he carried a weapon of war with a power that he knew not, and only Galen could truly know how dangerous that could be to him. He was never a coward though, and he would not become one in his old age.

The wind blew with a force that slowed Galen's pace as he struggled to walk through the pass that led him through the outskirts of the Fondland and to the Oblend. He looked over the pass and valley that led to the lake of Colossus. It would be three days till he would reach the lake, but he could see it clearly from the place on the hills of the Fondland. In this place, there was not near the amount of snow that had been dropped over the Myth forest, but the trek was just as hard because of the distance of his journey. It had dawned on him that he had not told the Order where it was that he was going; he, however, had no time to tell them. Galen had no time to tell the Order what it was that had been given to him and that he had succeeded in his goal to retrieve the key from the Musician. He could not tell them that he was going to meet the Colossus—a people that he had not seen or had any relations with at all. They had kept out of the business of the Order, and the Order had kept out of the business of the Colossus; but these were desperate times for the Order, and Galen knew that he would have to call upon something that had not been called upon before to save the world.

As far as Galen knew, the Colossus were a people that originated from the second world, and it was the humans that had taken the second world around the parts of land that the Colossus and the Requiem had not yet taken. It was that reason that they have stayed in peace for centuries, but now there would be a human knocking at the massive gates of the Colossus without knowing what action that would be taken against him if any at all. Galen was not going to betray the trust of the Musician, though the Musician would if he were in his place. *No*, he thought to himself as he scaled the tall mountain pass. He would not betray the trust that the Musician had placed in him and not take his possessions to where Galen knew that he really would find answers.

Pillars of stone greeted the entrance to the boat docks that led to the Colossus Lake; the water was cold but not frozen over, and so the boats were in operation. No human had come so far up to the land of the Colossus because they were afraid due to the stories that had been told about the ancient people that could crush you with their bare hands and not worry about the moral implications. Galen knew those stories were not true though, the giants were not so harmful, at least the Colossus were not. The Requiem, however, had proven to be a different breed altogether. Galen knew that the stories had been circulated by the Colossus to keep the pesky humans out of their business, as one of them had put it, without knowing that Galen had been nearby, listening to their conversation. No, they were not so much like humans in that they had the ability to be vicious. It was not in their nature to act in such a way. The Colossus were a different kind of giant. They were gentle and funny; and they, like the inhabitants of York, were isolationists, but without the hostility toward anyone that came through their borders. Thoughts like these were comforting to Galen as he scaled the hills toward the lake of Colossus. He could see the large men lifting the large fish from the lake and using them and preparing them for their markets.

Each second-world fish was about the size of Galen in length except for the mighty ones. He remembered one of the Order telling him how good it was that they had settled into this land—the land of the second world—because everything was so much larger than before in the first world and much more accommodating. Galen could remember the man from the Order telling him that the Requiem and the Colossus occupied exactly half of the known earth at the time of the settlement of the ancestors of the Order, but he was not so sure about the sayings of those men now that he had seen another truth; and he knew that the only way that he could get the truth would be to talk to a people that had always been there and had seen the first settlers and had written their history and who once had relationships with those ancient people. He knew that he would find answers where the Musician had advised him to go, and he had wondered why it was that he had not thought of it himself. Whatever the case, Galen would go across the lake and spend the first day in the markets of the Colossus and request a meeting with their king.

Pillars stood tall and supported the tents that had been set up permanently so that the fishermen would be sheltered from the wind that blew across the lake and valley. Galen's sword hung down low to the ground as he shuffled his way through the inches of snow that lay just from the beach of the lake. The waves were small and gentle on the shore of the lake, and the light from the sun shone brightly on the crystal-clear water. Tall men and women huddled around tables that stood over six feet tall from the sand. Black Stone Tower stood great and tall, and a gigantic wall covered and protected the entrance to the lake from the east, but it was now only a monument to the way of life of the Colossus.

Galen touched the side of the huge tower that reached into the clouds. Just one monumental building block of stone covered four times the length of Galen's body in all dimensions of the stone, it looked like each stone was carved out of the blackest coal that Galen had never seen before. It was, however, not made of coal. Ages of lore of the tower told that the stone was indestructible, and it looked as if the stone had never come under siege though it had been attacked over twelve thousand times through the ages of the existence of the Colossus. Galen reached out and touched the black stone that was far from smoothly polished. There were what appeared to Galen as layers of the stone that looked as if it had been forged and twisted just as the metal of a sword would have been tampered and folded for strength, and though there was much lore about the tower, there were none that told of the making of the great tower of dark power. Galen always wondered why it was called that by the Colossus and why it was considered a misfortune to enter through the archway that led to the tall, monumental corridors—corridors that spanned through into the depths of the Black Stone Tower. Perhaps the truest of the lore was kept hidden deep in the secrets of their ancient castle city behind the great Black Gate that paved the road to the path through the Colossus Mountains. Galen was unsure about the secrets of the Colossus, but he knew that he would soon find out everything he needed to know about them. He looked out across the lake and recalled the first time that he had come to the place of the Colossus; it was not a good memory. He was not worried about the memories that he would make anew though.

Galen walked along the icy sand toward a great ship that was ready to leave for the city of Colossus. He would need to book a safe passage through the waters and into the gate, and to do that, he would be required to talk to the captain of the giant ship.

The fire was tall unlike any other that he had seen before. Galen felt the warmth of the thirty-foot fire pervade across the tall hall of the Colossus. He had been in the city for hours and had already had his life threatened three times. He, though, knew that they were empty threats by soldiers that had nothing to do but keep guard over a peaceful people; and as he had heard some of them say before, it was not what they had signed up for, to be a soldier and have nothing to fight with, nothing to protect against, no suspense. Galen thought it served them right to sign up to a post that would be an inactive one; but nonetheless, they, through the years, were becoming more agitated at the thought that they would never see a true fight. Galen was, however, there to relieve them from their stresses, reassuring them that they would soon have a great evil to fight against, to protect their king against; and the prospect of having such a thing would settle them a bit. It was the silent threat that had been made on his life in one of the busy market areas that had worried him—the one where he was almost accidentally stepped on by, what seemed to him, one of the largest and heaviest of the Colossus. He had known that they were all different sizes, some small in their race and some larger than others; but it had never occurred to him that he would almost be killed in such an undignified way as accidentally being stepped on. If Galen hadn't noticed and used the Legacy to push the large foot off the top of him, he would have no knowledge that could be derived from the Colossus, and his mission would be all but accomplished.

Galen rubbed his hands together and felt the warmth of the fire that stood in the fireplace that was directly in the center of the hall. There were many that stared at the man-child that had dared to enter into the vicinity of the Colossus. They, however, stayed silent to the question as to the reason that he was there; and as the tall men and women stared at Galen as he roamed about the hall, they could see the large sword that hung on his hip and the keys that he had dangling from his neck. The giant men and women watched and drank their large wine glasses and stood prim and proper with their cloaks that were the size of a human's tent. Galen thought that he would never be afraid of them, but it was the way that they stared at him that made it harder for him to accomplish his mission.

He had spent the better part of his life trying to find the root of all evil but only found himself with the knowledge that where there is good, there would always be evil there in the shadows to threaten that good; and it seemed to Galen that for every good and righteous thing that he felt, desired, and experienced, it would always be repaid to him in the equal amount of evil. At times, Galen had seen the reward of good before the consequences of evil; but to him, they pervade each other; and without one you could not have the other. At times, the evil would prevail and in others the good; it was the same for Galen—there would be no end. Though he thought this, he would not stop fighting for the good to encompass the world at this time. He loved all sorts of people but could not dare to think that they had the ability for such destruction; he cared for them but could not see why there was a lack of nonjudgmental compassion, and to this conclusion, he found no end.

It was dark in the castle of the Colossus, and the day had faded into the gloomy night-light that shone through the tall windows of the hall of the Colossus. Galen didn't bother to look at the light source because he knew where it originated. The Colossus were, for Galen, much too queer a people, and he found their silent expressions toward him unnerving. The place that he had known before had changed, it was not the same to Galen, and he could not place the feeling that he felt; however, it was not one that was comfortable. That he knew to be the truth. He held his cloak closer to his body as he felt the piercing glares of curious Colossus as they stood and talked about things that Galen had no interest in, but he could not help but listen to them as they spoke in case something that he needed to know came up in someone's conversation.

His steps were loud as the sound of them fell upon the massively tall and wide pillars of the hall. His feet were not in the best of shape as he paced back and forth near the large fireplace that sat center to the hall. Every now and then, Galen's thoughts were interrupted by a large laugh that would come bellowing out of one of the man-giant's mouth because of something that one of them said to the other. It was more difficult for him when there was a great silence that would be corrupted by such a thing as a giant laughing and talking loudly, but for the most part, the hall was much like a library.

Galen was becoming more and more agitated by the delay in his meeting the king; perhaps it was because he was a mere human and not considered a true part of their world. The light from the fires that blazed at each torch that sat on the walls and near the entrances hissed and crackled as they shed light on the blue-and-black stone that was the Castle of Colossay. It was much like a dream to Galen walking through the huge places of the Colossus castle. It was as if he were a mouse that was scurrying from place to place as the real people stood around him and watched him in disbelief that he had somehow managed to penetrate their place of living. Now that the humans had lived in their world for so long, though, whatever evil the humans would encounter, the Colossus would have to deal with also. Galen hoped that the king would recognize that fact and understand that it would be in all their best interest to tell Galen the truth about their past and the reason that these things were happening. The truth is all that Galen would accept, nothing more; and he would remind himself to tell the king that fact just as he had made it clear to the Musician.

Tall doors opened and closed as people of the city entered and left the confines of the hall. Galen had stopped pacing by now and was sitting in a chair that one of the Colossus guards had broken down two sizes for him. He thought that that was the kindest gesture for one who would be foretelling a fate of doom to the king. It was not the exact reaction that he thought would come from the Colossus because of their queer nature and their incessant staring at him. The soldier had placed the chair in front of the fire; Galen thanked the man and pulled the pipe from his cloak pocket and began to puff away at it.

Galen thought that there was nothing that could warm the soul so much as a good smoke could, but because it was not a good habit to have as a Colossus, Galen was only able to take a few puffs, and then the sneering people that were in the smoke's reach convinced him to snuff his filthy habit out for just that moment. Galen knew that it was not in his best interests to have "such a habit," as he so often put it; but in his defense, he felt that after all that he had been through in his life it would probably not be the smoke that would be the death of him, he would have a right to indulge himself occasionally. He was often corrected by Mary on the matter, and oddly enough at that moment, he found himself not only being counseled by the sneers of the Colossus in the hall but by his own countenance; and so, moments later, the pipe was near the sword and, once again, in the small pouch of cloth, which he had sown onto his cloak deliberately for the use of putting the pipe there. *Someday, I would tear the pouch off.* Galen thought to himself as he shoved it back into its place.

Galen, reminded of his situation, could not fathom how he could be so deep in thought about his pipe and his habit at this time and then realized that it was his nervousness about his visit to the king that had brought it on. He told himself that he would not mind it any longer as he stared into the fire. Galen was thinking about the Order and how it had been three days since the last time that he had seen any of them, and he was beginning to miss their company. He knew that Talon would keep them safe at all costs, especially Cypress. Galen noticed the way that they looked at each other, and he knew that they would be good for each other if they would not allow the events around them to taint the true love that they so obviously had.

Galen knew that they were cleaning up the tomb of the city of Asscatan and that it would soon be livable as was the castle of Pastel the first time that it had been found by the Order. He could see that there was a great future for the Order, and he was ready to live the remainder of his days as the guardian of that future, that he knew was his lot in life, his purpose. Galen stared into the flames of the fire and thought about his life that he had led; and whether he thought that it was a good one or not, whether he thought that he had accomplished anything that could be considered worthwhile. Only after he accomplished his mission of saving the human race from their own stupidity could he really feel as if he had accomplished something that was great. The task had been placed into his hand and the Order's.

The large doors to the center chamber of the hall had been opened; two Colossus soldiers stepped out of the doorway with their weapons and their armor ready to escort Galen to the king of their kingdom. Galen got up out of the chair that the Colossus soldier had made for him and began to head in the direction of the escort. The sight of the Castle of Colossay was like no other for Galen; he felt so small and insignificant. In reality, however, he could reduce just one of the soldiers to a pile of ash if it came to him having to defend himself with the Legacy. He did not want to harm anyone though, and he had a feeling that he would not be required to do such an un-Orderly thing.

Galen thought about the sword that had been given him by the Musician and wondered if there was any connection that would arise with the telling of the story of keys, if the Colossus king had such a story.

The voices of the soldiers that had come to escort him echoed through the huge hall that Galen had been waiting in. He was not afraid, he told himself, as he entered through the large passageway to the chamber that lay near the entrance to the king's chamber. Galen was glad that he would no longer have to deal with the prying eyes of the other Colossus when he entered into the private waiting chamber that led to the king. The tall men watched the very small man and his cloak pass slowly underneath their arms as they held the doors open for him to enter the chamber. There was a giant that was lurking in the shadows of the chamber room that Galen had not seen when he entered; to Galen, he was a large statue that did not dare to move. All statues in the chambers of the Colossus were statues that had been painted; they did not enjoy the colorless statue. But this one was not a statue at all, just a well-placed sentry that slowly haunted each step that Galen made. It was the strange feeling that Galen got from the room that made him feel uneasy; he was completely startled when the sentry pointed to the small chair that had been brought out of an old chamber just for the occasion of the visit of a human. However, once the fear had subsided, Galen sat in the chair that was exactly his size. This was the place that had been the most comfortable to him; though the guard traced his every move, he knew that he was only doing his job, and he appreciated the effort in making the place more comfortable for him. Sitting in the chair, Galen thought about his opening words that he would tell the king when he would first enter the king's chamber. Suddenly he realized that he would not say anything at all; he would show him the key and graciously ask if he knew anything about it.

"Yes, that is what I shall do," Galen said out loud as he folded his hands together in front of him.

The sentry took a sharp look at Galen underneath his cloak hood in response to the voicing of his thoughts but said nothing to him.

The room was not in the slightest bare; it had many markings that Galen did not understand that told of the Colossus history and their conquest of the other worlds. They were not bloody, though, and Galen was astonished by the showings of conquest through the use of the ancient game—the game of the seven-year war. Galen looked at the markings and only recognized those things; it was a crucial point in his knowledge of the Colossus that he had not seen before.

He had, in no point in his life, seen the inner waiting chamber of the king and had never seen the markings such as the ones he was now looking at anywhere else in the city and was absolutely astonished at the thought that the Colossus had given such respect to the ancient game of war that Galen knew so well. This was the game of conquest that Galen would be required to teach the young ones of the human race later on in his life before those games would be put into play. He knew that he was now in the right place to find answers about the past, and he was confident that he would be helped to see the truth about the earlier period of the Order through the eyes of the Colossus. It was when he had made this conclusion that the sentry opened the doors to the chamber of the king.

Galen slowly walked through the chamber doors and across the chamber floor to the bottom of the stairs of the king's throne. He kneeled in respect for the king, but as he did, the king stretched out his hand and gestured for him to rise and not pay obedience to him.

"Do not do such a thing as this, my friend. You are a king amongst your people as well," the giant king said to Galen as he placed his hand back to rest on the arm of his chair.

Galen quickly rose from his knee and grabbed hold of the key around his neck, thrusting it in the air with his arm out in front of him. The key of the Musician glistened in the light of the fire from the torches. The king leaned forward in his chair and took a closer look at the key squinting; then after seeing it, he gasped.

"I see you have a key of the Ancients. Where is it that you have found this treasure?" the giant said as he returned himself to his normal position with an expression of fear in his eyes.

"I have come for answers to my questions that you, great king, may have within your grasp," Galen said to him, not answering his question about the key.

"You have come to the correct place. What is it that you would wish to know?" asked the king.

"Do you have such a treasure in your midst, and what is it that you know about the keys of the Ancients and the people themselves?" Galen asked, still holding the key out in front of him.

The king smiled a large smile and raised himself from his chair while gesturing for the sentries to leave the room. He walked to a chamber that was hidden behind a place in the wall behind his seat, and gestured for Galen to follow him into the hidden chamber, which was filled with very large books. The king reached out to the highest book that had been placed on a shelf, and brought it down so that Galen could look at it. Before the book was brought down from its shelf, however, Galen could already see the huge carving of the symbol that lay in the center of the large door in the hidden chamber of Pastel. Galen gasped and thought that he should have known that there was a reason that the door was so large, and he should have realized the puzzle together at that very moment; unfortunately for him, he had not. Galen knew that not all was lost though, he was here in the castle of the Colossus, and the secrets of the Order were about to be revealed to him; finally, he would have rest in knowing the whole truth about the matter, and he would be able to carry on in his mission that the Order had set out to do before the finding of the secret chamber of Pastel.

The king laid the book in front of Galen on a round table that he could barely see over; he had to climb onto the chair that sat near the table to get a good look at the book. It was incredibly old and was bound with many skins of gold and stone, and there laid in it the gold key of the Colossus. Galen stood on the chair and looked at the key; quickly he whipped his head around to look at the king.

"You must tell me all that you know about the settlers from the first world. It will mean the survival of both our races," Galen said as he looked straight into the eyes of the king.

The king slowly blinked his eyes in approval and sat at the table next to Galen.

"There is a legend that is no longer told about your people. A legend that told of a people that settled here long before the known race of humans that roam the second earth at this time. It was said that they were a people of visions who lived in places that were hidden to the eye. No giant ever found these places, and they were considered lying lore. However, this book was found in our own castle and was suppressed by the oldest king of the second earth that we have knowledge of. His name was never uttered in respect for him and his position. He placed the book here and told all kings after him that it was not to be taken from its place. Only now have I been given reason sufficient enough to disobey that command." The king paused for a moment so that Galen would understand everything that he was telling him.

"I have found those places of concealment, and this key is a key that opens the door that was made for your kind," Galen said, still staring into the eyes of the king.

The king's eyebrows lifted in response to Galen's statement, and then he continued,

"The ones that I speak of were not like you. The Colossus considered them a more beautiful race of humans, and they lived for hundreds of years at a time. They were said to be passionate in whichever choice they made of their lives whether it be for good or for evil. They were said to have either returned to their original time dimension or what they called the third dimension, another world. But the most common eventuality of the story is that they, in the end, killed themselves off by their war and violence and left the places of concealment behind."

Galen was astonished at the information that there was another race of humans that had come before the Order's descendants, and it did make sense that they were the ones who had built the castles of Pastel. It was the third dimension that worried him. In all his studies with the Order, he had never been told of a third dimension, and there in the map of the Order that told of the convergence of time, only had two worlds of convergence. Galen was thinking of these things as the king watched his expressions on his face. Galen realized that there perhaps was a third world but that it was not a part of the convergence and that perhaps the Ancients had found a way to pass through the barriers of time as the Dark Lord had been doing for the past months. It was beginning to all make much more sense to him. Galen picked up the key and looked at the king for permission. He didn't have to ask; it was the expression on the giant's face that told him that he could take the key and do with it what he must to find the whole truth.

To be Continued

IN BOOK 2

Made in United States
Troutdale, OR
12/18/2024